I0675337

# Thirst

## Amber Alferoff

Published in 2009 by YouWriteOn.com
Copyright © Text Amber Alferoff

First Edition

The author asserts the moral right under the
Copyright, Designs and Patents Act 1988 to be identified
as the author of this work.

All Rights reserved. No part of this publication may be
reproduced, stored in a retrieval system, or transmitted,
in any form or by any means without the prior written
consent of the author, nor be
otherwise circulated in any form of binding or cover
other than that in which it is published and without a
similar condition being imposed on the subsequent
purchaser.

Published by YouWriteOn.com

# Prologue

Thirsty for land, but enjoying the ride, a raindrop falls from the sky. It has fallen to Earth before, as snow, as hail, as tears of joy, and despair. As blood it has flowed gently through bodies and burst from wounds. It has boiled, in ancient seas and modern kettles. It has frozen, in every mountain range, both poles, and a billion freezers in between. This rain has formed ice-comet and amniotic fluid, plants and people, fish and sea, passing from one to the other with the ease of a lover.

The raindrop reflects the young man by the loch. He lifts his face, opens his mouth. He does not know that this drop has travelled from the south, dropped from a bridge over the Thames by a girl laughing with her sisters, but as it falls onto his tongue, becoming part of him, he knows it is the sweetest, strongest, brightest water he has ever tasted.

# A holiday?

Five months after the accident the people of the Sight stopped waiting. As dusk became dark, Kade's mother's wake began. The permanent members of the Sight gathered on the courtyard of the lodge, halfway between the loch and the mountain top. The flagstones felt soft, as though he might melt through. His hand gripped a small ceramic pot.

He stood frozen still until he was released by the silent flight of an owl across the courtyard. With a shiver that was nothing to do with the cold he began to walk. The others followed. In silence, each preceded by a halo of their own breath, they made their way through the trees that flanked the tumbling river, past the willow pool, to the loch. In single file they waited as Kade poured oil into each pot.

At nightfall, he lit the first lamp. As everyone huddled together to light their own flames, snow began to fall. They looked up, twenty faces in the night, watching snowflakes and listening to the waves break. Then the moment seemed right and they set their lamps in the water. Kade was last. He stared at the flame unable to say a final goodbye, then lowered it into the water and gently drew his hand away. The most acute part of his mourning was over: now he had to learn to live without her. He felt incredibly sad and, he was ashamed to say, free.

Islands of light flickered on the water. When he had pictured the wake, the tide had carried the lights away, but now the loch returned them to the shore. The waves extinguished each flame, except one, which lodged itself in the pebbles of the beach. His tears fell on the settling snow.

A week later he was nineteen. In the evening there was a sedate party in the lodge kitchen. The presents were packed with thoughtfulness. The children gave him handmade bundles of feathers and ferns, tied with ribbons and decorated with shells and moss. There were a few books – *Scottish Legends*, a self-help about grief. But it was the big present that forced him to acknowledge how much had changed. As he unwrapped the wetsuit he knew he would not wear it. The people would be disappointed. It would have taken them weeks to gather up enough money to buy it, but he would not be going back into the loch, or the willow pool, or the caves.

Cigarette smoke stung his eyes, attracted by the tears he was trying to hide. Thanking everyone for the wetsuit, but unable to meet anyone's gaze, he retreated to the courtyard. The people of the Sight knew how to read the signs of someone who wanted to be alone, and would not follow.

Outside, he felt better. The waning moon was rising. He felt some of its bright coldness and silence inside himself, and some of its optimism.

Initially after the accident he had been purposeful. The first thing he did after reporting her missing was rip all the pictures off the kitchen walls in a trance of frenzied anger. The next day, calmly, he whitewashed over the yellow paint. Afterwards, he had walked downhill and closed up the tipi that she had lived in for the past twenty years. Once he had laced the door shut, stillness took over.

For months he had returned to the willow pool every day, finding solace in the volume of the waterfall, which masked the loudness of his inner confusion. Then fear emerged, quiet and determined. Would anyone wonder if his mother's disappearance was due to him? Would anyone come asking? Gradually, though, as the flowers died and the bracken browned and curled in on itself, and no one asked him anything, and his mother did not return, he became intensely sad. He wept under the willow. As the trees on the ravine edge became black against the sky, he became hardened and brittle, snapping easily. Then snowfall came and softened him. 'Now what?' he had asked. 'Now what do I do?'

As usual, he had laid an evening fire in the thick-felt yurt his mother had constructed with him when he was fourteen. As he had reached for the old newspapers he kept for kindling he found himself gripping the travel pages of The Scotsman. A picture caught his attention: the Ganges and its beach, both oozing with people. *Kumbh Mela* said the headline, *Gathering of the Tribes*.

Suddenly he knew what to do. She had always promised to take him. She had said that if there was any trouble they would go straight there because in India you could get off the grid, as well as off your head.

After that Kade had moved fast. 'Hey Tom, I've got a present for you,' he had called uphill from the yurt's doorway.

'Whatsat?'

'My Action Men.'

'Yippee!' said Tom. 'I mean, cool!'

It meant a lot for Kade to give away the Action Men. They were a symbol of his struggle to balance his life and the normality of the rest of the world. Of course Tom coveted them. Action men were normal; they went down well with the village kids from Kittim, giving kudos that a Sight kid rarely experienced in the wider world. They could also carry a child into other adventurous worlds. Being able to use his imagination had been vital to Kade. His mum was never keen to take him anywhere. She'd found him totally unpredictable, and was bewildered by the strength and suddenness of his emotions. He remembered screaming in cafés, bursting into tears for no definable reason, dancing with joy at odd moments. Things had improved when his mum had made a policy of always carrying water from the well for him to drink. She'd taken him around Britain a bit. But for many years he'd had to entertain himself. His mum had liked him to climb trees and swim. He begged her for an Action Man, arguing that it rained *a lot*, and he needed something to do indoors. She finally relented when he held up an Eagle-Eyes at the village jumble sale and said 'Please please please,' tears of disappointment at the ready. Later he added to his collection with an Action Man in diving gear, and his mum seemed happy.

'C'mon then,' he said to Tom. The men peeked out from a basket hanging inside his yurt, as though on a balloon mission. 'There you go.' He swung the basket over to the boy, who gave him a big hug round the legs and ran off. Kade was pleased. Giving them away felt better than he had expected.

Hands trembling he reached into another basket and extracted the bone needle.

When he sold it later that week it fetched *plenty*, so he booked his ticket and called his friends to see if he could rustle anyone up to come with him. They all said they couldn't. He wasn't surprised. India would have too much in common with the Sight, which all of them had left as soon as they could, breathing sighs of relief at never having to see multi-coloured mohair or hand-painted shoes again, nor smell the aroma of Nag Champa incense or burnt lentils. Kade himself was not the greatest fan of the Sight's fashion sense, or some of the cooking, but before now he had never felt the pull to leave. The loch, the rivers and the well kept him close, as though they were magnetic and he were a collection of iron filings.

Now, on his birthday, in the courtyard under the moon, he unfolded the newspaper. Hundreds of people bathing; a belief that water cleanses the spirit as well as the body; a place, he hoped, where someone might be able to explain the Tasting.

# Mangos and hibiscus

'Hello! Hello! Are you there?' It was so tricky to get through. Brooke played with the tiny wooden hibiscus flowers on her necklace. Her fingers smelt metallic, and of coconut, traffic and hot stones. 'Samantha?'

She watched the parrots flying between the power lines and the orchard, settling on golden-green mango trees. Seven days in India and she was doing fine. She liked being here, liked the people and felt at home at the Kumbh Mela, the biggest festival on the planet. What did they say, a million people? Twelve million? But she missed her sisters. It seemed so long since she had stood shivering in her family hallway in Rayton clenching a towel round her, having leapt out of the bath to sign for her tickets.

'Morning Brooke. Whatcha got?' Charlotte had demanded.

'Ticket to India.'

'Oh yeah, course.' Charlotte had pulled her long ginger hair into a middle parting and made a peace sign. 'Like, going to find yourself eh? I'm glad mum and dad never took *me* to Glastonbury. I reckon you caught some kind of infection that's turning you into a hippy.'

'I'm no hippy. I'm going to research myths.'

'Yeah right,' said Charlotte running back upstairs with the hair straighteners. 'Yogurt weaver.'

'Carrot features.'

Her little sister might well be right though. Brooke had had a great time, most of it in wellies and a tutu, on that one trip to Glastonbury when she was five, before her parents became straighter than Charlotte's hair.

That's where the seeds of the plan were sown. The *plan*, which had picked up steam in her mid teens, had been to drive overland to India with a group of friends, smoking loads and wearing bright clothes that looked nothing like school uniform. As it panned out, none of her friends had even been willing to venture near Indian Airlines, let alone travel overland through Arabia. Never trust a hippy, they said sagely.

Here she was, though, at Hippy Central. Laxman Jhula. Down the road was Rishikesh, where the Beatles had gone Way Back When. All about were yoga temples, long skirts, tie dye and smoke. The hippies were so authentic that they spoke only in broken English – even if they *were* English. They were tanned all over, except under their heavy layers of jewellery. Quite probably they had grown their dreadlocks from scratch, rather than had them done by a hairdresser. Brooke loved it. People at home could not fathom why she would want to take a year off university to travel rather than finish her course, get a job, house and Audi. They just didn't understand, thought Brooke. No-one at home *got* her, and she badly wanted someone to *get* her.

'Hello?' she said again, picturing her voice as the zeros and ones of binary digital code. She saw the code travel along the phone line, shoot into space, bounce off a satellite, arrive back on earth, into another phone line, into a phone, and then change back into sound, vibrating the tiny hairs and bones of her sister's ear. She pictured Sam's synapses instructing her fingers to pick up the handset. Simple really.

'Hi?'

'Sam!'

'Brookin! How are you?'

'Fine thanks.'

'What's India like then?'

'Lovely. And hot.'

'Where are you now?' asked Sam.

'I'm on the balcony of my guest house.'

'And?'

'Um, there's loads of people. There's a snake on the pavement.'

'A snake?'

'Yeah. It's HUGE.' The snake had freaked her out totally when she arrived. Big enough to swallow her whole, it had hidden, somehow, in its stillness. Brooke had only noticed it when she was right beside it and had jumped, quietly, inside her skin. 'There's a bloke in a turban sitting next to it.'

Sam laughed. 'They're probably laid on by the government to increase India's authenticity.'

Brooke giggled. 'You'd love the menus.'

'Good food?'

'Good typos.' She told Sam about the *Girl Backed Bense Tossed*, *Scram Bled Egg* and *Social Pakoras* they served in the nearby café.

'Cool ... '

'How's the flower business? How're mum and dad?'

Sam filled Brooke in, then asked 'How's the studying going?'

'College seems so far away.' Brooke thought about her degree, and the freedom she felt when she'd decided to suspend her course and gather water-myths in India. Anthropology had seemed such a juicy subject, but had become so dry. She had yawned through lectures on the economic systems of the Bantu, the exogamy of the Pomo, and even the sexual practices of South Sea Islanders. Her job, too, had initially seemed so interesting, but instead of a *lifesaver* she was simply pool security, blowing her whistle and watching people turn their heads predictably, like guilty otters.

'Brooke? Are you still there? How's the water-myth project?'

'Okay. I mean . . . the people here . . . um, it's like being *in* a myth. I'm sure it feels like everyday life for them, but the attitude they have to water is just so magical, so refreshing.'

'Don't get too carried away Brooke,' said Sam. 'Make sure you do some work for your project.'

'I will.' Brooke felt herself drifting away from the phone call. There was movement in the mango orchard.

'I better go Sam.'

'All right darling. Have fun. Take care.'

'You too. Love to all'

'Bye.'

'Bye-bye.'

Brooke waited with her rupees as the phone-Walla totted up the cost. She paid and went to her room. As she swung open the door her movements were gentle, although she was unobserved. Conscious of her grace, she felt kind towards her body. She went straight to the balcony and looked out at the mango orchard again.

Amongst the trees was a man, near enough for her to see his vertebrae and the dark curls at the nape of his neck. His arms hung gently at his sides. Slowly he spread his fingers and closed them, spread and closed. He seemed captured by sensation. She guessed his eyes were shut. The moment she realised he was beautiful he walked on. Suddenly she was lonely.

Dusk arrived and her loneliness deepened, but she savoured the melancholy, knowing it would pass and would do her no harm.

Later, as she slept, the man from the orchard wandered into her dreams, claiming a space in her mind.

The following afternoon as she sat in the typo-café she saw him again, running along the silver sands of the Ganges. His pace was fast and aquiline as he slipped in and out between the boulders on the beach. She was transfixed by his lips, his hair, his footprints: red, black, silver. She thought she saw him smile and began to smile back. Then he was gone.

# Stealing feelings

That girl is lovely, thought Kade as his feet pounded the sand. There were a hell of a lot of pretty girls here, between the Indians and the westerners. But there was a brightness about that one. Aye. Maybe he would see her around again. Lust quickening his pace, he ran with the water's flow, chasing it. Downriver he approached Ram Jhula, the second suspension bridge.

He could still taste mango juice. He was getting used to India, and was relaxed enough to scrump for mangoes. At first he had been overwhelmed: out of his depth from the moment he had stepped from the Indian Airlines flight into a furnace of heat. And the crowds! Edinburgh had been bad enough. He was not used to busy. India was busy *and some,* with all the smells, people, colours, wonders and hassle that people had described to him at the Sight, but more somehow than the sum of its parts. The backpackers' area of Delhi was frightening, but then he had sussed it out: Simultaneously wholesome and deliciously sleazy, all the young travellers carefully tended to and given – or let into – just the right level of experience for them, be it shopping or degeneracy. Kade was not worldly, but he had never been naïve. Never had the chance.

On the train from Delhi to Haridwar he had chatted with inquisitive Indians. 'Yeah, so I've always been really into water,' he explained, to blank expressions. 'So I'm here for the Kumbh Mela.' The people smiled. 'Not sure what Kumbh Mela means, but I'm hoping to meet some interesting people and go swimming and stuff, what about you?' He listened with interest to people's stories, and even tentatively shared a bottle of water with a young man his own age, who showed Kade the method of pouring a stream of water into his mouth without the bottle touching his lips. 'I'm impressed,' said Kade, and gave the man a fifty pence piece, which seemed to simultaneously confuse and please.

As the train neared Haridwar, Kade said his goodbyes and went to the open doorway. He was followed by a fellow traveller, an Indian who had been watching him, and who, with a surprising amount of authority for a dreadlocked man in an orange lungi carrying a trident, said, 'You. Stay on the train.'

Kade looked out at the tracks speeding by and agreed. 'Fine idea. Yes. I'll wait till the station.'

'No. Stay on the train and go north. Go to Laxman Jhula.'

'Why?'

'More shanti – peaceful. And more westerners.' The man was insistent. 'You are not ready for the crowds.'

The train approached the city from a hilltop and Kade saw a scene more akin to a movie than to anything from his life. Below was a river of people, a torrent. They filled every street he could see, hiding the Ganges behind flesh and cloth. Kade looked back at the man with a bemused frown, and then grinned. 'You may well be right.'

'Yes. Right,' said the man, and jumped onto the platform, running and waving.

So Kade had continued to Laxman Jhula, a place named for a bridge.

Crossing Ram Jhula, he turned left and ran against the river's flow. Flicking sweat onto the tree-lined avenue, he ignored stares from the young families and groups of men in checked shirts who populated the many benches. Generally he did not get stared at much, being a dark-haired man. Not compared to the young western women who were transformed into celebrities by India. It was only when people saw his eyes that they stared, but they did that in Scotland.

The street became steeper, lined with workshops and professional beggars. He bought some toll – puffed rice – and placed a helping into each dish held out by the old men and women that waited, one on each step of a staircase. Next he turned left onto Laxman Jhula and began to cross the busy pedestrian bridge.

He had run a square now, as he often did at home, from the Lodge, down alongside the falls to the loch, along the stony shore and then up the other side of the field, alongside the other burn. Thinking of home reminded him that he would have liked to have called on the new people across the loch. They had arrived as he was leaving, and called themselves the Waterfolk. He'd seen the smoke from their fires, and the shine from a solar panel. Not that solar was much use in the Highlands. A windmill powered his stereo.

Halfway across the bridge, he stopped. There was the girl again, in an open-sided café on the hill. She had a flower behind her ear like a Tahitian woman, but she did not seem Tahitian. Her hair was auburn, perhaps she was Scottish? She could be from the village next to Kittim for all he knew. He wanted to find out. He ran on, heading for the café.

When he got there she was gone. Staring at the half finished bottle of soda at her table, he wondered if she had left in a hurry. An idea flickered. He could Taste where her lips had touched. The idea grew, and the bottle developed a gravity of its own, pulling him near. It was an intrusion, but she would never know, and he could not resist. He touched the bottle to his lips. Tasting anticipation, excitement and desire, he closed his eyes in pleasure, unexpectedly reminded of a rainy night by the Loch.

'Hi,' said a spicy-sweet voice behind him. Startled he dropped the bottle onto the table. Spilled soda fizzed loudly.

'Hi!'

'I left my bag here.'

'Oh. Right.'

As the girl reached for her bag, she brushed his arm with hers, seemingly unintentionally. His whole body – in fact the whole café and all the hills – tingled in response. 'Thanks,' she said with a smile. She touched her hand to the wooden flowers at her neck, seemed about to say something else, then turned and left.

'Oh lass … '

# Fire

Pleasure ran through Brooke. When they had touched it had felt so, so right, and the feeling ran from her arm to her soul. But her mind kept interrupting. 'Perhaps he was short of a few rupees,' she told herself. 'Or maybe it wasn't my drink after all.'

A few days later she was still wondering, but now there was something to take her mind off it, and him, and his lovely eyes.

All the customers at the Full Moon Café sat outside near the river. The food was cooked indoors on a gas fire in a hut made of newspaper wattle and daub; dry, translucent and glowing. 'It's a fucking tinderbox,' said Brooke.

'It's certainly the most obvious health and safety hazard I've ever seen,' said Anya, the Swedish girl she'd just shared dinner with.

'Just look at the curtain.' They giggled at the incredible danger of the flimsy piece of cloth that served as a door, flicking in and out of the doorway, flirting with the cooking flames. 'It's like a dragon's tongue,' said Brooke.

Inside, the solo chef rushed around, preparing every meal and drink. Brooke felt for him, especially as it was so calm outside, with groups of people chatting in the evening warmth. The sky was cloudless, the stars like seeds amongst the foliage of the trees. A stream trickled past. Brooke enjoyed her ice-cream pancake. She had made a friend, though Anya was leaving the next morning, and she had finally done some research into myths. A trip to a temple had yielded a conversation with a multi-necklaced priest who told her about Krishna claiming 'I am the taste in water.'

As Anya passed Brooke a joint, she caught sight of the man from the orchard. She said, 'Oh, that's him,' just as the kitchen ignited with a seemingly relaxed inevitability. In seconds the flames licked the trees and grabbed at the stars.

People either froze, ran away from the fire, or towards it. Anya ran away, Brooke towards. She grabbed a plastic bin, plunged it into the stream and threw water onto the base of the flames. Dozens of others did the same. She refilled the bin. As she soaked more flames she saw the man from the orchard next to her, fire shining in his eyes. Her heart leapt. He smiled. 'There's gas cylinders inside!' someone yelled, and the crowd picked up pace.

With little fuel, the flames were quashed within minutes. Some people collapsed by the river, breathless. Others continued drenching the ashes, bringing the heat down. Brooke was pleased to see that the chef was all right. She found Anya by the water.

'Well, that just proves that believing something bad will happen does NOT prevent it,' said Anya.

Brooke sought the man from the orchard, and saw him walking towards the footpath with his arm around a girl. Brooke hoped he was helping her with an injury. Anya gave Brooke a hug, and they walked home with the smell of burning newspaper in their hair.

After the fire, Brooke kept looking for him, hoping he had not left town. She did not know him, but she missed him. Then, one Tuesday morning, as she paused on the bridge to photograph the hills, she thought she saw him. Excitedly, she pressed the shutter, catching him between two boulders on the riverbank. Hurriedly she placed the camera in her bag, lifted the hem of her long dress, and ran after him.

The route was an old pilgrims' path which followed a steep tributary of the Ganges. She reached a wooded area, flanked by a temple, a dog and an old holy man with long dreadlocks. All seemed asleep, even the temple, its heavy roof pulled over it like a blanket. Little boys in grey shorts and girls in flowery dresses played by the water's edge. Uphill the path became natural stairs made of earth, roots and slabs of stone. The canopy of leaves became denser, noisier, and more luscious. The water in the river was white now, pouring down in tiers of falls and pools. She moved fast, momentum building in her step until she thought, just for a second, of a future with the man she was following, lost her footing, grasped the branches of a shrub above and, saved from falling, looked up to see a hibiscus bush in full red flower.

# Watersprites

Everything was moving. The water rushed over his body from his toes to the nape of his neck, then flowed to the pool below, over the fish, and onwards into the valley, singing, touching, bubbling and whispering; allowing the succulent maroon-pink rocks of the gully to guide it. The water was warm. He had never imagined that a river could be warm. The leaves of the trees, and the ferns and balsam, nourished by spray, collected the light and turned it green. The small stones of the shingle path whispered every so often, moving with a slow velocity left by the last walker half an hour, or a million litres, ago. Bees and dragonflies fluttered and darted, pulled by the scent of nectar. Birds swooped, resting on air currents, wings outstretched. He drank from the pool, and the water did not interfere with his feelings, so fresh was it from the snow-melt.

'I'm lonely,' he thought. 'I want someone to know me – to know my secrets, to believe me. But I'm afraid. I want to be ordinary, *and I don't*. I want to tell, *and I don't*. How are you Kade? people ask, and I say, Aye. Fine, but I want to say, I don't fucking KNOW. Other people's emotions are shoved into my taste buds with every fucking drink! There's no room for *my* feelings!

'I'm lonely. I want to quench my thirst. I want to have fun. And I'd really like to see that girl again.'

The young trees down the hill swayed. Someone was arriving, quietly and gently. Please let it be her.

Bright colour emerged from the forest like precious metal emerging from ore. Her hair was the colour of iron-rich water, her skin golden in the generous afternoon sun, her dress platinum, and her walk as mesmerising as mercury. In her hair she wore a blood-red flower. It was her.

She looked around as though confirming that the place really was as lovely as her senses declared, then swept her hand down the back of her legs to gather her skirts and sat by the pool twenty feet below his. From her bag she took a book and pen, then changed her mind, placed them beside her and closed her eyes. Dragonflies encircled her toes.

Kade could have watched her for ages, but it occurred to him that if she noticed him there she might find it a bit creepy. There had been a few 'tourists' at the Sight who were clearly only there to watch the girls. He had played his part in moving them on. So, quietly, with the agility of the waterfall itself, he left his pool, climbed the side of the cliff and slipped into the warm jade of her pool.

She looked up. Time dissolved. They were anyone, anywhere. They were gods and animals, and they were rivers, seas, rocks and earth, forming each other over and over again.

'Hello,' he said.

She smiled. 'Hi.'

'I like your necklace.'

'Thank you.'

He joined her on the pool's beach and sat with his legs tucked to one side. 'Did you get it here?'

'In London.' She paused, pushing a lock of hair behind her ear, then gave him a mischievous smile. 'I wear it to keep me safe from watersprites.'

'What's so wrong with watersprites then?' *Does she believe in watersprites?*

'Nothing wrong with watersprites.' She glanced around as if someone might be watching, put her finger to her lips in a hush gesture, and whispered, 'But they need to be kept in their place. If they follow you home they cause mayhem. Turn taps on, blow plumbing, cause floods.'

'Have *you* ever had a watersprite follow you home?' he asked.

'Not sure,' she said touching her necklace. 'Don't think so. Have you?'

'Loads I reckon.' He laughed. 'So how does the flower help?'

'People use hibiscus to protect themselves.'

'Really?'

'The Andaman islanders, who live about two thousand miles over ... ' she looked up at the sun, then pointed over his shoulder, 'that way ... ' As she drew her hand back her little finger brushed his bare skin. Pleasure danced through him. ' ... have a ritual to keep watersprites in their proper place. They kill a turtle, on hibiscus leaves using a hibiscus-wood spear.'

'Sounds a bit extreme. Does it work?'

'Never tried it myself,' she said with a laugh. 'They never get hurt by tsunamis though. So maybe.'

'Are you afraid of water sprites?' he asked, seriously.

'No. Are you?'

'No.'

'Good.'

'I'm Kade,' he said.

'I'm Sarah Brooke. People call me Brooke.'

He heard 'Brook' as in stream. 'Lovely name.'

Nodding thanks, she dipped her feet into the water. 'It's funny, you know. They might not know about the myths and rituals of the Andamans, but in places with a big beach culture people often wear hibiscus. Well the print anyway.'

'It is kind of surfy,' said Kade, reaching forward and touching the carving.

Brooke continued, slightly flustered. 'Like Australia, Hawaii, Goa, even Brighton. They're all decked out in it. Well, that's what I see on the telly and stuff anyway. I've only been to Brighton. And here.' She looked over to the waterfall, turned to Kade, and smiled.

Okay thought Kade and put his feet in the water next to hers. There was a moment of stillness as she noticed his webbed toes. Then she said 'Oh wow! I bet you can swim really well with those.'

He breathed a sigh of relief. 'Yeah.'

Changing the subject as smoothly as he could, Kade said, 'So you're quite canny then? Bet you know what Kumbh Mela means.'

'Yeah I do,' said Brooke, giving a slow smile.

Kade stared at her for a few seconds, while she said nothing. 'Tell me then,' he said, laughing.

'Okay. Back in the day, at the beginning of the universe, the gods had a big old barney over a pot – a *kumbh* – of divine ambrosia.'

'Back in the day? A barney? That doesn't sound very, um, religious.'

'I get bored of all the solemn language.'

'Okay then. So the gods were having a fight over some rice pudding?'

She double took. 'Rice pudding?'

'Ambrosia.'

'No! The kumbh was full of nectar,' she said, giggling. 'Four drops were spilled. They became four cities and the Kumbh Mela is rotated between these.'

'I see.' Kade raised his brow. 'And Mela? Does it have some sacred significance?'

'Sort of,' replied Brooke. 'Roughly translates as party.'

'I LIKE YOU,' he thought so loudly that he was sure she would hear.

Brooke stood up and lifted her dress, revealing a white swimsuit with a silver hibiscus print. The surge he felt in his blood made him dizzy. She dived in. When she surfaced, the hibiscus flower from her hair was lost to the pool.

He jumped in and they swam and laughed. They moved to the back of the pool, where there was just enough room to sit behind the waterfall. Their conversation felt intimate, a strange conversation to have with a stranger, but normal somehow. In India, like at the Sight, people launched into seemingly deep conversations with people they had just met. But as Kade reached for Brooke's hand, he felt nervous. She spoke first. 'You know,' she said against the roar, 'during the Kumbh Mela the veil separating the material and spiritual worlds is at its most transparent.' He nodded and they moved forward and allowed the waterfall to pour over them. It felt like gentle electricity.

When they finally decided to leave, they took a stepping stone route down through the gorge. A warm breeze accompanied them to town where they stopped in at Brooke's guest house for a drink. Kade got a hell of a shock from a giant snake, but kept his cool. Brooke invited him up, and they walked across the courtyard to her room, eliciting amused grins from the guest house employees. 'Butterflies,' he heard one of them say. He asked Brooke if she had heard too.

'Yeah,' she said. 'Here they call westerners butterflies because they think we flit from one partner to another like a butterfly goes from flower to flower.' She turned to him, and gave a broad smile.

'I ... I'm not a butterfly,' said Kade.

Brooke kept smiling. 'Do you want to meet up tomorrow?'

# Drinking water

Brooke watched Kade pour water from the metal carafe as they sat in a busy canteen-style restaurant that specialised in South-Indian food, almost foreign in this northern state. She could not get over how beautiful his eyes were, even in the strip lights. They were aquamarine. God he was gorgeous, sexy, interesting and interest*ed*.

He raised the glass to his lips. Was he going to *drink* it? Was it purified? She felt nervous and exhilarated as he took a sip, breaking Rule Number One of all the guidebooks. It seemed like a rebellious gesture.

'You can't tell if it's okay by tasting it, you know,' she said, passing him her bottle of mineral water. 'Here, have this instead.'

'No, I'm alright with this,' said Kade. 'I kind of can taste if it's okay. Thanks.'

'Suit yourself,' said Brooke in a mock-moody voice.

Kade smiled, then asked, 'What are you doing in India?'

'Well, I just always wanted to come here, and I got fed up with waiting for someone to travel with. I wanted to learn about Indian culture. I even had thoughts of living with an Indian family and learning the lingo.' She paused and looked down. 'But I didn't organise it before I left, and when I arrived I got really into the backpacker culture. I mean, you just meet people from all over the world here, don't you? People that would never go to England. Or Scotland. Too cold or too expensive.' She took a sip from her water bottle. 'But the main reason I'm here is to work on my degree project.' She paused. 'Actually, the main reason is to have fun.'

'What are you studying?'

'Water myths.'

She swore she heard him gulp.

The food arrived. Masala Dosas, and little white idlis – rice cakes that looked like flying-saucers. Brooke tucked in, really enjoying herself. Kade was the first person she had met here who she felt totally comfortable chatting to, as well as being the most gorgeous man. Ever.

'So you came for the Kumbh Mela?'

Brooke nodded.

'It's crazy isn't it? I've never seen so many people.'

Brooke nodded again. It was the largest gathering on Earth and it was all about water. Yet, at this moment, Kade interested her more than a million water myths and the whole Kumbh Mela.

They ate in comfortable silence for a few minutes.

'Did you know that in the seventies the beggars here went on strike?' asked Brooke. She'd heard it on a bus.

He laughed. 'No! How can beggars go on strike?'

'It's true. They weren't being given enough money so they refused to take any. The other Indians were worried about jeopardising their reincarnation chances and upped their alms.' Kade's laughter tickled her spine.

The waiter came and took the plates and they each ordered a chai.

'I must have come to India to meet you,' said Kade.

'You're ... ' said Brooke, thrown by his sudden seriousness, 'really lovely.'

'*You're* really lovely,' said Kade, blushing.

The chai arrived, hot and flavoured with cardamom and rosewater.

That evening they returned to the waterfall, carrying bedding. The stars drew their attention, filling any immediate need for words. They watched the big star systems, the planets and the satellites, those fast-moving bright-twinkling man-made stars. They saw the lights of planes flying far overhead. Kade put his arms around Brooke.

'There's Aquarius,' said Brooke.

'There's Mars,' said Kade, 'glowing red.'

'And there are the stars that live in the trees,' said Brooke, pointing out the fireflies. There were two or three in each tree, doing effective impressions of the stars on the horizon.

The air hummed with the songs of frogs. Bats flew above. Brooke and Kade stargazed and pretended that they held each other for warmth, even though the night was sultry. As the moon rose they hung Brooke's mosquito net from a branch and gathered a mattress of ferns. Brooke unzipped their sleeping bags and then zipped them together, making one double. They were glad the zips were compatible. They got in, and cuddled up, each comfortable.

'I feel calm with you Brooke,' whispered Kade. 'You're funny, you're beautiful. I want to learn much more about you.' Then he kissed her.

# Story

The Taste of the kiss still filled his soul as he opened his eyes. The morning was misty but Brooke's skin was scented with sun. 'Will you tell me a story?' he asked, once he knew she was awake.

'Once upon a time there were three bears ... ?'

'Nae. A water story.'

'Once upon a time there was a little hydrogen molecule called Kade and he was all alone. He was floating through the forest and met an oxygen molecule called Sarah Brooke and they lived happily ever after?'

Kade smiled and kissed her neck. 'I suppose I meant a water *myth.*'

'Okay. Floods. *All* societies have flood myths. The Jews made an Ark. The Nordics hid up Yggdrasil, the tallest tree in the world. The Mayans hid in caves. It's as if the world's waters broke, ushering in a new age. People had to innovate big-time. They had to think about what they ate, how it grew, for the first time.'

'That sounds more like fact than any myth,' said Kade, slipping his arm around her waist. Very tentatively he asked 'Do you know anything about people breathing water?'

'Babylon,' said Brooke.

'Is it a story about the police?' Babylon was standard slang for police at the Sight.

'No silly. Babylon the place – not the Rastafarian take on it. Anyway, Babylon, as lovely as its name sounds, was a bad place. The people had lost their way. Then one day, out of the Eritrean Sea ... '

'How do you know how to pronounce these words Brooke?'

'Talent. And a memory as deep as the ocean. Careful what you say to me Kade, because I am a woman and women remember everything their lovers ever utter.' She paused, and smiled. 'But I won't throw it all back in your face if we have an argument.'

'Good. Go on.' She called me her lover!

'Then one day, out of the Eritrean sea came a character called Oannes'

'Why are these myth characters never called John?'

'Well, there is one called John, as in *the Baptist*, He's in the Bible. Anyway, be quiet if you want to hear this story.'

'Okay.'

'Oannes could breathe water *and* air. He emerged from the sea and he taught people all sorts of things. He had the body of a fish *and* the body of a human. A fish's tail and human feet.' Under the covers Brooke stroked the sole of her foot against the length of Kade's calf, and down to his toes.

'He taught people how to plant seeds. Did you know, by the way, that each plant is ruled by a star system and if you plant them at the right time their survival rate is ninety-eight percent and if you don't it's fourteen percent?'

'Where did you learn that?'

'I don't know. I just know it. Why can't you just believe me?' she said, pretending to be annoyed. Kade stayed quiet.

'Oannes taught the people about reading and writing. That must have blown their minds. I wonder how *differently* people think if their brains aren't filled up with reading and writing. I mean, the Incas didn't have a written language and they ruled an empire as big as the Roman, but I can't imagine what it would be like not to have the symbolism of written words.'

Brooke was babbling. It made him feel warm towards her, and he could picture her as she must have been as a little girl – sweet, talkative. 'Maybe you *can't* imagine what it would be like *because* you are from a literate society.'

'Could be.' She kissed him on the cheek and continued. 'Anyway, Oannes also taught the Babylonians – that word feels lovely on my tongue – the Babylonians how to build great buildings. He taught them geometry. And their land became great. Then Oannes disappeared into the water again. Amphibious, you see.'

Brooke stroked Kade's feet again. Inside his rational brain, a deeper more ancient part unfolded, did a little dance across the rest of his mind and then slept again, tired from trying to conjoin his intuitive abilities to his rationality. This Oannes character, who was he? Why did Oannes make him tremble, just a little? He pulled closer to Brooke, closer and closer, until he was fully in contact with her sweet waters of fertility. He made love to her like the tide.

'Who are you?' he said as the final surge flowed from him to her, 'Who are you?'

'I am Sarah Brooke'

'But you are something else too. I'm so lucky I met you.' He kissed her, tasting her happiness.

# A dip

When Brooke and Kade left the waterfall, they followed the water's route to the Ganges, heading for a place where a sacred bathe was taking place. As she breathed the mountain air, Brooke was struck by the contrast between her expectations of India and the realities. The Ganges she knew from films, television, photographs and her own imaginings had low banks laden with clay-coloured houses and temples. The water was dark and languid, heavy with people and row boats. But the Ganges she walked beside flowed fast between steep woods. The water was aquamarine, like Kade's eyes. The soundtrack was not the soaring sitars of her imagination, but birdsong, Indian pop, revving mopeds and the river's rush. The boats were white water rafts.

*This river*, known by the locals not as the Gan-jeez, but the Ganga, was an unexpected river. *This man*, beside her, was an unexpected man, and the enjoyment of being with him gave her a lightness that felt entirely new.

As she walked on towards the sacred bathing area, Brooke's happiness with the present moment grew until it filled her mind, leaving no space for memories, or plans.

Down river the water became darker, wider, smoother, the banks full of families enjoying picnics. A sacred dip was taking place. There were so many people that Brooke could not see where the river met the beach. She smiled. It felt familiar: the Ganga was now a British seaside resort during a heat wave.

One family stood out amongst the noise. They were signing to each other. Brooke watched them talk, their conversation open to all, but a secret. Then Kade did something unexpected: he signed something to the youngest child, a boy of about ten, who was briefly astonished, then signed back to Kade. Brooke did not know what they were signing, but it seemed to be along the lines of many conversations with interested Indians. 'Whereareyoufrom? Whatdoyoudo?' It was beautiful to watch. Clearly they were not speaking quite the same version of sign language, but were getting across what they wanted. She felt left out.

Eventually Kade held his palms together, bowed his head then waved and the family moved on.

'Wow,' said Brooke. 'How come you could talk to them?'

Kade spoke excitedly, 'Well, sign language travels more easily across cultural borders than spoken language. If you get a group of signers together from different countries they'll be able to communicate sooner than if they're speaking English and Japanese and Hindi, or whatever.'

'But how come *you* can sign?'

'Oh, my grandmother, Lila, taught me and my mother.'

'She was deaf?'

'Yeah. Deaf with a capital D. She lived in a community of Deaf people.'

'Wow.'

'It's a whole other language, not a translation of English.' He drew a circle in the air. 'More…conceptual.'

'Did she speak?' Brooke asked.

'She could read but she didn't speak at all. Was never taught. She went into the community when she was a child, before the authorities decided to make deaf people talk. Lived there all her life.' He paused. 'I remember her hands. They were lovely hands. She always wore bright purple nail varnish. Said it was for her older friends whose eyesight wasn't great. If you're deaf and you lose your eyesight you've lost a language too.'

Brooke had never considered that. She'd never thought of sign as being anything but a second-best language. 'Tell me more.'

'Shouting is silent, whispers are visible across crowded rooms, grammar is spatial and time is indicated against an index finger.' He tapped his index finger three times, at the stem, the knuckle and the tip, then smiled. 'Lila and her friends used expressions they had made up when they were children. A secret language.'

'Sounds like a fun place.'

'Yeah. But most people were old, and a bit...'

'Institutionalised?'

'Yeah, and lonely. Their sons and daughters had moved away 'cos they could hear and speak. I mean, my mum was pretty bored growing up there. She left as soon as she could. My granny was sad that the place had driven her away. There was this notice in the kitchen my granny *hated*. 'You don't have to be deaf to live here, but it helps.' As far as she was concerned it wasn't deafness that kept the community together, it was Sign Language, and you didn't have to be deaf to sign. She always said that my mother may not be deaf, but she was Deaf.'

What a story, thought Brooke. Her family seemed boring in comparison. 'Talk to me then,' she said.

He replied with his hands.

It took her a second to get it. 'I really fancy you too,' she said, as she looked into his river eyes. They nearly kissed, but then remembered that kissing in public would invite some disapproving looks.

Gradually the beach came back into focus. The crowd had moved round, and it was clearly time to go in the water. 'Shall we?' asked Kade.

'Yes!'

They allowed their bodies to be pulled into the tide of those bathing for their spiritual health.

Kade looked around, taking in the scene, feeling startlingly happy. He wanted to dance in the water, to dive in deep, even drink the Ganges. He wanted to Taste it.

Kade submerged. The river here, he knew, was clean compared to downstream. Those that bathed here believed that the Ganges cleaned everything. They believed that the river washed away all dirt, but is so holy it remains clean itself. He thought this was misguided, but nonetheless he did dare – he dared to Taste the Ganges.

He nearly opened his lips, and then stopped. If it wasn't right – if he got sick or tasted too much sadness – it would affect him for ages, and could ruin everything. And *everything* was a lot of fun.

# Save

A fortnight later, Brooke and Kade sat high on the boulders of the beach, just outside the Full Moon Café, which had been rebuilt after the fire exactly the same way as before. They drank lime sodas, and chatted about other places in India.

'What about Goa, or Kerala?' asked Brooke.

'You know, I don't really want to go to the sea,' said Kade. 'Too salty.' He looked down the beach, where an Indian man and his son, aged about twelve, were playing with a camera. In the black water nearby a woman – the wife and mother – waded out fully dressed as the women did here. The wife turned and smiled at her family, but they were concentrating on the camera. A moment later, the wife called out, but the rush of the water and the bells from the temple blocked her sound. The wife called again, struggling to stand.

'Jesus!' said Brooke. Before he knew it, Brooke had leapt down from the rock and run barefoot down the beach. Her lime soda bottle lay smashed between the boulders. Kade watched, heart pounding but the rest of him motionless as Brooke scanned the water. The river ran faster as it neared the centre. The woman had been spun into a deeper faster pull. Her head submerged then her face appeared, searching for air, finding panic. Brooke dived in. The woman went under again. Kade's own breath pulled into him painfully, as though he were breathing for two. His hands formed fists. The water was smooth and unhurried. Brooke swam hard and grabbed the woman, snatching her from the desires of the river's centre. The woman's hands gripped Brooke, sharing humanity's will to live. Kade breathed out. Then the woman's grip weakened. Her face was ashen. Brooke hauled her onto the beach and thumped her chest through her pink and gold sari until a rush of water spread onto the silver sand and sunk out of view.

The father and son put their arms around the woman, then the husband, with tears in his eyes, gave his wife a life affirming kiss on her lips. With that Kade got the feeling back in his body.

'I love you,' he said to Brooke, though she was out of earshot. He jumped from the rock and ran to her, wrapping his arms around her panting body. Brooke blinked the water from her eyes, looked up at him, and he lost his words.

The family thanked Brooke and told her there would always be a place for her if she chose to come to Ontario, and they invited her for dinner at their hotel. 'Thank you,' Brooke said. 'But I feel exhausted.' She nodded to the woman. 'And I'm pretty sure you need to sleep rather than socialise.' The family agreed.

Kade, stunned into silence by seeing Brooke rescue the woman, could only think of love.

'And I just want to be with you,' whispered Brooke as they made their way to the guest house.

# Flying

The café had the sharp scent of lemon and ginger and was, unusually, without music. Brooke savoured the sun's warmth on her feet. Kade gave her a slow sexy smile and squeezed her thigh. Today was their one month anniversary and after a celebratory morning in bed they were breakfasting on yak cheese sandwiches in an open sided café, with an entertaining view along the suspension bridge.

Tourists milled across. A portly man and wife, him in a white shirt, her in a green sari, were peeling oranges to give to their children. On the safety rail above crouched a family of monkeys. The woman bent to pass an orange to her toddling daughter, but in a clatter of railings one of the monkeys dived down and stole it. With professional precision the monkey was back on top of the railings within seconds, eating the orange at high speed, unmoved by the child's tears. Brooke and Kade giggled at the monkey's audacity. They liked to observe things together. They had seen the mugging-primates in action before.

'That'll stick in that kid's mind for sure,' said Brooke. 'Do you remember much from when you were tiny?'

Kade shrugged. Brooke switched to a French-Russian psychiatrist accent. 'Vot iz yourr eaarliest mem-mory Kade?'

A thought traced a smile onto his face. 'Water. Something to do with water.'

'Uh-huh?'

'Ice. I remember being given an ice cube to suck by my mum. I didn't like it. I threw it away. Bad Ice, I said and threw it on the floor. It smashed.'

The woman in the green sari soothed her daughter.

'What about you Brooke?'

Brooke hesitated, and then said, 'I remember flying.'

'Where were you going?'

'Down the stairs.'

'Oh, I thought you meant on a plane.'

'No. I used to fly downstairs,' said Brooke, frowning to herself.

'Maybe you just slid down the banisters so fast it felt like flying.'

Brooke smiled. 'No I really think I flew.'

'But you can't have done Brooke.'

Brooke's smile erased itself. She had never mentioned that memory to anyone. In a voice half-insistent, half-faltering she said, 'One day, when I was about three I was standing at the top of the stairs. It was the straight wooden staircase in my first house. It was very yellow. A ray of sunlight lit the stairs. The dark wood banister was gleaming. Suddenly I was inside the sunbeam, then at the bottom of the stairs. I didn't touch the banister or the stairs.'

'Brooke, you might be a bit of an angel, but you haven't got any wings. You must have been pretending.'

'Well, I *do* remember it,' said Brooke, crossing her arms, not appreciating his back-handed compliment, feeling like the toddler who had been mugged by the monkey. She had only just revealed this memory, and already it was being doubted, taken away. She had not expected that of Kade.

The thing was she was not sure if it was true. Did she remember a real event, or did she just remember imagining it so vividly that it felt real? Anyway, Kade could *act* as though he believed her. That would be more fun than cynicism.

'What was so memorably bad about your ice then?' asked Brooke.

'It tasted sad.'

'How can ice taste sad?'

'It just did.'

'Oh come on, you must have just imagined it,' said Brooke in revenge, but not in jest. 'How could ice ever taste sad?'

Kade shrugged his shoulders.

Brooke wanted to challenge him further, but she let it lie. Children do say funny things, like 'bad ice,' or 'naughty chair for hitting me.' She remembered saying 'the snow tastes happy,' one Christmas and everyone had laughed.

As the mother on the bridge compensated her toddler with sweets, Brooke tried to work out a scientific explanation for a child flying. The best she could think of was 'Why not?' The world was so unbelievable anyway, with satellites and planes and computers and dreams and strange animals, why couldn't children fly sometimes? Especially if they had not yet been told they could not. 'Look Kade, I think I'll go and do a bit of shopping,' she said, and left.

'What the hell was I doing?' Kade thought, loudly. Who the hell was that guy in the café who dismissed Brooke's first memory as being impossible? Just the kind of person who has pissed me off all my life.

After having a go at himself for a while, the realisation of how much he had to lose came into focus. Everything rested on the way he revealed his secrets. He had to reveal them, and soon, or it would be too late: Brooke would never really know him and so never really love *him*.

It was all making him increasingly nervous around her. He missed Stirling and *really* missed his mother. He wanted to still his whirring thoughts. Just a chat with someone who knew him would do.

There was a way to have a conversation, of sorts. He popped back to the guest house, took a bottle from his rucksack, and returned to the Ganges.

Three elderly Sadhus were playing percussion on the beach. Kade was used to seeing these guys now, with their dreadlocks and slim bodies covered in ashes. He loved the way each of them carried a trident, just like Neptune. To the music of these old men, he gathered some water in the bottle, and sealed it with candle wax. Ganges water for Stirling.

Kade had met Stirling just before he'd left for India. A week after his mother's wake, just after he'd been given the unwanted wetsuit, Kade had stood on the flagstones of the Sight's courtyard. A huge noise began to ricochet between the clouds and the loch, and Kade had looked up to see a man skilfully riding a large white motorbike down the steep track.

The biker reached the courtyard and drew to a halt as though landing. With a solid leather-clad stride, he stepped onto the flagstones. His biker-suit had little devil-like faces on the knees. His helmet was black.

Excitement took the edge off fear. Many visitors to the Sight were sort of beginner-hippies, into the kind of talk Kade had heard since he was in his cradle: astrology, crystals, gentle things. This man looked better-defined, *more of a man*, than the others he knew. It was not just the clothes and motorbike, it was the confident energy that pressed forward as he approached, visor down.

Kade imagined a friendly smile and a haircut smarter than anyone else's at the Sight. He imagined this man to be the kind of boyfriend he might have wanted for his mother, if she'd had to have one. But it was too late for that.

Gloved hands reached up and undid the chinstrap. Carefully, the man lifted the helmet. Dark-brown skin appeared. A black man? Kade had not expected that. As the helmet continued to lift he saw lines on each cheek. Scars from an accident? From torture?

No. They were tribal scars. He had seen something similar in a book. Then came the man's eyes, large and interesting, and his brow, with four deep lines, this time given by age, not a blade. Finally came a shaven head and the man was out.

'Hello,' he said, in a voice that rolled over the hills and into the valley. He removed his gloves and held out his hand, 'I'm Stirling.'

Kade looked through his dark fringe at Stirling, hesitating at the way the name didn't quite fit the face.

'My mother found a British coin when she was pregnant, apparently,' said Stirling, winking, and they shook hands.

'I'm Kade,' said Kade, mesmerized at the blueness of his own veins. When he looked up, Stirling's expression was expectant. 'Oh. Right. Yeah. Means something to do with dwelling near the marshes I think.'

'Pleased to meet you Kade. So who do I see about somewhere to sleep?'

'That'll be Ursula.'

Kade showed Stirling in, proud to be able to introduce such a visitor. The table was strewn with forlorn birthday party remains: chocolate cake crumbs, streamers, and half drunk wine. Two people also remained: Ursula, the Sight's owner, sat with an old friend from Kittim. They did not look up. Kade felt embarrassed about the mess.

'This is Stirling,' he announced, as though he had known Stirling for years.

Ursula turned her head slowly, then stood up quickly. She was usually too stoned to move so fast. 'Hi,' she said, her voice a touch huskier than usual.

'Stirling is looking to stay,' said Kade.

'I don't mind camping,' said Stirling. Kade and Ursula double took. It was January.

'He can stay in the yurt with me.' Kade turned to Stirling, 'There's a fire and sheepskins.'

Stirling smiled. 'I'd be honoured.'


Kade was happy to have a guest. In the yurt he lit a fire, slow burning and sweet scented, using wood from a rosebush that had recently died. He tended the flames until the yurt's rounded walls glowed. There was something about Stirling's openness that put him at ease, though he knew that such forwardness may have made others uncomfortable.

'I'm from Namibia,' said Stirling, settling back and answering unasked questions. 'A country of sand dunes and coast. They call it the skeleton coast. My Dad was a consul to Britain and I lived in London from age ten. When I came to

England I was amazed to see how much water fell from the sky. In Namibia, some people – many people – have to walk for hours to collect water.'

Kade pictured Namibia, a place where he would not be able to pick and choose the water he drank. He imagined all the water there to taste happy, because people were so grateful for it.

Stirling continued, 'My parents wanted me to be a doctor or a diplomat, but after eight years in London I just wanted to be a normal English kid, so I went travelling, looking for a vocation. It was in Bangkok that my career started.'

'What do you do?'

'I'm a water dealer.'

This conjured up images of someone saying, 'I can fix you up with six quarter pints, a couple of drops, and a litre for the weekend. But nothing on tick.'

'Mineral Water?' Kade asked.

'No. My water's not for drinking in particular. It's just for. . . *having*. I sell it in terracotta pots and the punters do what they like with it. Some put fish in it, and the richest clients bathe in it. I've got one guy who orders a bath full every week and I'll have no idea what water he'll want. Gets a kick out of washing in Polar one week and Amazonian the next. He really wants some deep-sea water, but it's impossible to bring to the surface. The pressure explodes the container, you see.'

'So you pick water up in one place and sell it in others?'

'Zactly.' Stirling rummaged in his bag. 'Here.' He passed over a leaflet. '*Water of Life,*' it was titled. '*Let secret knowledge from other lands heal you.*' It told how buying '*Water from Caribbean Waves*' can make your living room feel sunnier, and how '*Exclusive Water from Alpine lakes*' is imbued with '*herbal wisdom*' and '*may contain attractive and authentic pieces of fern and peat.*' Stirling could get you water from the place you were brought up: '*The Sacred waters of the Ganges*' or '*Genuine Manchester canal water.*'

'I might live long enough to do water from the moon. Or even to bring moon-dwellers water from Earth,' said Stirling, and laughed.

'How did you get into such an unusual line of business?'

Stirling sat back into the sheepskins. 'Basically, well, like I said, I'd travelled to Bangkok and seen the oxygen bars. People paying for air! And I'd noticed the little ornamental fountains in the hotels and I'd watched as mineral water appeared in shops all over the world. Meanwhile, I found time to be a struggling actor and made some seriously affluent friends.' He raised an eyebrow. 'And I saw all the crap people buy. Gold balls that tinkle when you shake them. Inside, assure the makers, is a diamond.' Stirling mimed shaking a little gold ball, listening and looking satisfied. Then he threw his hands into the air in exasperation. 'Little tanks of blue oil and water that sway in the corner of offices, for no apparent reason! And crap little pieces of shipwreck, worthless, except for the story attached.'

He leaned towards Kade, 'People don't pay for anything real, Kade. They pay for the ideas they can attach to things. It was the shipwrecks that got me – inspired my business. 'With all this environmental stuff going on,' I thought, 'why bother with the artefact? Sell them the water straight.' Beef it up with tales of local scenery. Marry it with a bunch of people trying for the cleanest way to feel good they can find that week, and make a *lot* of money. Better than dealing coke.'

'Yeah,' said Kade, lost for words.

It was surreal, but it certainly made sense. Perhaps normal people could feel something from water, even if it was not as powerful as the Tasting. 'What are you doing *here*?' he finally asked Stirling, who smiled mischievously.

'I do *believe* in what I'm doing you know. I believe water from different places has a different feeling to it. That well by the courtyard, I read about it in this book. Here.' Stirling had passed him an old red leather bound volume with '*Springs of Scotland*' embossed in gold on the spine. Kade turned to the page bookmarked with a crow feather. There was a medieval-looking etching of the well outside the lodge. '*The sacred well at Tayside is renowned far and wide for fine flavoured invigorating water.*'

Kade sat forward. 'Are you here on business? I don't think we would want to sell the well water.'

'No. Not business. I'm here on a personal project. Some fun. I'm making a collection – just one bottle's worth altogether – of waters from sacred places all over the world.'

'Can I see?' asked Kade, extremely intrigued. Could he Taste?

'Sorry. I've just recently had the idea. This is where I'm beginning.'

That night Kade slept with a smile on his face. He had not asked Stirling why he was making such a collection, or what he would do with it when it was completed. He just liked the idea, and felt he had met a kindred spirit – a travelling salesman water-dealing African biker friend.

Early the next morning, Kade had left Stirling snoring and climbed up the river rocks to the willow pool, to sit on its tree-sized island where the winter was quieter, stiller and warmer. Parts of the waterfall were frozen, forming glittering miniature caves. Deep inside the pool, was the one true cave, its entrance invisible.

After a while listening to the rushing water, Kade heard leisurely humming. Stirling appeared and strode over the stepping-stones to the island. He smiled and, using his hand as a cup, drank a few sips of water from the pool, then clapped his palms together, said, 'Right. That's enough water in me. Now for me in the water.' Shedding his clothes he jumped into the pool.

Kade laughed.

Stirling grinned. Treading water he yelled, 'Feeling invigorated by proxy eh? That's the first time I've seen you really smile. It might never happen, you know…'

Kade's smile left.

'I'm sorry,' said Stirling. 'Must keep my mouth shut sometimes.' He climbed out of the pool, dried himself with his shirt, put his clothes on and joined Kade under the willow. 'Something already *has* happened, hasn't it?'

'My mother d...well, I don't know if she's dead. She disappeared last August. We were diving in ... ' He hesitated. He *wanted* to tell Stirling everything, 'We were diving in the loch.'

'I see.'

'They never found her.'

'What about you? Were you hurt?'

'No I was fine.'

'Was she a good mother?'

'Yes.' Kade nodded, assuring himself. 'But she left a lot of questions.'

'And you want some answers,' said Stirling. 'I went seeking answers once. You know last night I told you I went travelling?' Kade nodded. 'It was just after my mother died. She'd been sick for a long time. Blamed it on living in a damp country. After she was gone I went off on my own. Couldn't stand to be in the place where she'd died. Have you thought of going away?'

Kade smiled. 'Aye, actually. I'm off in a couple of days. To India.'

'Perfect. A hot place. You can dry out those tears.'

Kade looked down, made shy by Stirling's interest in his life and his grief. But anticipation was building. His trip to India made him more excited than his mother's promise to take him cave-diving.

'Have you been before?' asked Stirling.

'No. I nearly went with my mum when I was a kid. I got stabbed in the leg with a compass at school. It got infected.' Kade stopped abruptly.

'So the trip was cancelled?'

'Yeah.'

But the stabbing was the reason they were *going* to India, not what had stopped them. The school took him for some blood tests without parental consent. His mum was all ready to go, even got him a passport, but nothing came of it. Perhaps the tests were normal.

'You'll have a great time.' Stirling clapped him on the back.

'I hope so. There's a Kumbh Mela there at the moment. A big celebration on the banks of the Ganges. I'm headed there. I can't wait.'

'The Kumbh Mela! Of course! While you are there, do you think you could do me a favour? I wanted to go, but it clashes with a bike race,' said Stirling.

Kade smiled slowly as he realised what the favour must be. 'Yes.'

Stirling smiled, shaking with cold. 'Thanks.'

Now, crouching by the Ganges, Kade held the bottle close. How would Brooke react if he told her *everything?* If he wanted her to really know him, he would have to.

When he returned to the room he found Brooke in bed. Lying down beside her he whispered, 'Not just anybody can fly you know.'

# Neptune

Ambiguity bothered Brooke. Anthropology lecturers had told her that myths were created to make ambiguity digestible, but this was no help as she woke from shaky sleep with a pebble of tension in her stomach. 'Not just anybody can fly,' could equally mean Kade did believe her, or did not. She was not sure that she believed *herself.* She could feel misunderstanding snarling at the edges of her life with Kade.

She wanted to chase away the ambiguity, but knew that putting Kade on the spot brought the threat of tangled conversation. Instead she got bossy. 'We're going into town today.'

Outside on the sunny street she felt better.

'So shall we fly or take a rickshaw?' asked Kade, and a smile broke out onto her face. She put her arm out to hail a driver.

They travelled along the side of the Ganga, past the yoga temples and restaurants, past the fields and woods, to the city, the thousands of canvas tents, the temporary homes of millions of pilgrims, cooking, cleaning, bathing, laughing, eating, smoking, preening and praying. 'Wow, an in-tents-city,' whispered Kade.

There were eight people in a rickshaw designed for four. Brooke was on Kade's lap, feeling his gentle arms round her waist and something slightly firmer pressing against her bottom. Physicality felt good, tangible. Opposite them a young Indian mother sat similarly on her husband – transport being a rare chance for public touching. Their four children, all boys, filled the other seats and spilled out onto the floor of the tiny vehicle.

The wife was practising her English. 'What is your country?' she asked Brooke.

'England. London,' said Brooke. 'Well, near Watford.'

'England,' said the wife. 'India is very crowded country compared. No?'

Brooke wished she had a photo of a rush-hour tube to show the woman.

'And is your father a businessman or a serviceman?'

'Um,' thought Brooke. 'A businessman.'

The husband began to address Kade. 'And you are also from England, London?'

'No. I'm from Neptune.'

'Ah, Neptune. My cousin has a shop in Neptune.' The man smiled. Two bullshitters, thought Brooke, laughing quietly.

The man continued, 'And is your father a b…'

'My father is a fisherman.'

A *fisherman*, thought Brooke. She never would have guessed. She had never even asked. Kade and she had missed out asking those kinds of questions early on and now, somehow, it seemed inappropriate, like asking someone you have known for weeks to remind you of their name.

'Are you married?' the wife asked, pointing at each of them.

'Yes,' said Kade.

'No,' said Brooke, and they all laughed, except the children who were entranced by the herd of water buffalo outside.

# Who what when where

When they left the rickshaw, Kade and Brooke ordered some cardamom milk at a little shack café. The heat had risen. The breeze carried scents towards them. The incense reminded Kade of home, as did the floury heat of chapattis cooking, and the river's magnetic scent.

Outside the café, a father chased his infant son down the street, gathered him up in his arms and kissed him. The boy looked at his father with big eyes outlined in kohl. He sees his father as a hero, thought Kade and wondered how many years it would be before the child was disappointed.

'Is your father really a fisherman?' asked Brooke.

He knew she would bring it up. 'Dunno,' he said, trying to sound casual. 'I never knew him. My mum said he was a lifeboat man. She said he drowned saving someone from drowning.'

'You don't sound like you believe her.'

'It doesn't make any difference to me. It was so long ago. It doesn't really matter.' As he spoke, he wondered if that were true. 'I think my mum just wanted a baby, and not a bloke.'

'Oh.'

Kade knew Brooke would start asking him questions about his mother next. He interjected, reluctant to let his past intrude on the sweetness of their relationship, his sadness on her happiness. 'How about *your* parents, Brooke?'

'Dad works in an office and mum helps out part-time at a nursery.'

'Plants or kids?'

'Kids.'

'Any brothers and sisters?'

'Yes. Two sisters. Samantha and Charlotte. I'm in the middle. No brothers. What about you?'

His heart pounded. He would have to let the past in. Until now he had been swimming. Now the water had turned, throwing him hard against the bank, exposing him. But the words flowed easily, as though impatient to be spoken. 'No sisters. No brothers. And I don't have a mother either. Not anymore.'

Even once it was out, the past did not grip him and frighten him. He wasn't back in the caves, nor was he underwater. It was okay to tell Brooke. Relief felt physically good.

'Oh, Kade I'm sorry.'

'She died. In a diving accident.' Then it hit: the feeling of being cheated, the sadness, the *guilt* took hold of his consciousness.

He felt Brooke's hand on his and was startled. He was almost surprised to see her face, so different from his mum's. Her eyes were reddening with tears.

'When?' she asked.

'Last summer.'

The wave pulled out again, ready to smash his mind towards Scotland, to the caves, to the sickening moment when he realised his mother was gone, and the moment he realised he could breathe…

A waiter walked past and Kade lunged for the man's forearm, pulling him towards him, pulling himself back to the café. 'Two coffees please.' The waiter nodded, unperturbed.

Kade looked at Brooke. Despite her slight smile her expression was nervous and sad. She was not asking, but she needed more explanation, so he obliged. 'After my mother dis ... died, I stayed in Scotland, waiting for her. They never found her body. I thought she might come back.' He paused. 'I came here to try and come to terms with it. I don't really want to talk about it. Not right now.'

Brooke wiped her eyes. 'Okay.'

The coffee was bittersweet, a parallel to his feelings.

# Heather and rose

Brooke did not ask more about his past, but Kade felt sure that she would be there for him if he wanted to speak about it, and the gentle way they moved through their days together continued. He felt comfortable, she was kind and intelligent and his last scratches of wariness lost their itch.

One evening, he was lying on the bed wearing only shorts, allowing the ceiling fan to hypnotise him. Then the lights went out and the fan slowed and stopped: a power cut. Both Brooke and Kade breathed out, feeling the quiet and the dark. They lay still for a minute then Brooke got up and produced some candles.

'Scented. From England. I was saving them for a special occasion,' she said. 'But you'll do.'

He smiled.

'This one's vanilla,' she said, from the window. She came closer. 'And rose for by the bed.'

Kade watched as she lit a match. He stood up, kissed her, and went into the bathroom. While peeing he noticed she had put a candle on the cistern. He took out the lighter that he carried (finding 'Yes' a more conversational answer to 'Have you got a light?' than saying 'No I don't smoke,' although he had never smoked in his life). He lit the wick, releasing the scent of heather, and was reminded of Scotland, albeit Scottish gift shops rather than hillsides. He washed his face and ditched his shorts. Caffeine cruised in his veins and he felt very awake. Glancing in the mirror he was taken by how tanned he had become.

Back in the room he surprised himself. 'We are very different you and me,' he found himself saying. 'You have a happy safe normal family and I have a different kind of family. I was brought up on a permanent campsite for people you'd probably call alternative. It's called the Sight.' He explained the wordplay to a wide-eyed Brooke as she sat on the bed. 'I know, pretentious name, huh? Anyway. I went to school there, but the teachers were always changing – coming and going. Most people were. There were a few who stayed for a long time, like the owner, Ursula, and me. Most people my age moved out as soon as they could. But I never wanted to leave the land. And the water...'

Brooke stroked the hem of the white slip she wore. 'Was this in Scotland?'

'Yeah. On a mountainside, by a loch.' He joined Brooke in stroking the hem of her slip, and ran his hands up her thighs. 'There are two rivers. One running down each side of the main field, reaching from the mountaintops to the loch.' Brooke giggled. 'In one there's a waterfall that fills a huge pool and in the middle there's an island where a willow tree grows.' He intertwined his fingers with Brooke's and kissed her neck. 'I want to show you someday.'

There was quiet between them for a while. Perhaps Brooke was contemplating this invitation. She would like it there. She would enjoy the Sight without getting too hooked-in to whatever people were claiming to be the True Way that week.

'We'll camp under the willow, cook fish under the stars, and swim in the bubbling water.'

'Like we do here,' said Brooke. She lay beside him with her index finger by his heart. She parted her lips, ready to be kissed. He kissed her, Tasting her intrigue. Then, gently and quietly, close to her ear, he said, 'In the willow pool there's an underwater tunnel and at the end of the tunnel there are caves.'

Brooke let out a gasp.

'And in the caves,' said Kade.

'In the caves?' asked Brooke.

'Are monsters!' He growled and grabbed her tight. He rolled on top of her and she guided him closer until he found the grip and wetness he desired. He moved inside her, gently holding her wrists to the bed.

Outside the window, the beginnings of a storm prickled the air. Kade turned Brooke onto her hands and knees. Watching her spine undulate expectantly, he moved into her again, deeper this time, stronger and harder. He pressed his palm against the wall as he felt her swell to meet his hardness. The sweat at her nape twinkled dark red in the candlelight. Her body quickened. They moved fast, loud and wet. Kade began to come as he saw the sweat appear on her back like rain, some from inside her, some falling from his brow, then he felt her flicker as the final tides pulled them down onto to the bed sheets.

The first thing Brooke noticed the next morning was Kade's handprint glistening on the wall next to the bed. The air was fresh from the storm rains that had broken as they had fallen asleep. Rose scent lingered from the candle that was now a pile of wax. She was surprised to find Kade still asleep, so in tune had their bodies been the night before. He wore a gentle expression and for a moment she was mesmerised by his long lashes, his dreaming eyes, and his parted lips. Mela. Mela might be a good name for a child. Mela Brooke.

But not a good name for an STD. Brooke's condoms were languishing in her rucksack pocket. 'Condoms don't work in the drawer,' she remembered Samantha saying as she had slipped some into Brooke's hand luggage at the airport. 'We've been good until now, Sam,' whispered Brooke.

Poor little Mela wouldn't have a grandma, or grandpa or any aunts or uncles – not on her dad's side. But they could take her to this Sight place and the willow pool. Was Kade serious about them going there? This was not just a holiday romance, was it?

The rain began again, making Brooke want to pee. As she got up she could feel her moisture from the night before. On trembling legs she walked to the heathery-scented bathroom. She dripped red ... red ... red. Her period. Little Mela was forgotten. She had not had a period until now in India. They could halt due to the sensory culture shock, said the guidebook, so she must be feeling more relaxed now. She cleaned herself and the splashes on the floor. Then she woke Kade and they began again. He did not mind the blood but the sheets were a goner.

# Kuano and crannogs

The days became hotter, and Brooke told Kade stories. She had no secrets herself, and so shared with him the world's secrets, wrapped up in myth. She told him more about Noah's Ark and all the stories where people escape from a great flood by building boats or climbing the tallest mountain or living in the boughs of the tallest tree in the world. She told him stories of the legendary river Sarasvati, who was also the goddess of speech and music, and who flowed from her Himalayan source, a fig tree, carrying gold in her bed, past forests populated by Apsaras – nymphs – but now no longer flowed at all, or else flowed just at the edge of human perception, or had simply become the Ganga.

She told him of the boy lost in infancy to the Kuano River who returned at fifteen with a green tinge to his skin and the ability to fish and dive better than any human, and who reached for fish and frogs and chillies with his mouth. Kade was very interested in that one. She told him how, before the boy was born, a holy man had drowned in a well he had dug to invoke the goddess of the water. The spirit of this man was said to be something to do with the boy's existence, along with his living mother who claims he was conceived – against her will – during a thunderstorm.

Kade told Brooke about the wooded Viking burial ground near the Sight, with autumn beech the colours of Viking hair. He told her about the iron-age Crannogs – round thatched homes built in the shallows of the loch, reached by a little pier – that had been recreated as part of a history project. Crannogs offered protection from insects and invaders, but possibly not watersprites.

Getting involved with the building of the Crannogs must have been fun for him and the other kids of the Sight, thought Brooke: something to do other than hang around. Not that the Sight sounded particularly boring anyway. He had told her about the tree houses there, and the parties that rocked him to sleep as a child, and about chasing chickens, and being chased by kids from the local village.

Fun stories. But there was stuff he was not revealing. When he spoke, his eyes moved as though his mind were navigating an obstacle. She wanted to know. She *really* wanted to know. One morning, as she watched him sleep, the urge to question him became impossible to ignore. She laughed at herself and her desire to know *everything* about him. But was she going to ruin her cool by making that obvious? No. She was going to buy him some food and give him breakfast in bed; a gesture, performed by thousands of men in thousands of movies and even a few in real life, which had always struck her as being a power game. The man was always showered and shaved, in a suit, back to daily life. The woman, with messy sex-goddess hair, naked body entwined in sheets, still in role from a night of lovemaking, was always woken with champagne and kisses before she had even brushed her teeth or had a pee. It seemed unequal.

Unlike such men, her leaving him sleeping was not a power thing. It was a recognition that it was important not to pry, and it might not be wise either. She dressed, whispered, 'once I know, I know,' and left the room.

Kade and she had created a bubble that kept out most of the contemporary world. The bubble was kept taut with myths and legends, themes rendered timeless by their appearance in the lives of people in all time and all places. It was not a mask, talking about such timeless things; it was about simply being together, allowing safety and trust to form. In the bubble Brooke was the messy-haired woman in bed, and Kade was there with her, messy-haired too. Neither had left and returned. Neither had let the outside world in. She really liked it, but now she had noticed the bubble, it had gone.

Everything had become more real. She gritted her teeth, feeling locked into Kade, unable to have thoughts without him in them. The patterns of the moles on his back, three like Orion's belt, the long shape of his fingernails, the backs of his hands, his feet, his voice, his touch: a mythology of his body had imprinted itself on her. She thought of her own mythologies: the colour of her hair, which led her to feel kinship with Ophelia, Boudicca, and even Ginger Rodgers; the way she had taken her surname as her first; the hibiscus. As she walked down the street, Brooke suddenly felt overwhelmed by all the nuances and feelings people secretly carried. Billions of people, each as discrete as snowflakes; no one ever really knowing anyone. She wanted to know what Kade was holding back, but even her own mythologies were too much for her sometimes. Was she ready for someone else's? Perhaps she would not get the breakfast. Perhaps she would have a day by herself.

# Patterns

When Kade woke and Brooke was not there he decided to go out. There was no food in the room and his stomach had got the better of him. He headed for the yak cheese café with the view along the Jhula. If she crossed the bridge he would see her.

Today there was music – loud reggae that amazingly was not Bob Marley, the ever-favourite of cafés trying to attract young western travellers. The café did a fine breakfast that mixed Tibetan, Indian and western food, and was busy. He ordered momos and a mango milkshake. Cows were happier up here in the hills eating grass than those in the backstreet dairies of Delhi where the cows famously feasted on cardboard, producing miserable milk. Enjoying the meal, he wondered if the mangos were from the nearby orchard where he had walked that day, just before he met Brooke, a lifetime ago.

A group of three westerners – two women and a man – came in and sat on the sarong-covered sofa next to him. They were Scandinavian, he thought, but not all from the same country, so were speaking English. One woman was older, and did not have on the usual backpacker gear of flip-flops, toe-rings, mosquito bites, cheap clothing and random bits of coloured string and silver tied on ankle, wrist and neck. She was smart in a safari-skirt and red lipstick kind of way. Her being older and smarter made her stand out, and the younger scruffier two had obviously taken her under their wing. In her hand she held a big glossy book. Lying it on the low table, she began to talk the young couple through its photographs.

Kade could not look away. The book showed close-up photographs of frozen water drops. 'You see,' said the woman, pointing to a picture of water crystals that looked just like flowers, 'this is where he has put homeopathic camomile into the water and look! It looks just like camomile flowers!' She turned to another page. 'Here it's cat's claw, from the Andes. Don't you think this crystal looks like Machu Picchu?' The others nodded, wowing. Kade wondered what Machu Picchu was, and was still struck by the camomile flower picture. He had considered, back in Scotland, whether the Tasting worked anything like homeopathy. The idea that something could be active in water, even if science could not detect it, made sense to him, obviously. But growing up at the Sight, especially under the influence of a particularly sceptical science teacher, made him doubt that homeopathy was anything more than a placebo. Ironic of him to be so sceptical given his abilities, he knew.

The woman realised he was watching but did not seem to mind. 'Here is a comparison between water that has been talked to kindly – people saying Love and Gratitude, and water where people have said, You make me sick I want to kill you.' The difference between the pictures was pronounced: one was a sparkly hexagon that raised his spirits; the other looked like pockmarked metal. On another page was a trio of pictures of a river. *Upstream* was a perfect hexagon, its edges fernlike and soft. By *midstream* the hexagon had disintegrated and seemed unsettlingly like a portrait of an angry moustachioed face. *Downstream* looked arid, like a deep pothole on the surface of Mars. Industry had taken its toll.

There were many photographs, each illustrating that the way water was talked to, and the way it was treated, affected the shape it took when frozen. Water that was not cared for froze in an unformed and often ugly chaotic shape. The most beautiful were the spring waters and those that had been spoken to sweetly, which formed hexagons, with shell-fern edges, soft and definite. How would the water from his well look?

The woman closed the book – *Messages from Water*.

'Pretty cool,' thought Kade, 'Pretty cool ... ' As open-minded as his upbringing was, in some ways it had been sheltered, and he *had* thought that many of the more new-age ideas were not part of the wider world, but – as he had realised since coming to India – they were. And they kept spreading. He got up to leave. On his way past he stopped beside the woman and the couple and said, 'I can Taste all that you know.' The reply was three smiles, free of scepticism, and Kade grinned back, feeling positive.

He left with a bounce in his step. As he walked he saw water everywhere, taking many shapes: water flowed down old walls inside cascades of leaves; as flowers it shot straight up through roadside cracks; it reached skywards in the boughs of trees; more quickly it walked down the street, inside people, supporting every cell. Plant-shaped water. People-shaped water. Enjoyment rippled through Kade's mind like a stone thrown in a lake. What was the Earth but a drop of water rolling through the universe? He walked for hours.

# Secrets

He wanted her to come back.

A gecko walked up the yellow wall. The colour reminded him of the kitchen walls at the Sight.

*Secret,* he thought to himself. Secret. Seekret. Seek-ret. See-krut. Sek-reet. Sounds like secrete. Like sweat evaporates off a guilty person, secrecy pours out of the holder and evaporates into the room, scenting the air with feelings but revealing no facts. He inhaled the aroma of his secrets. I have the means to change the way Brooke looks at the world. The power to rearrange the way she arranges reality.

Brooke wasn't sure. She couldn't tell by touch.

'It is silk,' insisted the salesman, gripping the other corner of the red and gold cloth. He was old, with short features, his nose only just big enough to balance his heavy black specs on.

'I don't know, could be polyester. I don't wear polyester.' She didn't like the oily feeling of synthetics.

'Silk. Silk,' said the man. In a professional-looking gesture he tore a thread from the cloth, produced some matches and lit the end. The thread burned rather than melted and the man had proved that the cloth was, at least, not a hundred percent polyester. She smiled at him and he smiled back, as if to say he forgave her for mistrusting him.

'I'm going to get a tea and think about what I want.'

'But you can have tea here,' said the man. 'No pressure.' He gestured towards two wicker chairs that overlooked the street and the river beyond. 'Sit. Sit.'

Brooke accepted the man's offer. The man called to a boy who he seemed to know, gave him some rupees and said 'Do Chai.' The boy walked away.

'My name is Ashok,' said the man.

'Brooke'

'Pleased to meet you Look. Thank you for visiting my shop.'

'It's ... ' She paused. Ashok raised his eyebrows, waiting. Brooke smiled, ' ... really nice to have a Brooke around.'

As Kade paced, his heavy breaths gradually coated the windows with condensation. The lights outside became gentle blurs of colour, like a harbour from the misty sea. His thoughts rang loud in the quiet room. His instinct was strongly in favour of telling her. This instinct had flowed through him, fuelled him, since he had first seen Brooke, but never so strongly that he had been unable to contain it. He wanted to tell her, but was afraid of her fear and, he admitted to himself, part of him enjoyed having this secret. If he shared it, it would not be his, it would be theirs.

The boy with the rupees bought two glasses of tea from the café across the road. Brooke noticed that he actively ignored the westerners there. The two men, sitting on chairs, both wore wooden beads, short dreadlocks and pseudo-wise expressions that forced their puppy fat in new directions. Three girls sat quietly on cushions, seeming obedient, as though the men were their gurus. Brooke had thought they were actually pretty cool, until one man clicked his fingers above his head to call the waiter. That click dissolved the scene, and any depth dropped away, revealing smugness and shallowness.

Kade was different, she told herself. Did have something real. Wasn't just pretending at depth and feeding her false hints to keep her interested. She was not certain she wanted to know his secrets, but she liked that he had shown her he had them.

As dusk dappled the room, Brooke's red notebook shone up from the bedspread. Kade flicked on the light.

Brooke had not hidden the book, so it could not be very private. Had she left it there to entice him into reading it? He fanned the pages with his thumb, enjoying Brooke's handwriting, big and expansive at the beginning of the book, but becoming smaller and more precise the longer she'd been abroad, as though she realised that the fewer books she filled the less she would have to carry.

The boy delivered the tea. Brooke knew accepting it meant she was obliged to buy something but she did not mind. No need for salesman-style chit-chat now. This was a good place to sit and think.

Dusk brought a coolness that made her feel at home. Night would come, she would buy something from this shop, and she was on a path with Kade that she could not get off. Warning signals burned dimly somewhere in the distance of her mind but Brooke was too consumed to heed them. Perhaps it was being far from friends, or perhaps it was the headiness of India, but any doubts about Kade were washed away before Brooke's consciousness could address them.

Kade felt as though he were reading a secret code.

*Only by encapsulating a multiplicity of subjectivities can we arrive at anything resembling objectivity.*

This was English, but not a way of using words that he could easily understand.

*The near-universality of flood myths implies that a truth became myth in order to travel through time, space and culture.*

What?

*Myth as effective a method as DNA at passing information from generation to generation.*

He chewed his nails.


Ashok gestured towards the teashop. 'Sadhus. Very interesting to foreigners.' Three Sadhus sat under a tree by a small fire. Her eyesight was not perfect and it was now dark. She struggled to focus on the shine of their tridents, and on the matt ash that covered their bodies. One lifted a white bowl to his lips. As her eyes finally focused, Brooke felt a wave of disbelief. He was drinking from a section of human skull.

She wasn't repulsed, but it was an extremely odd thing to see.

Ashok noticed her change of demeanour. 'He is an Aghori Baba. Exception that proves the rule, as you say. For initiation they find one human skull and cut.' He brought the flats of his hands to the side of his own skull. 'And use to drink and eat from. Sometimes they go to a funeral pyre and take a piece of flesh and eat. Most people are frightened of them. People think they make curses.'

Brooke's mind gripped this new information and squeezed. Ashok was suddenly more than a cloth salesman.

'You are afraid also?' he asked, with a head wobble.

'Only a little,' she replied, with a wave of her hand as if warding her fear away.

She bought the cloth, and walked home reminded of the world of myth and symbolism she had wanted to immerse herself in.


There were pages and pages of words that would not go into his head.

*Myth inhabits the boundary between fact and fiction.*

A picture of a mermaid caught his attention. It was heavily drawn, as though Brooke had traced it over and over, deep in thought.

*Mermaids are boundary-blurring creatures, inhabiting the in-between places – the beaches, reefs and rocks, from where they tempt sailors across the boundary from life to death. The mermaid's mammalian beginnings and Piscean endings challenge traditional boundaries between species, yet the mermaid's status as mythical creature informs and confirms those same boundaries.*

He closed the book. Brooke explained things so differently to the way he did, explained so much *more*. They just did not teach you to write like that on a rainbow painted bus in a car park near a loch. For the first time in his life, he wished that he'd studied harder, gone to university.

At the sound of footsteps he dropped the book onto the bed. Brooke opened the door, flushed and excited, the whirring of cicadas singing her in. Onto the covers she unrolled two swathes of sari cloth, dusty red and pale blue-green. A land infused with a river.

'Aren't they beautiful?' she said, as though she and he had created the fabric together.

He could not tell her yet. He wanted to know more of her first, before things changed. Since opening her book his desire to tell her had waned, but his anger waxed and he did not know why.

# Fireflies

The next afternoon, after a morning of chatting about Bollywood, how great jam and peanut butter chapatti sandwiches were, and how they preferred swimming to yoga, Kade sat beside Brooke on a verge of grass by a wide dusty path that looked like turmeric.

Hundreds of people moved past, walking into town to cleanse themselves in the Ganges. The song 'Take me to the river' played in Kade's head. The café speakers, meanwhile, gave out the sound of high pitched female singing, and the hills echoed with the enthusiasm of unpolished brass bands. Across the street, green pastures rose into brown crags. In one peak nestled a temple, which would have been perfectly camouflaged if it, and the whole crag top, had not been painted pistachio green. The same colour was embedded in saris, hats, and mopeds, lending an ice-cream freshness to the scene.

'Why are you in India?' Brooke asked suddenly. 'I know you are, kind of, trying to leave bad memories behind. But why are you *here*?'

Dozens more people passed the café. Mothers and fathers and children and holy men walking to the river.

'I'm on the run, kid,' he joked in a gangsterish tone. 'This is the safest place to stay off the grid.'

'Off the grid?'

'I just wanted to get out,' he said, consciously uncrossing his legs as he realised how tightly they had been crossed. 'I didn't like having my name and my photo on all those different things. I felt they were trying to pin me down. I wasn't sure of their motives, and I was – I am – young enough to slip through the net.'

'Isn't that just paranoia?'

'Maybe a bit, but it's more something I just wanted to do. It felt right to do.' And mum always wanted to come here, he thought of saying, but kept quiet, unwilling to provoke a flurry of questions. Not here, or now. He did not want to talk about her.

Brooke thought 'That's not all, is it Kade?'

The secrecy was beginning to really bother her, but she didn't say anything. She just stared at his hair, highlighted reddish in the sun, and his earnest handsome face. He turned away.

She began to take an interest in her water bottle, which featured a cartoon maiden collecting water from a stream.

'So you didn't come for the Kumbh Mela then?' she asked, finally.

'Yes, I did,' he said loudly, without turning to her. 'And that's what I want to do. Be here. Not chat with tourists about the same old shit all the time.'

'What!' thought Brooke, gripped by the desire to throw her drink in his face and shout at him. Why did he have to be so defensive and plain bloody rude? But she did the elegant thing and simply walked off quietly to join the crowd going to the river. To try and wash away her anger she would immerse herself in the jubilation.

Kade only realised Brooke had gone when he turned to her to point out a girl in the crowd who looked just like her. But there's no girl like Brooke, he thought, and then winced at the corniness. What do you do when your girlfriend walks off? He didn't know. But he would be a gentleman about it, reasoning that Brooke would be in a vulnerable state and this was a foreign country and he should tail her to make sure she was all right. He lost her immediately. The crowd had thickened, wanting to be at the water for the next ritual bathe, and Brooke was hard to spot in her headscarf and local colours.

Brooke walked down the street for a mile, the recipient of concerned looks. People seemed worried that someone would be unhappy at their happy gathering, but no one hassled her, and she was given some food that someone had made specifically to give away to strangers. Gradually her anxiety lessened.

The day cooled and Brooke began to remember who she was without Kade. How come her whole life was taken up with him? She barely knew him. They had met in February and it was only April. The serious way she had been taking things suddenly struck her as silly. Her anger and frustration dissipated into the atmosphere. Stopping, she watched the holy men, offering healing and knowledge, and the middle-class mothers, buying ice cream for their children.

Perhaps Kade's secret was that he had no secret! Like a coming-of-age ritual where the deep secret that the adults have been keeping is that *there is no deep secret.*

No. He *did* have a secret and he *was* going to tell her, but he and she were acting out this whole play for each other. It was a complicated exchange. They had spent weeks avoiding stepping on each other's toes. Tiptoeing round the secret.

'Ice Kreeeem. Ice Kreeeem,' said a man passing by with an ice-cream cart. 'Cheapest and Best.' Brooke bought one and agreed that they were indeed the cheapest and best. She ate it at the side of the street, opposite something that called itself an ashram, but was more like a cross between a Disney cartoon, a fairground ride and a casino. A huge blue Shiva towered over one side of the entrance and a huge Hanuman, the monkey god, empowered the other. The fibreglass interior of the building gave the impression of a cave. It seemed to be for kids, a kind of starter-ashram. When she finished her ice-cream, Brooke crossed the street, paused between the gods and went inside. Dotted around the faux cave were shrines and waterfalls. Despite its artificiality it was as enchanting to her as it was to the dozens of children there. When she left it was dusk.

Behind the ashram was a busy path through some greenery. She walked over, entranced by the fireflies that lit the bushes like glowing berries. She sat, for quite a while, by the gnarled trunk of a small but ancient tree.

Eventually Kade saw her in the field, under a knotted and twisted tree that looked as though it had grown out of a fairy tale. As soon as he saw her, he knew he would tell her that evening. He watched her from behind rusted barbed wire for a moment, before walking up the path lit by moonbeams and firefly light.

'Brooke?' he asked. He was about to add 'are you alright?' when Brooke smiled and walked towards him, a firefly on her outstretched palm. The words spun round in his head. 'What if I tell her, what if I tell her, what if I tell her?' His heart joined in: 'Tell her, tell her. Tell her?' He felt serious, sincere and confused, aware he had consciously decided to tell her, but also aware that she was enticing it out of him.

She was looking at the insect with wonder. 'It's amazing isn't it?' She moved closer to Kade so the firefly was between their chests. 'You know, I don't even care how it glows. It's just that it does glow that's important.'

Pleased about the firefly, she was wanting to share it, wanting someone else to enjoy it as much as she, realising the situation was magical. She was being only Brooke and not all the pieces of others' personalities that people pick up on the social path and confuse for their own. Things people say when they are off guard; nagging and shouting and bitching; things discarded for a good reason; things that should have been disposed of properly. It seemed she had disposed of them all. She was unguarded and still none of them came out, because none of them were there. Only her, him and the fireflies.

He liked her happy. If he was going to tell her, he was going to make it fun. He felt like he was on the edge of an Olympic diving board. And then he dived.

'I have special powers,' he declared, and then his heart sank. What a stupid opening. The whole Mela was full of people with special powers, or claiming to have special powers. Special powers might have sounded exotic in some places, but at a Kumbh Mela they were ten-a-penny. Kade had an image of

71

himself as a superhero, in a tight nylon suit. 'The Water-Taster' uttered the gravelly voice-over introducing the superhero into the cartoon.

But while this stream of bright images hurtled by, Kade was sailing on calm waters. He had decided. He was going to tell her. She could make of it what she would. The difference between Brooke and everybody else was that Kade was interested to see what Brooke would make of it.

'Special Powers huh?' Brooke smiled. 'And you think the authorities might be after you? We better go and hide under the bed sheets then.' She carefully replaced the firefly on the tree and pulled Kade close. Then she ran and he followed. They ran through the warm evening, through the camps, past white canvas tents lit by supper fires, through storms of incense, past Sadhus with dreadlocks to their knees, past an astonished film crew, past trees and banners and temples. They emerged by the guest house, panting.

# The Tasting

They burst into their room with their arms around each other. Brooke felt great. Really exhilarated.

'I can taste emotions in water,' said Kade, loudly and seriously.

Silence filled the room. Kade's statement hung in the middle. Brooke felt dizzy. She pulled away from Kade. 'Wha ... ?' she said, and lowered herself to the bed. She focussed on the floor, trying to catch her breath. Her skin prickled. She was hyper-aware of how little she knew about Kade. He was unworldly, vulnerable even. Had India, she, and all the water myths been too much for him, made him imagine crazy things? If only she could concertina time, suspend it, so she could figure out the best way to react.

'You're joking,' she said eventually, and slowly looked up, wanting him to be smiling and say 'Yeah, course I'm joking,' wanting him to wrestle her to the bed: to show he knew her because he knew how to tease her. But he stood stock still, waiting for her reaction, her approval, her comment. Whatever else, she thought, he certainly was handsome.

She realised she loved him.

A deep breath shuddered through her as she tried to encompass all the emotions ricocheting around her. Then a laugh escaped. God, why had she felt heavy-hearted and paranoid? 'Lighten-up,' she told herself, and a smile followed a thought.

'You're synaesthetic!' she said, praying she had hit the nail on the head.

'I'm what?'

'You've got synaesthesia, haven't you? I've always wanted to meet someone with synaesthesia.' Kade looked questioning. 'Loads of people have synaesthesia.' Her voice felt high, false. But as Kade slowly blew out a stream of air and sat down next to her, relief seemed to fill the room. 'It's quite common.'

'Why did no one ever tell me?' he said, almost to himself.

'Maybe no one you know's heard of it. You had a pretty sheltered upbringing by the sound of it.' Brooke moved further back onto the bed and crossed her legs in front of her. Kade frowned, tilted his head and looked upwards, thinking.

'What exactly is synaesthesia?'

'It's what happens when parts of the brain aren't differentiated properly. The senses overlap. Your grandma, the Deaf one, the parts of her brain that looked after sight and touch and stuff might have taken over the part that would usually hear. It's a bit like that. Can you taste colours too? See scent? Smell sounds?'

'No.'

'So what is it you can do? Taste emotions in water?'

'Yes.'

'Water has emotions? That's cute.'

'No, I don't think it's water experiencing the emotion – though I'm not sure – just that water carries people's emotions and I can taste them.'

'I've never heard of that.' Brooke smiled at the concept, feeling a lot better.

'Are there any myths about it?'

'I don't think so. Anyway, they are just myths. Metaphors. They're not exactly *true.*'

'Oh.'

'So what's it like then? How does it feel?' asked Brooke.

'Wonderful and dreadful,' said Kade. 'And absolutely relentless. It's in everything I drink, 'cos water's in everything. The water in soft-drinks and plastic bottles tastes of processing. That kind of blurs the emotions. Sometimes I like that.' He walked over to the window and gazed out, one hand gripping the metal grille. 'The Tasting ... ' he began, then paused and looked at her. Silence threatened them again, but Kade fought it away. 'I call it the Tasting, with a capital T. It's been with me for as long as I can remember. That bad ice story? I wasn't making it up. Whenever I drank I felt emotions that weren't mine. I thought it was normal. I thought everyone did it. Kids are like that aren't they?'

'But not every child has that kind of imagination.' She brushed her cheek against his.

Anger tinged his voice. 'That's what everyone said. They said I had a good 'imagination'. I insisted it was real. They waited for me to grow out of it. Some even seemed frightened when I talked about water carrying emotions.'

'I'm not,' said Brooke. This was enjoyable, the game they were playing. All these layers of truth and lies and imagination to wade through. What child dismisses a fairy tale for being unrealistic?

'Is it like happiness tastes sweet, anger spicy, bitterness bitter?'

'And then I translate it?'

She nodded.

'No. I *feel* it. It gets a bit much sometimes. Quite often.'

Then, to himself but audible, Kade said 'Water, water everywhere, no space left to think.'

'I'm going to light a candle, okay?' said Brooke. Kade nodded.

In candlelight they lay side by side, looking up at the ceiling fan. Kade's tone lightened. 'Water in glass bottles is usually alright. Perhaps water's long-term relationship with the beach mellows it. Glass used to be sand you know?'

'Course,' she said. Against her better judgement, Brooke brightened at the words 'long-term relationship'.

'Course. You know most things.' He smiled.

'What do you like to drink best?'

'Anything that hasn't been drunk for a long time. Wild water. Rivers, lakes, wells. Water that may never have been drunk by humans, like from glaciers. I like the well-water on the Sight.'

'Why?'

'The emotional flavour. How can I explain?'

'Try.'

'Tap water is like being stuck in a crowded street. Well water is like taking a country walk.'

If this was true ... thought Brooke, 'Then city water must have thousands of emotions in it.' Kade rolled onto his front and turned to face her.

'Each batch is different,' he said, and laughed. 'Once, in Edinburgh, I found I had a sip of completely loved-up water. I ran and filled up the bathtub, and drank from it for weeks.'

'Cool.'

'Actually I think it froze in the end.'

She laughed.

'I always wondered what it's like for astronauts who see their pee turned into drinking water everyday.'

'Ugh'

'I want to drink water from the moon, or other planets.'

'Kade?'

'Yeah?'

'You're making me thirsty.'

Kade swung the water bottle over to her. 'I used to get people to bring me water when they came to the Sight. I've tasted sorrow from a well in Ukraine, fun and excitement from a tap in Tanzania, serenity from St David's in Wales and anticipation from a tap in Ibiza. Once I got a bottle from a French well that was a mixture of terror and humour. I found out it was from a town that had poisoned itself with hallucinogenic rye bread in the fifties.'

'Really?'

'Yeah, but the emotions were only just perceivable. Water from springs has a calm that comes from passing over rocks and through rivers since it was last inside a human. However jagged the original emotions all become as smooth as the rocks of a river.'

'That's very poetic,' said Brooke. 'Can I ask...?

'Yes,'

'Are you employed by Evian?'

'No,' said Kade, a bit too seriously.

Brooke took a big gulp from the bottle and washed it round her mouth. 'Mmmm. Freedom and excitement, leaving an aftertaste of cinnamon and high rises on the palate.'

'You're taking the piss,' said Kade.

'Nice turn of phrase.' She winked.

They stared at the fan for a while more. Brooke was not sure what to think. She had chased away the fear, but the worry that he was a little bit mad, at least, remained. 'You know, I like your story Kade.'

'My story is true.'

'Nah. You're pulling my leg with this one Kade.' He was pulling it very well though.

'No.'

'Prove it,' said Brooke, tilting her head and smiling in a friendly but challenging way. She swung the water bottle towards him. 'What's in this one?'

'I'd rather not drink any. I'm enjoying being here with you. I feel happy and I don't want someone else's emotions getting in the way. Some stranger's emotions, I mean,' he said. 'I like the taste of yours.'

A shudder flew up Brooke's neck, leaving her head buzzing so loud she was sure Kade would hear it. It was the sound of belief opening up in her brain. 'Kissing!' she exclaimed. 'You can taste the feelings of the person you kiss!'

Kade answered her with a long gentle sexy kiss. The most intense kiss of her life. Love spiralled around her body, but the love danced close to less comfortable feelings.

He moved back. 'Doubt,' he said. 'Fear. And love.'

'I do love you,' said Brooke, with her eyes closed.

'I love you too,' said Kade, but Brooke could not look him in the eye. Her heart was pounding. She got up and went to the bathroom, washing her face as though trying to wash away the emotions Kade had described.

When she returned she said, 'But that proves nothing, except you are a good judge of character. I want you to prove your story.'

'Well, if that kiss proved nothing then there is something else you should know. Something I can prove for sure.'

'What?'

'I can breathe water too.'

'Oh come on Kade!' Brooke dissolved into nervous giggles. 'Perhaps your father is a mermaid?' He gave her a look. Shrieking with laughter, she clapped him on the shoulder. 'No! Of *course* he wasn't a mermaid!'

'Of course he wasn't.'

'He was a merman!' she spluttered, and rolled on the bed laughing, and then looked at him, surprised to see him standing still. Her gaze wavered and travelled to the floor, and then she looked away.

'Come down to the river,' he said. Intrigued at how far Kade might take this, Brooke agreed.

The clouds were in a hurry. The streetlights, bare bulbs strung on wire, snapped about in the wind. The trees billowed, and flying leaves made vortex shapes. The noise frightened Brooke, who was jumpy enough already. They followed the road, and walked down to the sand.

'Not here,' said Kade, and led her up the beach to a dark area where the water was like smashed obsidian. He stepped towards the edge.

'C'mon Kade, let's come back in the day.' It would be crazy to enter that water. Had someone put something in his drink? She felt for his hand, but Kade stepped forward into the shallows and Brooke began to fill with dread.

'I'll be fine.'

'No. Really. Stop.' Stop this all.

As he stepped towards the water, Kade had a feeling of bad timing, but it did not stop him. So used to feeling the anxiety of others, he couldn't be sure that this anxiety was his own. He felt Brooke's presence behind him, her strength and her lack of belief. He was bitterly disappointed that she had not believed him, but he understood her need for proof. He would illustrate his abilities to her no matter what. He would force her to believe.

The Ganges carried on past, hiding its currents under its black surface. Kade waded into the flow. The water gripped his calves, and he paused. He looked down at his reflection. His life was full of reflected emotions. His image rippled beneath him, cold, undefined, made up of little pieces, each tiny wave another facet.

He dived down, ridding himself of his reflection. He heard Brooke cry 'NO!' but didn't stop. He would prove he could breathe underwater.

As he breathed in Kade felt a stronger terror than ever before. Fear, pain, panic and disbelief jolted his system like an electric shock. He tried to escape. Bursting to the surface, he swam to shore as fast as he could. He had to get the taste out of him. The terror, the hormones, the emotions, the blood, sweat, urine and saliva. The water tasted of dying.

He pulled himself out, grabbing handfuls of sand, afraid of slipping back in. He retched. Aggressively, he pushed the water off his skin and beat it out of his hair. But it was too late. The Taste of horror was in him. On all fours he tried to gain control of his breathing. He stared angrily at the river, which moved at the same pace as ever, hiding all. The wind had died down and the water's surface was silky and innocent. He retched again, shoulders straining like a wild animal.

Then he felt Brooke's hand on his back. He collapsed on his side in the sand, and began to cry. Brooke lay beside him, put her arms around him, held him close and stroked his hair.

They lay there together until Kade had cried all his tears. When the sand flies became too territorial, Kade and Brooke rose and walked away from the black water. Brooke silently comforted him all the way to the guest house and put him to bed.

When he woke Brooke's arms were embracing him and her hips pressed against his. He was not sure if she was awake or asleep, but either way she would hear his words. 'I couldn't breathe the water because I tasted something terrible,' he whispered, then went back to sleep.

Mid-morning they woke again. 'You're so strange,' whispered Brooke, sleepily.

Yeah, thought Kade. I am. And you are kind. He had not breathed water; not had to cope with Brooke's reaction to his abilities. But she had coped with his reaction to the terror in the water. They had been through fear together. She might not have taken his words all that seriously, but she was careful with his feelings. He felt safe.

But troubled. He stood and dressed, wanting to get away from the bed's safety, with its smooth dreams and sweet scent. What was the source of the terror, the fear? It was the sharpest he had ever felt.

'Come on,' he said walking out of the door. 'Let's get a chai.'

On the way Brooke trotted after him, out of rhythm with his determined pace. 'Are you okay?'

'Yeah I'm okay Brooke. I just want to find out what happened.'

'What do you mean *what happened*?'

He ignored her, felt more purposeful than her, more *knowing*. She dropped behind him, catching up as he was asking the chai maker – who knew everything – what had happened.

'The last white-water raft yesterday,' said the man, lifting his ladle high and pouring a ribbon of hot tea into the pan of brown-white froth. 'Went over. A western man and woman die.'

Brooke gasped. She turned towards him, astounded, mouth open, lips glistening, eyes wide. The blackness of her pupils reached back miles. Inside swam his reflection. Slowly she blinked, swallowing Kade's reflection. Then she turned and ran.

He gripped his skull, trying to keep his anger inside. A growl of frustration forced its way through his gritted teeth. He had lost his mother, and now he had lost Brooke.

He wasn't sure how much time had passed when the chai maker tapped him on the shoulder, bringing him back to himself. He raced to the guest house. Her passport and her traveller's cheques were there, along with all her clothes, so she would have to return, if just to leave him. He spent an exhausting few hours trying to work out what she was thinking, before realising no matter how much he thought about it, he would not *know*. He fell asleep and had a vivid dream about diving down through the seabed and emerging into another sea.

He woke to the Taste of his own exhaled anxiety in the humid air. He staggered out of bed, reached into the deepest part of his rucksack and drew out the diamond ring. He held it to his chest, checking with himself, then opened the pocket of Brooke's rucksack, dropped the ring inside and pushed it down.

Brooke could come and get her stuff if she wanted. If she wanted to leave him he would understand. It would break his heart, but he would understand. Now at least she would have something of him.

Kade left the guest house, compelled to get away from the river. Unlike the Ganges, level and steady regardless of its contents, his feelings did not flow. They flickered like rising heat, displaced by other people's feelings every time he tried to quench his thirst.

As he climbed he became increasingly resentful of the second-hand emotions that bound themselves to his life. They were invisible to the people he met, but formed a separation, a barrier, a fucking *moat*. The gulf between Brooke and him was widening. He kicked a rock. For anyone to really know him they would have to know this aspect too: the towns and cities and rivers worth of emotion that formed him moment by moment. He was bombarded by the emotional voices of thousands of people, yet was alone. No one could understand this, not even Brooke.

It had always been difficult with girls, since he could Taste how they felt. The Tasting had intensified around puberty. His first proper kiss happened during a game of true dare, double dare. 'True Dare, Double Dare, Love, Kiss or Promise?' they'd chanted. He'd not expected to be picked, but someone dared a girl to French kiss him. She was loud and popular. Or rather she was brash, bitchy and showy and used to tease him about his feet. He'd thought she would refuse the dare, but she took it. When they'd kissed he'd been surprised to feel affection, and he'd realised that the Tasting wasn't just from drinks, but from kisses too. He'd been so freaked out that he'd not kissed anyone for a long time.

Years later, drunkenly in the woods, he'd found himself about to kiss again. This time he'd liked the girl, a lot. But when they'd kissed, he'd Tasted reluctance and disgust. He had been so taken aback – he'd really thought the girl liked him and had no idea why she had kissed him if she didn't – that he had not kissed anyone again.

Not until Brooke. Brooke was the first girl he had slept with. Whatever else he told her, he would not tell her that.

He spoke to her, in the hope that somehow she would hear. 'With you the Taste came subtly. Perhaps it was knocked aside by the surprise of being kissed by a beautiful girl, or maybe your feelings were harder to differentiate from my own. 'I really like this' was the feeling I got from you, Brooke, and the feeling I had myself. How you felt was how I felt. Desire, comfort, fun and love. I did not know where I ended or you began. You made my world bigger Brooke, I love you.'

Gradually his feet began to find comfort in the dryness of the hill. At the top he stopped and sat down. His mouth was parched. Good. The midday sun shed no shadows. He stared into the sandy soil, held its grains in his fists, and thought about how he felt.

When he finally stood up to leave, the shadows were cast. Walking downhill he watched the valley open out before him, saturating his vision with green, with a glittering snake of a river swimming to sea, through time.

He found Brooke sitting on the bed, writing in her notebook, drinking a bottle of water he had rejected, sweetly unaware of the onslaught of emotions it would have made him absorb. He was so relieved to see her he wanted to rush over and cuddle her, but something in her demeanour formed a barrier. She looked up, her expression tender and tense. 'How are you?' she asked. Kade glanced around the yellow room. The lines were so straight, the bed so square, the table so sharp, the walls so ridged.

'Can we go to the river?' he asked.

She looked at him.

'I won't go in.'

'Sure, let's go.'

They walked to the water and sat side by side on the beach.

'I feel as if ... ' He took her hand in his. 'Confused. I just seem to be made up of bits of other people and my reactions to their feelings.' He looked at her, hoping she had the answers.

'I understand,' said Brooke. 'Lots of people feel like that.'

Kade let go of her hand and fell back onto the sand, relieved. Of course she couldn't really know how he felt. She couldn't *really* understand. Brooke would never *know*. But that sense of himself as an amalgamation of other people's feelings ... maybe that wasn't so unusual? Maybe he wasn't so strange. Some people were ultra-sensitive to other people's feelings even without those feelings being literally forced down their throats every time they had a drink.

It occurred to him that he'd not asked her how she was. Why hadn't he asked Brooke how *she* felt, rather than just worrying about what she thought of him? He sat back up and took her hand again.

'How do *you* feel Brooke?'

The wind played with Brooke's hair, spinning ochre shapes into the air. Her face wore a slight frown. On her cheeks and nose tiny freckles hid amongst the tan. Sand was caught in her eyelashes. 'But you know how *I* feel, don't you Kade, when you kiss me.'

'I don't know what you *think*,' he said, recoiling from her edge.

She looked away, sighed and said, 'I think we are playing a big game. When I met you ... when we met ... it felt so right. And these stories you tell me, they are beautiful and magical and enchanting. My imagination fell in love with yours. But I can't really believe your stories. I think you're going a bit crazy. I can't play along. I feel like I'm caught up in your fantasy. I've lost myself, and now I feel like I've lost you. I find the stories distracting, like a mask hiding what is really happening to you.'

Kade was lost for words. Then he saw a boat out on the river. 'Let's go somewhere else Brooke. Somewhere else in India.' A change of scene was what they needed.

'Okay,' said Brooke. 'Where shall we go?'

'Where do *you* want to go?'

'Varanasi.'

'Okay,' he said, although he had secretly wanted her to say the mountains. He began to pack.

She didn't believe him. But he loved her.

# Dead see

They caught the next train, arrived in Varanasi that evening, and booked a boat trip for the following morning. While Kade slept, seemingly peacefully, Brooke lay awake. Belief and disbelief churned in her, covering and disguising each other, rising and revealing each other. Breathing water. Tasting emotions. Such crazy claims.

Could she believe water remembered emotions? If Kade *perceived* the Tasting then it was, to him, true. Should she encourage someone in fantasy? But what if it really was true, an undiscovered sense that some people had – a seventh sense?

Why her? Why had he decided to sleep with her, to fall in love with her, to allow her to fall in love with him, to tell her these things? She loved him, crazy or not, but fear danced with love, and reality moved in shifting unpredictable layers. Brooke knew she could not absorb much more.

The porter woke them before sunrise. Already the air was hot. Half asleep, they dressed and passed through the guest house gate into the misty morning. They stopped to buy a bottle of water. Brooke winced with annoyance at Kade's insistence at testing the water. *She* checked the water, the lid anyway, to make sure the bottle had not been refilled with tap water, but as usual Kade did his ritual of taking a tiny sip. He did not make a show of it, which annoyed her even more than if he had. The idea that she would choose a boyfriend with an obsessive compulsive disorder distressed her more than her choosing a showman, a weaver of stories.

Kade seemed cheery enough. Once he had decided the water was *emotionally safe* he smiled and kissed her on the cheek. 'Well, let's go. We've got nothing to worry about. They say that if people die here they miss out all reincarnation and go straight to Nirvana.'

It was a short walk to the Ganga. Kade helped Brooke into the wooden rowboat and they looked at the boatman, an old man with a calm presence who smiled, showing teeth stained red from betel nut. He used an oar to push the boat out and then launched into the rhythm of the morning.

This time the river was the one Brooke was expecting. It was still wide and flat, but here were the Ghats – giant steps for washing clothes, doing ablutions, selling soft drinks, begging for money for your funeral pyre so they didn't just chuck your body in the river.

Dusty-red and yellow buildings emerged through the mist as though they had grown from seeds that morning. Temples rang with singing. People went about their daily tasks, both in and out of the water. A man floated in lotus position, passing river water through his nostrils. His neighbour brushed his teeth. The scent of a thousand breakfasts wafted over the boat. A girls' swimming team made their way across the river. On the Ghats two women stood a sari-length apart, drying blue and white fabric in the sun. Next to them was a similar pattern of people, and on and on, until the funeral pyre flames at the first bend in the river.

The water looked inviting. Brooke reached to stroke its surface with her fingertips, but hesitated. The boatman caught her eye.

'True believers are never harmed by the water. To them it is always clean,' he said and spat a red gob into the Ganga.

'I'd like to Taste this water, but I wouldn't dare,' whispered Kade to Brooke, and she wondered, who was crazier? The people by the Ghats drinking the Ganges despite the risks, or Kade, who claimed he could taste emotions?

The mist became rippling heat and Brooke saw that living people populated only one side of the river. The other bank belonged to the dead, and the vultures. It was like a desert, with skulls and bones bleached white and picked dry. It was beautiful.

'Look! Human skulls!' said Brooke turning to Kade.

'They look like jewels,' he said. 'Like pearls.'

She loved him for seeing what she saw. His eyes were very bright.

'Your eyes look like jewels,' said Brooke. 'Living ones.'

Kade smiled and leaned to kiss her, but Brooke gently stopped him.

They passed a boat selling cola. 'How do you think it works, Kade? The Tasting.' Kade glanced nervously at the boatman. Quietly Brooke said, 'It doesn't look as though there is anything he doesn't know. Anyway, he probably doesn't understand much English.'

The boatman looked downriver.

'The science. That's what I want to hear about.' She wanted to see if he could come up with some hard facts. Try and pull him down to earth. 'How does water, you know, *remember?*'

Kade pushed his hair back from his forehead. 'I don't know Brooke. I just don't know.'

'You must have thought about it.'

After a minute he replied. 'Well, water remembers form, doesn't it? So why not other things? And tears are full of hormones. Maybe it's the hormones I can taste. They do seem to have a lot of control over people's feelings.'

'But really. How can that be the case after water has been filtered, cleaned, frozen, evaporated?'

'I'm not sure. I don't know how it works. I don't know what it's *for.*'

'Do you want to find out? If you want I could visit some scientists with you.' Her mind suddenly spun with theories. Could the Tasting be an ancient ability, from when we were hunter-gatherers, to help us survive? A skill that had been lost to our subconscious for thousands of years but now found its way back through Kade?

'No,' he said abruptly. 'No scientists.'

'But maybe you could do something with your ability.'

'No scientists. Look Brooke, just leave it. I'm not in the mood.'

'But ... something useful. Something more than just you and me...?'

'Shit. Something useful. Do some good huh? What does it matter? I never asked for this. I never wanted it. If I could get rid of it today I would.'

'But there must be some reason ... '

'There's not a reason for every tiny little thing in the world you know. Even if there is, knowing the reasons does not make you feel any better.'

Brooke was hurt. And she didn't agree. Knowing reasons *did* make her feel better. She looked away from him, but she couldn't walk off.

'I'm sorry,' he said. 'I didn't mean to ... Look, if I say one thing, will you leave it?'

'Yes,' said Brooke. For the moment.

Kade spoke as though he was measuring his words. 'Water from wells and streams and lakes usually seems happy, lively. As if that water has washed itself. Water that's been contained for a long time, like in bottles or the public water system, doesn't. It's like it's not clean, too full of emotions. So when I drink it, it pours the emotions into me as though it can't wait to unburden itself. It feels dirty on my taste buds.'

Brooke looked away. Kade continued. 'All these angry frustrated people drink angry frustrated water, then piss and sweat and spit it back into the same supply. I don't know if it's the water that affects the people or the people that affect the water. I don't know if anyone's emotions ever leave the water. All I know is it doesn't quench my thirst.'

The boat moved closer to the skeleton side. Brooke spoke slowly. 'So people's feelings are dirty to you?'

'No it's not like –'

'Did *I* taste dirty?'

'No.'

'I reckon if I did have the Tasting you'd taste the most dirty. I wish I *did* have it.'

'No you fucking don't.'

The boat swayed as the boatman paddled to avoid something. As they passed the obstacle, Brooke saw that it was a woman. Her chest was thrust upwards, her hips sunk down. Her arms were outstretched and her head was thrown backwards. Her feet were as white as snow. She was dead. Yards away, the girls' swimming team raced back to the Ghats, oblivious.

A real dead body. She had only seen one in horror films. There was something calming about seeing a real one. The dead woman did not turn her head and stare at Brooke like a horror movie corpse; she just rose and fell gently in the boat's wake. Brooke felt a sense of relief. Looking back at Kade, she was sure the presence of death would have halted their bickering. He was pale.

'Can we go back now?' he asked the boatman.

The boatman nodded and turned the boat. Then they heard a loud scrape.

'Get out. Get out,' said the boatman.

'Why?' asked Brooke. Was he *crazy* too?

'Pushing,' he replied and got out.

They had run aground. Brooke stepped reluctantly into the Ganges; glad she had no cuts on her feet, and pushed the boat. Kade remained in it, gripping the sides. His knuckles were as white as the dead woman's feet.

'I want to go,' he said when they were moving again. 'To the mountains, where the rivers are purer.'

They left the following dawn.

# Mountains

It started as a normal bus journey. Brooke had packed samosas, a pack of cardamom cream biscuits and a couple of bottles of water. The moon was high, and Brooke felt excited. They found seats at the back, Brooke by the window, Kade by the aisle. It was supposed to be a luxury bus, and had velveteen upholstery, but that didn't prevent the driver picking up hitching locals, and the road was far from luxurious. Soon the bus was bouncing about and the gangway was full of people. Brooke pulled her head scarf forward in a childish 'If I can't see you, you can't see me' gesture, and it worked. People generally ignored her and she ignored the people.

Talking about the Tasting had reached saturation point, but Brooke was not sure what else to talk about. 'I'm glad I wore a good bra,' she joked as the bus jumped potholes.

Kade glanced over, 'Yeah. Bus tickets might be cheap, but we'll probably have to spend a fortune on osteopathy when we get home.' He spoke dryly, as if forcing himself to make conversation. She decided not to force him.

With her knees shoved up against the seat in front, Brooke felt she could drop off to sleep quite easily. Kade, too tall for that, looked uncomfortable to her tired eyes, but seemed to be asleep.

They woke every stop, stiff and musty. For a while Brooke gave up on sleep in favour of staring out at the ever-changing view. As they travelled north, the scenery began to remind her of home. Not London, or Rayton, but the countryside of Britain. The road carved through mountains and dived through bends. The rock and ferns could have been from any mountainous place. But these were the foothills of the Himalayas, she told herself. Only seven hours to go until the peaks.

The night air was fresh and cool. Prising open the reluctant sliding window of the bus, she stuck her elbow out, and rested her wrist on the sill, taxi driver style. Kade still slept. She wanted to wake him to show him the view but he was twitching and his eyes were moving from side to side beneath his eyelids – dreaming. Brooke attempted to sleep again. She found she could manage a half-sleep if she pretended she was at sea and the twists and turns of the bus were the boat riding the waves.

The waves become rougher and rougher. The boat is caught in a storm. The sea is orange. There is someone at the wheel – she can see a yellow sou'wester and hat. Sure that she can command the boat better, and fearing for her safety, she moves towards the helm. The sailor looks round. It's Kade. His eyes, glowing amber, seem angry. As she reaches for the wheel he rotates it hard to the left. One of the handles hits her wrist and she reels backwards in pain, slips over the stern and into the sea.

'Ow. Ow. Fucking HELL' Brooke cried, waking herself and Kade. The bus window, which seemed so stiff when she had opened it, has slid closed and carried Brooke's wrist with it, scraping it on the metal frame.

'Bloody Hell,' said Kade. 'You're bleeding.'

Brooke looked at her blood. It was trickling out of her flesh not spurting from an artery, but the cut was savage and jagged. She held it tight.

'Here, hold it up.' Kade pulled her forearm towards the roof. 'Are you alright?' He looked at her intently, with eyes glowing in the dawn sunlight. Then, as though he couldn't help himself, he licked the wound.

Brooke jerked her wrist away. 'Your eyes,' she said.

He unwrapped his cotton scarf from his neck and wrapped it tight round her wrist. 'It's not an artery, you'll be fine.'

'But I'm *not* fine.' Her blood blossomed onto the orange scarf bandage, like the sun oozing up through the clouds. Red sky in the morning: shepherds warning. Brooke moaned like a woman mourning. She *was* mourning. She had trusted Kade, but now she didn't feel safe with him. Why did he have to lick her wound? Was he a vampire, an animal?

After a few minutes the blood slowed, but her thoughts did not. Why did he make so many things up? Couldn't he deal with real life? She had thought him so interesting, so fascinating, but now she was afraid. All the stuff about water – either he was insane or – he was too much for her. Why could she not have met someone normal, balanced? Someone she did not have freaky dreams about? She wished he would go away.

He did. The coach pulled into a town called Mandi.

'I'm going out for some orange juice,' said Kade.

'Do you think you've got time?'

'Yeah, sure.' He picked his way to the front of the coach and stepped off into the dusty depot as the rain started. I hope he doesn't come back, thought Brooke. Be careful what you wish for, thought another part of Brooke.

When the coach left without him her heart sank. She recognised it as another one of those times when the bad thing you've convinced yourself won't happen, *does* happen. But it did not feel too serious. She would see him again. She thought of stopping the driver, asking him to wait, but it did not seem urgent. They were five hours from Manali. It would do her and Kade good to spend some time apart – a few hours, a day, or perhaps longer. Being with him was like watching a movie with eyelids pinned open. Too much. Too quick. She remembered the hippies she'd met when she arrived in India, so many of whom seemed wise to her at first. It had taken her a while to install her bullshit filter. It did not always work, but the words of one particular man, Tree, remained quietly in her head until now, when they reached towards her, loud, still, and clear.

'I lived too much too young, Brooke. I had too much fun. It's hell knowing you've already had the best fucking time of your life. You can never create it again but you try and try. I fell deeply in love with a woman and with this land. Now the romance has gone. Be careful Brooke. Don't spend your energy all at once.'

She'd spent a lot of energy on Kade, trying to help him through all his wonderful delusions. Now she was simply going to be a normal backpacker. Get drunk, get stoned, go shopping, and go home. Go back to her studies. Tone down the intensity. If he did not want her, she would not want him.

Kade had his money, passport, traveller's cheques and a blanket. He went to the bus station tea stand and comforted himself with a chai as he listened to the rain on the blue tarpaulin and watched Brooke's bus drive away. He had tasted fear and anger in her blood and it was directed at him. To be feared like that was horrible. He could still Taste her, metallic.

Her interrogations had become too much. She was always asking him questions and they had a patronising taint. For him water was a feeling, not a theory. Talk could not quench his thirst. He was glad to be away from her and the way she said she believed him, when her kisses told him that she doubted him.

Yet he loved her and wanted to see her again. He would find her in Manali in a few days. It could be good for them to be apart, for a while. Over the past few months their hearts had been ablaze with feelings neither could properly express. Now they had parted like mountain streams.

# Chocolate and chilli

After Mandi the bus was emptier. It climbed uphill for three hours. Entrenched in her seat, Brooke sat as still as the eye of a hurricane: Any activity would unlock feelings too strong to hide. Every so often, she peeked into herself to see how she felt. Each time she received a different answer. She felt angry, sad, regretful, optimistic, relieved, and guilty. Was the empty seat next to her symbolic of the free space she would now have, or did it illustrate that something was missing?

A young woman from the seat in front peeked between the seats and gave a sad-for-you smile. The woman was a honeymooner, with the hennaed mehindi pattern on her hands from the wedding. Brooke smiled shyly and resumed looking out of the window, not very happy. Then the bus turned a corner and everything changed. Brooke took a deep breath at the beauty of mountains, forests, ferns, wild rivers, smallholdings and apple orchards.

Having done the hard part, the bus stopped for a café break. Brooke stood, stretched, unstuck her clammy clothes and walked down the gangway experiencing a quickening freshness, feeling more alert and optimistic. Through the windscreen a white-topped mountain, stood taller than any she had seen before. Supporting and echoing this mountain were many others. At their peaks they were difficult to distinguish from the clouds. Snow or cloud; both are water thought Brooke, aware that Kade would have said something similar. She jumped off the bus. The air was wonderful; so clean that it even seemed easier to see things. Her lungs trusted it.

Compared to those further south, the café's structure was more solid, more cold-weather hardy, more familiar. *Everything* seemed familiar: the ferns, the hills and mountains, the pine and apple trees, the roots forming staircases on the bank beside her. It could almost be the Lake District or Scotland. But this landscape was bigger, deeper and higher than its little-sister landscapes in Europe.

In the gully below the road, a huge river made a jade green trail as it travelled to the towns below. She wondered what kind of watersprites people said lived there.

In the café she bought a cup of tea and took it outside to sip in the bright daylight. The tea, like the air, was fresher. Mountain water, milk from local cows, and tea leaves from not so far away made a better cup of tea than reservoir water and milk from cows so hungry they munched cardboard boxes. Brooke was aware that this was another thought she would never have had before Kade. But he would have only thought of the water, and possibly the milk, she said to herself. What about the sugar? What feeling did that lend to the experience of drinking tea? What about the cardamom, cinnamon, ginger and cloves? She felt the heat and warmth from the sugar and the spices as a dense, sticky-warm sweetness. Brooke held the mug of tea to her chest and it burned her skin like the sun, just for an instant. She looked down into the valley. She would miss Kade, but was already enjoying being alone. What a wanker for deserting her anyway.

When it was time to get back on the bus, people climbed to the roof, planning to ride the two hours to Manali in the open air. She joined them and noticed Kade's red rucksack nestled between a husband and wife. Of course – he had left it behind. Left it for her to deal with. Annoyed at first, soon she was pleased, realising he would be back for it and so she would see him soon. Maybe she could even have a look inside? He had always left it packed, never showing everything. Was it fair to look? She would consider that question later. She felt light now. Maybe some sense of loss would sink in, but perhaps the Kade that lived on in her head was the version she preferred, and being lumbered with his nicely packed luggage was preferable to his badly packed baggage – his loose grip on reality.

Brooke arrived in Manali exhilarated. Riding on the roof was better than the best fairground ride. The passengers smiled with a sense of shared achievement at having completed their long journey, especially considering how many bus carcasses they had seen along the way. She climbed down, waved bye to the honeymoon girl, and helped catch the luggage as it was passed down.

When the activity stopped and the bus had driven away, all seemed still. Then she was blasted with a delicious aroma from an omelette stall next to her. She reached for her rupees.

As she ate her omelette she noticed a street-side map. It showed that there was a wood just up the road. She finished eating and lugging the bags with her she walked uphill through the marketplace, past traders with piles of floral mattresses, embroidered shawls and felt jackets, past photo-developers and ice cream-shops and more omelette stalls. Indian tourists, the honeymoon couples and snow-seekers, contrasted with the locals who were taller, more cosily dressed and had a streamlined quality to their faces. It felt like a new country.

Inside the wood the light was green. Brooke sat down and rested her back against a large mossy rock, welcoming the dampness it pressed into her shirt. Lugging two backpacks was hard work. At the edge of the trees, cub scouts learned about pinecones, and honeymooners took morning strolls. One couple kissed, which was rare to see in India. Brooke felt she could stay all day, but she had to find a place to sleep. Tree had recommended one, but could not recall its name. She began looking for the card he had given her. While rummaging she glanced at Kade's bag, wondering what was inside. Kade had been embarrassed by the bag's brightness. Its redness seemed incongruous with his wateriness. Lashed across the top was his sleeping bag. They had slept on it so many times. She remembered the feeling of the soft yellow lining against her knees, her back, her palms, her cheek, and of Kade's body, golden next to the yellow. As she unclipped the sleeping bag it released his scent, her scent, *their* scent. A strange combination, but somehow right, like chocolate and chilli, familiar and intriguing. She bit her lip.

As she opened the top of the rucksack, a bird, which had been perched above, flew away through the trees. Its wingtips skimmed the firs. That's how she felt with Kade, as though she could fly. Free and wild.

Reaching down past the clothes, she teased to the surface an A4 envelope full of papers. Wrapped around the rest of the papers was a page from the Scotsman. She checked the date. It was three years old. It opened out to reveal a full colour picture of bathers at the last Kumbh Mela. Refolded it, she reinforced the crease that divided the crowd. It was so quiet here in the woods compared to the Mela and its millions of people – throngs of people. It had been amazing. Humans and animals and barbed wire and smoke and religion and barely controlled mayhem amongst the islands of canvas tents. It was friendly too, but occasionally flashes of strangeness would flicker through the crowd. Once there was a lost little girl, and furrows of worry appeared on the brows of the devout. The child had been lifted onto the shoulders of a tall man, from where she shouted for her mother like a baby bat on a cave wall. The mother was found straightaway and the crowd had breathed a collective sigh of relief that no real panic had pervaded the Mela that time. But panic always felt close, as if anything might happen. She had felt safe with Kade, who seemed able to sense an atmosphere on the breeze before it changed for the worse. He had always managed to find a comfortable place in the crowd, where they were free from buffeting. With him she had avoided crazed cows and fresh fires. Instead, she had found groves of fireflies and groups of people dancing and offering food.

There was no one visible in the woods now, just the trees and animals. On the back of the Kumbh Mela picture were adverts for highland holiday lets: Loch Lomond, Loch Tay. She put the paper aside. There was a photocopy of his birth certificate. Mother – Aurora MacLeod. Nice name. Father – blank. Maybe he carried it round for bureaucratic reasons or maybe he kept it to look at when he wanted to give himself an occasional fix of pain and melancholy.

Behind the birth certificate was a bank statement. It was a new account. Statement issue one. There had only been one payment in of several thousand pounds, shortly before he left for India. She started to try and memorise his address, but suddenly felt someone watching her. She looked up guiltily and saw a group of funny long-nosed monkeys congregating on the rock opposite, half observing her. They weren't threatening, she reassured herself.

Brooke brushed aside the guilt, and carried on rummaging. There were a few photos. Why hadn't he shown her these? They were of a waterfall and a lake, or maybe a loch. There was a beautiful pool next to a willow tree, which shed a light as green as where she sat now. Brooke put the photos down, spreading them out on the moss and leaves. They looked at home.

Next was a silhouette drawing of a kind of tribal man, tattooed all over, with webbed fingers. Kade drew well, if it was by Kade. Behind it was a receipt from an auction house, for about the same amount he had in his bank account. Interesting.

Finally she pulled out a metal bottle, its stopper sealed with wax. She shook it. It was full of something. What was that for? It had a label, written in his handwriting. 'Ganges upstream,' it said. Why was he collecting Ganges water? So many unanswered questions. Why was she looking through these things anyway? He had left her and she had helped to drive him away. It was a relief to be without him. She almost admired him for doing the right thing. No messy break-up. She would lodge his rucksack in a café or a guest house and put a note in the poste-restante telling him where it was. She looked for Tree's card again and found it: River Guest House, Old Manali.

She lodged his bag at a chai hut, trying not to think she would never see him again, and then caught a rickshaw uphill to the old village, where River Guest House was located. Old Manali seemed like a mixture of Camden Town and medieval Switzerland. Velvety cows and wooden houses with pointy roofs were interspersed with cafés and shops selling falafel, noodles and party clothes. The driver let her off near a boulder with *River Guest House* written on it in red paint. Arrows pointed along a narrow path, carved into the hillside, about ten metres above a river. She walked on, wary of the drop to her left, amazed at the marijuana bushes on her right.

River Guest House was made of dark old wood. 'Beautiful,' whispered Brooke. The guest house owner, a handsome middle-aged man, smiled and greeted her as if he had been expecting her, then led her up the outdoor stairway and into a room at the end of the building. The room was cosy, all wood. Outside was a covered veranda overlooking the mountains, where a few people were sitting and skinning-up. Brooke could smell the rich smoke from a joint they had already lit. They were English and about her age. Brooke nodded hello, then lay on the bed and slept.

The next couple of hours, days, weeks, were spent smoking and giggling with her neighbours. They were from Leeds and their main conversation topic was what food they would eat when they got home. They had come up to Manali for a holiday at the end of their trip, which had been spent helping out in an orphanage in Rajasthan. Brooke enjoyed the ordinariness of their company. They were earthy and humorous, swapping quips and taking the mickey out of each other and out of India, especially the pseudo-spiritual side.

One day she told the girls in the group about Kade, making him comic, like a bad mistake she had narrowly avoided. They decided she was better off without him.

But he *could* be in Manali, thought Brooke. She was unlikely to have bumped into him as she had barely left the guest house since she had arrived. Supper and breakfast and endless games of carom and backgammon were all provided. She had watched the path almost constantly though, looking for him.

After about a fortnight, Brooke travelled back to town to check if he had collected his bag. He hadn't. But maybe he was in Manali but had not checked the poste-restante. He would only look there if he was expecting a letter, but he had not talked much about people from home, and who wrote paper letters these days anyway?

Maybe there was somewhere else she could leave a note? It was a passing thought, and disappeared with the next inhalation of dope.

The next day the people from Leeds had planned a trip to a series of waterfalls up the mountain, and Brooke was invited to join them. During the walk she went off her companions a little. They giggled and quipped and chatted all the way, leaving no space to enjoy the scenery. When they reached the first fall – a tall, thin, white cascade that fell into a deep jade pool – they did not stop talking despite the waterfall's powerful presence. They shouted about how pretty it was, but Brooke felt as though she were a guest in its presence. It reminded her of something, or somewhere she could not quite remember, and their voices chopped into her concentration. It was certainly more than 'pretty'. Kade would have appreciated it.

Brooke lagged behind the group as they climbed to the next fall. She tried, and managed, to allow in enough quiet to be able to feel the landscape. In the quiet she began remembering all the good things about Kade. There were lots. She had fallen in love with the way he saw the world and she missed that now. Kade would have loved these falls. If he came to Manali he would definitely visit this waterfall. Maybe she could leave a note for him here?

She found the perfect place. The top waterfall dived sheer off the plateau, spinning rainbow arcs with its spray as it pulsed onto the rocks below. It was too young to form a pool, but behind it was a shallow cave. She was thrilled. It hinted at secret worlds. Inside were offerings of sweet foods accompanied by prayers, tied to the walls. She wrote a note, and added it to the prayers.

*Dear Kade. Your bag is in the chai hut by the bus station and I am at River Guest House, Old Manali. Come and see me if you want. I love you whatever happens...*

100

Brooke stayed in Manali for a few more days, watching the path everyday, not daring to leave the guest house. Kade did not arrive. She gave up, angry with herself for pining and for failing to gather local water myths, for leaving a note in such an obscure place, and for hoping love would magically lead Kade to it. Why had she never given him her email address? She counted her money and found she only had enough left to go to the airport and go home. She was too full of pride and sensibility to trek back to the fall and leave her home address there. She stayed one final night in the mountains, desperate for Kade to turn up, desperately willing herself not to care if he didn't. The Leeds lot tried to cheer her up:

'At least England's clean and you can drink the water,' said one girl with hennaed hair.

'Ah, but did you know that London tap water has been through seven people before it gets to you?' asked Brooke.

'Yeah, I heard that when I was a kid, freaked me right out,' said the girl. 'But is it still seven after all these years? Wouldn't it be more by now?'

Brooke giggled and accepted the joint the girl passed. 'Maybe. But I thought they let it go wild after seven.' She took a drag. 'Or maybe all the water in London just stays there, going round and round, everyone drinking each others blood and piss and hormones like some kind of aquatic incest.' She stopped, shocked at herself for putting it so crudely. The girl looked momentarily embarrassed. Then a boy said,

'God. I'm glad I don't live in London. Pennine water is lovely. Fresh off the hills. It's so soft that you hardly need any soap 'cos any soap you use takes ages to rinse off.'

Brooke was amazed how easily water had slipped into the conversation. Soon she would be far from Kade, but she knew his influence would stay with her all her life.

'Not that there's anything wrong with London,' added the boy. The smile in his eyes hinted that, actually, of course there was.

They were sweet these people, trying to soften the blow of leaving. Even if they had no interest in scenery, they cared about other people. That wasn't bad. But people and place are not truly separate, she thought to herself. As soon as a person drank the local water they became part of the place. The people from Leeds had been healthy all the time they had been in India. They said it was because whenever they arrived in a place they had a lassi. The yoghurt in the drink, made with local water, counteracted any harmful effects of bacteria. Brooke had also remained healthy. Perhaps water liked her.

# Trees and rocks

The plastic tarpaulin roof of Mandi bus station tea hut gave a light as blue and gloomy as his feelings. Kade did not notice the Westerner in the corner until he heard a slow, high voice say. 'Hey man, you're travelling light. You just here for the day?' The man was about thirty, but wrinkled from the sun, furrowed with inner thought and greyer than his time. He was sipping tea and rocking slightly.

'No. I thought I'd stay in Mandi for a few days,' answered Kade.

'Wow. Seven years in India and I've never seen anyone but Sadhus travel as light as you,' said the man, then under his breath he muttered, 'Too much, too young, too soon,' and then louder again, 'And you don't even look like a hardcore hippy. Anyway man ... You don't want to ... What's your name?'

'John,' said Kade. He had given too much away recently.

'Mmmm, good solid name.'

'And yours?'

'Tree.'

A dyed-in-the-wool hippy, thought Kade.

'Anyway, er, John,' said Tree. 'You don't wanna stay in Mandi. Nah, you don't wanna stay in Mandi. Smelly. See that bus over there?' He pointed with one arm, nearly spilled his tea and quickly pulled the cup close again, as though it were a stabiliser. 'See that bus over there?' Kade was looking. 'SEE THAT BUS OVER THERE?'

'Yes,' said Kade. It was a public bus. Blue grey.

'Get that bus, travel for half hour past the Tibetans breaking up stones. Get off Resalwar. Much better. Three temples. One Hindu, one Buddhist, one Sikh. Noisy at dawn but nice. And a little zoo with deer. Weird. And a lake. Can't go wrong. And, if you're one of those do-gooders there's a couple of orphanages.' Tree paused thoughtful. Kade caught a glance of the public school-boy that Tree must have been. 'Actually,' corrected Tree. 'The orphanages are still there even if you aren't a do-gooder.'

Kade grinned. 'Okay,' he said.

'Well go on fuck off to Resalwar then. What are you hanging around with me for?'

So Kade went to Resalwar, past the Tibetans breaking up stones for road building. They were women, as were most of the labourers Kade had seen in India. The stones decreased in size as the bus approached Resalwar. Large piles of boulders became large piles of smaller rocks became large piles of shingle.

Resalwar, in the hills, was beautiful. Three temples surrounded a small lake. There seemed to be no other tourists. Kade booked himself into a guest house run by Buddhist monks. He thought about having a shower, but noticed that the shower water would fall directly into a live electrical plug on the wall opposite. Instead, he set off for a walk around the lake.

All around the lake he tried not to think about Brooke. There were plenty of distractions: a Sikh temple with stonework that looked like swathes of cloth, the Buddhist temple with its colourful flags, and a Hindu temple with a three foot high face of a white-bearded Shiva looking like Father Christmas, next to a life-size bull carved in black rock, with a stone snake at its feet. There were turtles in the water. Best of all were the teenage monks playing football in their wine-coloured habits. Kade felt like joining in, but was too shy to invite himself.

Behind the players was an art deco telephone exchange, and behind that was the deer park. He paid the entry to the park and wandered in. He passed the deer, which paid him no attention, and then he followed a path uphill, past a tiled bathroom sink and mirror planted incongruously in the middle of the wood. Finally, the path arrived at a picnic table, beside a series of small pools and cascades.

The river's movement churned up feelings that had been buried in the sediment of his mind. He suddenly felt homesick and lonely. He moved down to the water's edge and stopped, letting the purr of the cascades into his senses. The water shivered downhill, forming and reforming itself, curling and unfurling. Plants clung to rocks, perpetually watered under the spray. So fertile. But at the rocky edges the ripples turned to damp and the sweet scent became old. Unwashed crevices, spinning with flies, waited for the next snowmelt to refresh the foetid dampness. For now, the edges were only for snakes and leeches and other un-enticing creatures. Kade did not want his heart to become like these edges. He did not want it to become dried out, mouldering, craving the liquid of love. He wanted to feel like the deep fresh centre of the water, clean and self-cleansing, full and sure. He wanted to feel Brooke's giggles filling him up and tickling him, as the bubbling cascades tickled the pools.

He missed Brooke's giggles. Even before he left her he had noticed their absence. Brooke had not been relaxed in his company since he'd told her his whole story. She had thought him a liar; that he lived in a fantasy world. At first she had enjoyed sharing 'the fantasy' with him, but then it had overwhelmed her. That made him sad. He threw a stone into the white water, then picked up a fistful of shingle and cast that in too, noticing the illusion that rising out of each splash was a small black ball.

On his walk back to the monastery guest house Kade passed a stone wall, where each top-stone had a prayer or a picture scraped onto it: wishing stones. He found a blank stone and using a slate he wrote his own wish on it – *To see her again* – then placed it back in the wall.

As twilight arrived, Kade sat down beside the lake. Coloured light from the temples slipped into the lake water, making spiralling columns that seemed to reach deep beneath the surface. Pre-recorded prayers from the evening ceremonies sung out across the water from the temple loudspeaker. 'Ohm Namah Shiva. Ohm Namah Shi-vy-ah.' The tune was repetitive and Kade felt it slowly filling the part of his brain where his thoughts liked to run round. *'Why did I leave? – Why didn't it work? – Could it have worked? – Why did I leave? – Why didn't it work? – Could it have worked?'* The rhythm, the repetition of the prayers, hijacked the part of him that kept asking what he could have done differently. 'Ohm Namah Shiva.' It stayed in his head as he slept that night.

The next day he set off to catch the bus to Manali, but paused to watch the orphanage monks playing football. He was sure they were very spiritual with lots of inner calm, but the word that came to mind was *cool.* They had style. The older teenagers played in burgundy robes and any T-shirt in the orange-to-wine spectrum. They were either barefoot or wore top-brand trainers, donated by tourists no doubt. The younger boys, instead of football, were playing a Tibetan rounders, which involved knocking a stone off the top of a pile of rocks and then running. Everyone was playing something, except for one boy. He was tiny, only three or four years old. He sat still, by the lake's edge. Was he particularly holy, wondered Kade, especially contemplative? Was he some very high reincarnation? Maybe he was just unpopular.

'Namaste,' said Kade, looking at the back of the little monk's head. He had learned the greeting from the children he had met in India. The boy did not respond. Kade's shadow fell on the ripples and with his reflection Kade waved. The boy turned round. Kade looked into his eyes, which seemed to hold the knowledge of countless generations. Or, Kade wondered, was that just mildly racist claptrap, to think the boy was deep because he was Tibetan?

'Apke nam kia hai?' asked Kade.

The boy did not give his name; he just made a feral sound. A teenage monk approached. He wore a fluoro-orange T-shirt with a Chinese dragon on it.

'His name is Takla,' said the teenager in English. 'He can't hear you.'

'He's deaf?'

'Yes.'

Kade switched to sign and introduced himself. He saw a glimmer of interest in Takla's eyes, but it was clear he did not understand.

'He has no language,' said the teenager.

'None?'

'The teachers try and teach him to read, but it doesn't work. He can't even chant.'

No language. How amazing and how horrible, thought Kade. He remembered Lila telling him about two little Indian girls brought up by wolves. They were encouraged to talk, but they just howled and growled. Those girls, though, had a language – albeit Wolf. This boy had none. He had never said a word, never *signed* a word, and maybe never *thought* a word.

'Is it okay if I try something?' he asked the teenager, who was obviously protective of Takla.

'Sure,' he said and gave Kade a broad smile.

Kade sat down next to the boy, pointed to the lake and made the sign for it over and over again. After a while Takla smiled. Then he copied Kade. On seeing this, the teenager ran off and returned with the monastery teacher.

They sat and watched as Takla copied Kade, signing *cow, tree, football.* Takla was making excited noises. The teacher finally interrupted to congratulate Kade. Kade thanked him and explained that he had to catch the next bus, but the man implored him to stay. 'Can't you teach him more?'

Kade paused. He had just blown oxygen into the embers of Takla's soul and feared that the small flame would peter out if he left. He could miss today's bus. Sure. He had no way of contacting Brooke, but he could make contact with Takla. He must not interrupt the kindling of language in him.

Takla looked tired and Kade invited him, the teacher and the footballer to the café and bought them drinks. They rested and the teacher explained how Takla had been carried across the Himalayas as a young baby, by his mother, who had died of frostbite on arrival in India, so the baby had been taken to the monastery, with only a name.

Kade watched Takla watch them talk. Kade wondered how it felt to have no language then suddenly to understand, to copy, to speak? 'May I have a sip of your drink?' he asked Takla in sign. Takla offered his glass, the gesture of *asking for a sip* immediately clear. Kade turned the glass and sipped from the side Takla had. He could taste Takla's happiness but then he detected an aftertaste of sadness. Takla knew this was the end of his life before words.

The teacher described to Kade how some anthropologists had donated a video camera to the monastery 'to record our own culture.' Inspired, Kade spent the next week naming anything and everything to Takla, and filming it all in order to make a visual dictionary. Takla was happy and full of energy. By the end of the week he could name everything in sight. Kade wondered if his hand muscles were tired.

Kade tried to teach conceptual words, like *think, feel, love*, but Takla could not grasp what he meant, so Kade filmed them as best he could, to teach them to the teacher to show Takla when he was older. Kade knew that, although he could not say them, it did not mean that Takla did not understand these things. The kid had started signing in sentences, with grammar. That was the most important thing, Lila said.

In return for his teaching, Kade was given a room. Not just any room, but one usually reserved for high re-incarnations, and painted with the sky on the ceiling in blue and gold, and hung with tapestries of mandalas. He was fed with delicious noodle stews that left him nourished and contented, though he could not resist buying some deep fried sugar spirals and sharing them with Takla.

After nine days, Kade decided it was time to go, because nine days was nearly too long to leave Brooke wondering if he was angry at her, and it was just enough time for Takla to begin trying to teach his new language to the other boy-monks. At the bus stop, Takla hugged him. Kade was sure Takla understood when

108

he said he was going away. Both smiled and waved for as long as they could still see each other, and until the Ohm Namah Shivas could only be heard in Kade's head rather than through the speakers.

The prayers continued in his head all the way to Mandi, and played loudly as his stomach began to contract and moan. They reached a crescendo as the bus pulled into the shelter and he ran to the bins and vomited, much to the interest of six little stripy piglets and their not-so-cute mum. The prayers continued when he booked into the Rajmahal Palace which smelled of musty British colonialism, and featured rows of leather books, carved wood furniture, and even had baths in the rooms, complete with swords as towel rails. He stayed for three nights, cursing himself, until every last bit of sugar spiral had poured out of him.

A little lighter, he set off for Manali and the prayers were still playing in his head when he found the note behind the waterfall after a futile week of trying to spot Brooke around town. 'Ohm Namah Shiva. Ohm Namah Shivyah.' The tune and words seemed to be waterborne, as if the waterfall were playing them, as if water could record sound as effectively as emotion.

After reading the note, Kade allowed himself to feel excited. He imagined that Brooke was somewhere near the fall; a mythical character who only existed when Kade summoned her up.

What would he say? Would it be tentative or would they fall into one another's arms like the ending of a romantic film? He ran downhill, almost in time with the flowing water, and he hired a rickshaw to travel to Old Manali. The prayers rattled along with the rickshaw's engine as they rode past the forests.

Sitting next to the rickshaw driver was a shiny-haired boy of about ten. He and the driver were chatting away in Hindi, so Kade was surprised when the boy turned round revealing the freckled face of a European. The boy friendlily told Kade that his parents had decided to move form Helsinki to India, determined to start a life in a new place – and it had worked. Things had gone so well they had never returned to Europe. So free, thought Kade,

I am not that free. He knew he would have to return to Scotland and find what he was missing.

The prayers in his head helped keep him calm as he walked the narrow path to River Guest House. He tried to suppress his excitement, in case Brooke was not there. The path was narrow. On his left was a steep drop to the rocks and white water of the Beas River, to his right grew large marijuana plants, which looked at home next to the ferns and wildflowers. Far away, across the river, two mountains stood, their snow capped peaks revealing wolf-like and feline shapes. It was a big world.

He arrived at the guest house and managed to gain the attention of a bunch of people from Leeds for long enough to learn that Brooke had left seventy-two hours previously. 'For Delhi' they said, and then resumed talking about cheesecake.

'I wanted to take her to the snow,' he said, but they ignored him. Perhaps Brooke had complained to them about him, he thought. He set off. Glancing back, he caught the eye of one of the girls but could not read her expression. He hurried.

He returned to his guest house, then picked up his bag at the chai stand, paid for its keep, rushed to the bus station and boarded the first bus to Delhi. It was a public bus, already full. It set off as soon as he got in. Seated on his bag in the gangway, he peered at the mountains as they and he parted. He caught his breath and closed his eyes. The prayers were still in his head and he felt calmer as he listened. The prayers were present in Delhi while Kade wondered where Brooke could have gone, and they hummed along with the plane's engine as he returned home, having decided that Brooke, in going to Delhi with its forty-degree heat, was also planning to fly home.

# Flight IC408

He was *so* thirsty. The drinks trolley was approaching and he glanced behind to see how long he would have to wait: Too long. The plane was full and the passengers looked crumpled and sticky in contrast to the streamlined efficiency of the cabin's design. The lights shone dozy orange. In the seat behind, a fat woman had dribbled sleepy spit onto her stomach. Deciding that the more patient he was, the less time it would take for the drinks to arrive, Kade turned to the window. The cloying scents of reheated food and duty-free perfume were balanced by the freshness of the white clouds unfolding on the horizon. Kade hoped Brooke's plane had flown through the same clouds. Tigers and horses, old women and babies, kings and queens, chariots and dogs stared back from citadels of cloud. You're an idiot said a quiet voice in Kade's head.

The citadels were being gold-plated by sunlight when the drinks trolley announced its arrival with a splosh-ching sound. 'What would you like, Sir?' asked the stewardess in a part-waitress, part-cosmetics-saleswoman tone.

'Mineral water, please.' He hoped he could drink it: that he could use the innate alchemy of mammals and turn it into blood. If the water's Taste got in the way, it would be a hard flight.

'Sparkling or still?'

'One of each please.'

She passed him the water on a little tray. Thanking her, he took a tiny sip. It seemed innocent enough, not too strong, so he had another sip. It was European – Alpine. The main emotion was relief. He imagined Neanderthals, quenching their thirst in mountain streams as they walked to warmer lands.

Hours later the plane flew over the mountains where the mineral water had been gathered, but by then Kade's mind was completely focussed on Brooke. She took care of him. She was his lover. She was his goddess. He imagined Brooke and himself bedding down in the palace of clouds, in their own world, where nothing could harm them. His thoughts became desires, his desires tiptoed over to arousal and he and Brooke were rolling around from cloud to cloud, him inside her.

Kade was jolted from his fantasy by the loud English voices of two girls in front. Both reminded him of Brooke: similar age, similar accent. They were talking about finding a place to live and some part-time work before they had to start university. Reality. Brooke was an ordinary girl: wonderful, but ordinary, a backpacker trying to find herself. Instead she had found him. He had absorbed her, taken over her thoughts, and distracted her from her mission to find out about water myths. She had done no research in all the time they were together.

Perhaps it had been for the best to leave the bus that day in Mandi? Brooke had her life. She probably needed to be away from him to live it. All for the best. 'Ohm Namah Shiva, Ohm Namah Shiva. You're an idiot,' said his soul. He did not even know where she lived. Was it somewhere north of London? *Why* hadn't he taken an e-mail address?

The plane began to descend, circling over night-time London. The city was a huge monster, eating electricity and spewing out light. The plane gripped the tarmac. As the engines ceased humming, the Ohm Namah Shivas left Kade's head. He had forgotten the prayers were there, until they were gone. His mind left the clouds and his worries came raining down, but he did not panic. It was time for action.

# Euston

Nine hours between Delhi and England. Nine hours over the rippled landscape of Asia and the fields and clouds of Europe. Nine hours from one version of the twenty-first century to another.

On the bus from the airport to central London, Brooke felt overwhelmed by space and smoothness. The buildings shone. Such an abundance of pale stone and plate glass would dazzle or even blind in an Indian climate, but England's dull skies could afford the brightness. In India the powdery matt surfaces invited the gaze and the imagination. Here it was deflected.

Between the buildings were a few people, dashing about, *all* wearing dark blue. The streets seemed almost empty of life. Everything met at the edges, was squared off, cleaned and thought about. No intriguing chasms or tiny alleys. The pavements had clear beginnings and endings, no piles of rubbish, no children playing, no children *at all*, no animals, no street stalls. Not much room for the imagination. Brooke missed India.

It began to rain. The ride was smooth, unencumbered by potholes. The driver did not pick up hitchers. No one was hitching. The coach seats smelled of solvent spray. The strangest thing was that she could understand the chit-chat of people on the bus. Conversations were either boring or overly intriguing. Either way, because it was English, she couldn't help but eavesdrop: *'I'm not convinced by these new washing powder tabs,'* or, *'It was lovely. Top Notch. Big fuck-off steak by the Med every night. Cheap as chips,'* and, *'I'm on my way to collect the greenstone now. I'll bring it home to Auckland in a fortnight. We'll repatriate all the greenstone in the world eventually.'* When she had been surrounded by foreign language human voices had sheltered her from loneliness, yet had not interfered in her thoughts. Here her thoughts were pulled this way and that by the words of strangers. Repatriating greenstone? That one was too interesting to leave alone.

Brooke turned to the New Zealander, who sat in the seat across the aisle. Using her friendly-traveller voice, she asked, 'Excuse me. I hope you don't think I'm being nosy, but did you say something about greenstone?' He looked at her carefully, as though establishing what depth of answer would suit her. He was tall with green eyes and dark curls and reminded her of Kade.

'When all the greenstone is returned, Aotearoa will be in balance again.'

'Right. Good luck then,' said Brooke, not wanting to flirt. She began to move away.

'So if you have any Tiki ornaments send them to their home,' he said and smiled. She smiled back at this man with a mission, suddenly so unlike Kade, who, despite all the stories, did not seem to have a clear purpose in life.

Where was Kade now? He could be anywhere. Most likely still in India, having found a new girl to hypnotise. A torrent of jealousy poured into Brooke. She let it wash through her and away. What else was there to do with jealousy, she thought to herself.

The bus was caught in traffic. Orderly traffic: a tidy line of taillights, turning all the puddles red. Suddenly the whole scene seemed red: people outside wore red or carried red bags. The coach pulled up beside a big red postal van: the Royal Mail, a coat of arms, the lion and the unicorn. England. Where was his red rucksack? Would he realise she had searched it? She imagined him somewhere in the hills, in the mist, missing her.

The lights changed and the bus pulled up outside Euston Station. Brooke nodded goodbye to the greenstone man and walked past one of the old stone entrance posts. They were inscribed with all the destinations of the trains: Manchester, Leeds, Rugby, Stirling, and Glasgow. She walked through the glass doors. The white-flecked black marble concourse spread under people's feet like a night sky, with a quality that reminded her of India. But in India whole families lived in stations, doing all their cooking and cleaning there too. Such an expanse of floor would never be visible. Euston did feel busy though, but with ads and information on giant screens and discarded newspapers. All the writing caught her attention; headlines yelled MASSIVE FLOODING IN THE SOUTH EAST. She felt forced to read as well as listen, and wished literacy and hearing could be turned off at will.

The culture shock of coming home felt far greater than that of arriving in Asia. She braced herself. This was going to take some getting used to. She had experienced so much, but now here she was, back where she'd started, the only visible difference her tanned skin. People walked by, ignoring her. That felt really strange. She remembered Tree, the wise, under a ceiling fan in the heat: 'And then you go home and nobody gives a toss about your holiday snaps or your glimpses of enlightenment. They've probably just sat there watching TV the whole time. Don't expect them to be interested.' Her mum and dad would be though, wouldn't they? She could not wait to see her sisters.

From the secret pocket of her rucksack, she produced a cash card, its hologram as shiny and square as the buildings. She slid it into the hole-in-the-wall, typed in the code still etched in her memory, despite all the experience she had layered on top of it, and out popped crisp notes, as minted and structured as London. After buying a bottle of water to turn a note into coins, she phoned her older sister.

'Hello?'

'Hi Sam.'

'Brookkin! How are you? Is it hot there, cos it's really pissing down here?' Brooke looked out at the rain.

'Sam, I'm in London!'

Forty minutes later Brooke found herself in a van, pressed against cut flowers and a very affectionate sister. They drove straight to the pub at the end of Sam's street.

115

Brooke sat opposite Sam, gripping the stem of a huge white wine spritzer.

'Sooo, did you fall in love?'

Brooke smiled into her glass. All the time Brooke had been saving to go away, Sam and Charlotte had teased her that she was going to fall in love with some nutter-hippy and end up wearing hand-painted shoes, eating mung beans and living happy-ever-after in the jungle. Brooke had been sure she would not. But she had. Apart from the living happily ever after in the jungle bit, and the hand-painted shoes. And they'd only had mung beans the once.

'You're blushing,' said Sam. 'You *did* fall in love.'

'Yes, I did.' Brooke paused. 'And he *was* a nutter hippy.' She smiled again.

'Yeah?' said Sam.

Brooke leaned forward. 'Yeah. But second generation. Not all enthusiastic about yoga or dope or weaving yoghurt or whatever. Grew up in some camp in Scotland.'

'Wow.'

'And *really* a nutter.'

Sam looked concerned. Brooke continued, using a jokey, mocking tone. 'He said he could breathe water and when he drank he could taste the emotions water had, well ... ' She struggled for a word. ' ... downloaded. Said he could tell how I was feeling when he kissed me or ... ' Brooke took a gulp of wine ' ... went down on me.'

Sam laughed into her glass, said 'That's the most original chat-up line I've ever heard,' and gave Brooke a searching smile. 'Seems to have worked a treat on you. So tell me, was it all kissing in temples and sex on the beach?'

'No. A waterfall actually.' Brooke suddenly felt shy.

Sam softened her tone, 'When can we meet him? Are you still seeing him?'

'I don't know,' said Brooke.

'Like that is it? What was his name?'

'Kade.'

'And what was so great about him?'

Brooke took a big gulp of wine. 'Just about everything.'

# Thirst

Scotland was a grey and green blaze. Outside the train, the pale sandstone and concrete of Edinburgh blurred past replaced by rolling hills, craggy mountains, firs, lochs and the occasional small grey town. Soon he would be by his pool, the pool that was preventing him seeking Brooke in England. This metal train, and his train of thought, propelled him towards the pool. The forests and hills and towns all hurtled towards the pool. Every thought was about the pool. The thoughts turned to song, a replacement for Ohm Namah Shiva. 'That pool, that pool.' Rain lashed the train, adding rhythm. 'That pool,' he thought. 'The pool is why I couldn't give my love to Brooke. I wanted her to know all of me, but I don't know all of me. I have to go back. I have to find out what happened.'

Then other pools pummelled his thoughts: the orange-rocked pool where he had first met Brooke; the pool in Manali where he'd got her note. Briefly he recalled its beauty, and then remembered that that waterfall was too young to form a pool. No pool and no Brooke. He regretted leaving it so long before going to Manali to find her, but he knew he would not start searching for her in the labyrinth of South East England. Not yet, at least. The willow pool, on the other hand, he was sure of finding.

The train hurried on, the rain hurtled down and 'that pool, that pool, that pooo-oooo-l' became a classic in Kade's collection of internal tunes.

It was still raining when Kade alighted and stuck his thumb out for a lift. The drops were soft, a stroke on his cheeks, like a lock of Brooke's hair. He lifted his face away from the grey of the motorway to the sky. The rain began to fly at him horizontally, tasting of road. 'Ach, bollocks,' he said, and sought shelter under a fir on the embankment. Inside its circle of dry, the world was quieter. Sighing, he sat down. He had been constantly moving recently, and had rushed so much he felt like he had arrived in Scotland early. Miserable and excited he waited for his soul to catch up with his body. And as his soul caught up, it told him, again, the story of before he left for India.

Over dinner their conversation had reached no rhythm. Now it had stopped. Outside the night looked fresh: the silver moonrays reached deep into the loch, and reflected in the raindrops on the ivy that grew across the windowpane. But inside felt jaundiced as he sat with his mother, feeling angry.

The Lodge's communal kitchen was too bright. When he was a child the grown-ups had returned from town infectious with delight at their discount yellow paint. But deflation set in when they opened the tin. As soon as the paint had dried the grown-ups – his mother, and Ursula and the other crew that were kicking round back then – encouraged the children to stick their art on the wall. One of his was still there: the willow pool and the waterfall, rendered in felt-tip and glitter.

The others were at a ceilidh in Kittim, but he was wheezy and the prospect of teams of soap-scented giggling girls and red-faced men twirling sweat made his ribs grip tighter, so he had stayed behind and his mother had too.

She flicked through a local guidebook. That riled him. They had lived here all his life. She knew the area intimately, from the Viking burial grounds to the crannogs. Yawning, she pushed her hand through her raven hair. A single strand tangled itself into her diamond ring and broke free from the others. She unwound it and let it fall.

He shoved his plate away. He had caught the trout that morning, loving the feeling of the sun waking his muscles. Now all that was left was bones. He reached for the bottle of expensive mineral water that some French backpackers had left, lifted it and observed the kitchen, rain, loch, mountains, clouds and moon caught inside. He poured two glassfuls.

'Ta love,' muttered his mother, unconsciously signing simultaneously, causing a pang of missing for his grandmother, who had been more talkative than his mother, despite being deaf.

His mum was quiet, closed, some said. With her rare beautiful smile, and hair that shone, people wondered why she was single, but Kade liked having her to himself. They had fun together, swimming and diving, and they were the only people at the Sight who could sign, folding secret conversation into the air. But they never talked about big things, and that was why he was angry.

Of course, at a place like the Sight there were always people to answer the Why questions. But some things only his mother knew, like about his father, and the Tasting.

She sipped her water absentmindedly. All people drank absentmindedly, which infuriated him. The only water that he could drink with confidence was the water from the well. He regarded the French water. What would it do? He touched the glass to his lips, imagining – hoping – it contained the joy of can-can dancers, the courage of revolutionaries, or the calm of philosophers. But as it reached his taste buds, the saddest moment of someone's life entered him like a sob.

He spat it back into the glass and tried to suppress the grief it forced into him. But it was futile.

120

Swallowing tears, he thundered across the kitchen and poured his glassful down the sink, not caring about washing grief and anger into the water supply. No one else could Taste.

'What's up love?'

'AS IF YOU DON'T KNOW,' he shouted.

She looked as though he had struck her. Her voice trembled. 'What's the matter with you?'

'It's not mine. Not my emotion. I'm not sad.'

'Why are you crying then?'

'This water's full of grief.'

'I haven't seen you cry for years.'

He wanted to thump his chest and shout, 'I've been keeping it inside. I didn't want to upset you,' but he was not that dramatic. Instead he pointed to her glass and asked, 'Can't you taste the grief?'

She took a sip. The feeling of being humoured scraped through him. 'You were always so imaginative,' she said. Furious he grabbed the glass from her hand and hurled it away. It smashed against his picture of the willow pool. They watched the ink bleed.

When the silence had finished he said, 'Every time I drink, I feel emotions that aren't mine.'

'Maybe it's your hormones?' she offered, too quickly. 'Hormonal changes.'

Hormonal changes? That was almost funny. He was eighteen bloody years old.

'No. NO! You shouldn't keep things from people. Not things that matter. Tell me what the hell is going on.'

She took too long to speak.

'Maybe I should see a doctor,' he threatened. She had never let him see a proper doctor in his life.

'No!'

'Why not?'

She gave him a look as piercing as the midday sun. 'I thought it had gone away. When you were little, while you drank, you would cry and cry, or laugh and laugh. I could never tell why. One day you said 'Bad ice,' and threw the cubes across the room.' She paused. 'I thought it had gone away.'

'No. I just stopped talking about it.' He saw tears welling in her eyes. 'For fuck's sake don't cry. You're always bursting into tears unless everything is happy happy happy. You've got to tell me why this happens.' His tone sounded new to him, as though his voice were breaking for the second time.

'Well you certainly don't get it from my side of the family. Must be from your father.' Her tone was flippant but he could hear the fear. His father, the man who had disappeared under the water. Died.

Silence gripped them once more, then was broken by one of her teardrops splashing on the wooden floor. 'He wasn't a lifesaver,' she said, quietly. He felt heavy.

'And I don't know if he is dead.'

He felt light, like before a dive. 'What do you mean? Where was he from? Mum?' His heart felt hot. 'Why did you say he was a lifeboat man?'

'I wanted you to be proud of him.'

'Why didn't you tell me the truth?'

'Because ... I don't know the truth.'

'Where was he from?'

'I don't know. He signed. It wasn't an accent I knew.'

'He was deaf?'

'I think he could hear but he spoke with his hands.'

'Didn't you ask?'

'We didn't know each other for long.' She looked down, seeming to struggle to find the right words amongst her new-age vocabulary. 'We had a very strong spiritual connection, but we both knew ... It was like we met to conceive you. I didn't see him again.'

'Where did you meet him?'

'Here. I met him here.' Trying to sound upbeat, she said. 'I don't know what this water emotion thing is about. I wish I did. But I can take you to the place where I met your father.' She pointed to the picture on the wall, 'It was there.'

'The caves?'

'Yes.'

Only his mother and he knew about the caves under the willow pool. He was never to tell anyone else, she said. The caves were where magic met reality. She had never taken him there.

'Cave diving is the most dangerous thing in the world,' said Kade. 'Why do you go?'

'I go looking for your father.'


They tumbled into saturated sunlight. Cold held their bodies, crept into their wetsuits. Only skin divided the pool from his blood. Kade's mother smiled as best she could in her mask, and beckoned him. Exhilarated, he swam down to the mouth of the tunnel. She tied a nylon thread to a rock, and with another thousand feet ready to unravel, she swam through the entrance.

He paused to look at the limbs of light, flickering and unfolding, and his mother was lost from sight. Stomach muscles contracting, he grabbed for the length of nylon. Then she switched on her head torch and cracked her glo-stick, releasing phosphorescent pink. He cracked his yellow glo-stick, and followed into the underwaterland that had been promised for so long.

The tunnel was too narrow for him to turn. He swam carefully, wary of bumping his tank. He became aware of air pockets at the roof, and realised he was swimming uphill. For a long time he swam, too excited to be scared. Then his calf cramped. He stopped and manually moved his foot. Stubborn blood flowed again and he relaxed. He took off his fins. He did not really need them anyway.

Now he was too far from his mum. He couldn't call. She couldn't come back. A rock scraped at his side, breaking his glo-stick and he shed yellow globules. Breathing heavily, dangerously, he turned on his head torch. Battery power awakened his own power and the tunnel opened up under his light. At the apex was his mum. He increased his pace until she took his hand comfortingly.

He looked at the underwater path they had just travelled. The blackness was interrupted by yellow globules, like cat's eyes for passing pike.

She released his hand. 'Are you ready?' she signed.

'Yes,' he signed, before his mind said no.

'Mind your head.' She took her tank off, but kept the DV in her mouth so she could breathe, and motioned for him to copy. He gave her a questioning look, but her hands were occupied and she did not answer. She pushed the tank upwards through a small tunnel, and then followed it. He did the same.

He emerged into air and chalky green light that was like daylight in a wood. His mother hauled him up. He removed his DV and gasped. 'Where are we?' he asked and was startled by the loudness of his voice. She pointed upwards to where a beam of daylight filtered through a shaft.

'We're inside the mountain.' She leaned towards him, nudging him with her shoulder. 'And look.' She pointed to another pool that looked brighter than it should. 'Do you want to go on?'

'For sure.'

'I love you, you know,' she said as they plunged down into a wider cave.

Fast dark shapes loomed towards them. Not pike. People. Other divers? Maybe Taste them. He removed his DV and swam forward to see if he could tell what they felt, who they were. But pain crushed his thoughts as he hit an overhang. He felt his eyes close as consciousness drifted away.

Kade woke in the first cave, alone. Compounded realities pounded his head. Moonlight whispered from the small hole in the roof. He raised himself up, nauseous, confused. He heard water moving and spun around, then jumped in fright. A person was climbing into the cave.

This was not his mother, and was not mountain rescue. The man – he was naked and the shape of his maleness was clear – made unintelligible words with pale intricately marked fingers.

Must be asleep, in a lucid dream, he told himself. But the moon looked real and his toes felt cold. Cold had never dared be dreamed before. A silver dolphin danced on a chain around the man's neck.

He woke flat on his back feeling that she hadn't gone. She was somewhere, watching over him. He felt none of the happy achievement he had anticipated before the dive, but he felt okay. The sun shone in, a beam touching his outstretched hand. In this cave, he had dreamed of a man with a visible bloodstream, and a familiar presence.

Stiff in the wetsuit, he stretched, feeling like his flesh could crack like decayed rubber. His fingers touched something small, hard and cold, too

125

geometrical to be natural. It was a ring. His mum's ring? No, different, older. As old as a diamond ring could be and still be delicately made. Looking to where he had found the ring he saw something light-coloured and narrow. It was shaped like a large needle and made of bone, horn, or tusk. It felt warmer than he expected, and was engraved with a mountain and lake, forming a circle. He held the two objects before him, wondering.

He saw his pack and tank, seemingly placed purposely against the cave wall. Putting the ring and bone carving in his pack, he examined the tank. It was scratched and dented. He wanted his mother. 'Mum,' he cried, 'MUM!' No reply came.

He tried to think straight. It was morning when they had entered the willow pool. He had seen the moon, and now it was daytime again. If his mother had made it out, she would have alerted the authorities and they would have rescued him already. But no friendly voices called to him. No one knew these caves existed. And the chances of a passing hiker hearing his yells were lower than the chance of hypothermia. He could not stay here.

His tank still worked. Steeling himself, he entered the tunnel that led back to the willow pool. His mother's guidance thread was gone. He swam on.

When his air ran out, sense twisted into him as though waterborne. He discarded his tank and swam forward, scraping his fingernails on the tunnel roof until he reached an air pocket. He held himself in place. Trying to obliterate images of panic, he panted, filling himself with stone-scented air. He set off gently, swimming on his back, fearful of smashing his face. He forgot about his mother as his survival instinct took over. Fight or flight. Fight or swim. Another air pocket. He willed rich oxygenated redness into himself and swam on. His blood flowed loudly, objecting. He reached about for air, even the smallest amount. There was none. He scrambled at the rock, pulling himself forward. There must be another air pocket! Red became purple. Fear tasted magnetic.

He saw distant daylight and tried to power towards it, out of the willow pool, but his lungs were flat. They were desperate to breathe in. 'Don't,' he told them. 'Don't. I'll die if you do.' Thoughts spiralling like a hurricane, he forced his body to move forward, towards life.

His instincts fought each other. 'Inhale,' said some. 'No, no,' said others. 'It's water. It's WATER!' But there was no time. The desire to breathe overrode the instinct for air. His lungs heaved. He tried to swallow, but his insistent lungs drew the water deep. His vision turned blue

People said that drowning was the most pleasant way to die. That's what he would do; drown in the fluid of Scotland's caves. No, he could make it. People could have lungs full of liquid and still survive.

He gulped in more water. Blue became purple, then red. He was still swimming, breathing in the edges of heaven. If this was death, it was good. He felt vital. He swam on. Another breath. In. Out. In. Out.

The hurricane of thoughts began to clear. Kade could see the willow pool. He swam hard and finally the tunnel released him into the wider water. He shook with relief, waiting to float upwards, but with lungs full of liquid he was as heavy as water. He gripped the soft plants at the wall of the pool, hauled himself up and fell into the air. On his hands and knees he coughed for his life.

Realities had switched. An instinct, left over from when all animals breathed water, had whispered to him not to be afraid, to allow his blood to take oxygen from water. Or had he been drowning and managed to save himself? Spiralling thoughts consumed his oxygen more rapidly than holding his breath, and he fell into flaccid exhaustion.

Alertness crept back slowly. He became aware that he was clenching the earth under the willow, he noticed the cold air scratching his lungs, then the noise of the fall crashed through his mind.

He hauled himself up and stood above the pool, arms crossed, challenging it. He had to go back in. He had to find her.

He entered the pool, but as he slipped below the surface, fear penetrated his cells, turning him from a brave man into a scared teenager.

Trembling, ashamed, he left the pool

Five months later they had held her wake.


The rain stopped, bringing him back to the motorway. He slipped down the embankment and stuck his thumb out.

At first, grief had soaked him, drenched him, slowed his every movement. Gradually its intensity diminished, replaced by guilt. Now he was freer, but would always be ashamed that fear had stopped him going straight back into the willow pool.

He arrived in the village of Kittim at dusk and walked the last four miles to the Sight. As he turned off the road and started down the track, his spirits were lifted by the weaving smoke from people's fires rising to join the mackerel sky. A near-full moon turned the loch silver. He was happy to be home.

Who was there? People came and went and returned so much that he probably wouldn't know exactly who was around until morning. In the evening people retired to the Lodge and to their tents, tipis, yurts, caravans and buses. He looked forward to them emerging with the daylight. This time *he* had left and returned and could tell stories to the others.

Damn, he had not brought any presents. All he had were a few stones from the Ganges. Precious things to him, and millions of Hindus, but not necessarily to the people here. Maybe to the land, though. He would take one to the willow pool and drop it in. He would take one with him when he dived there, to bring him luck. He had met Brooke by the Ganges. It had taken a whole beach full of Ganges stones for that kind of luck. He missed her, but he had to do this.

With a whoosh of bike wheels, Sky and Timmy appeared on the drive, holding their handlebars like horse reins and neighing as they halted. They were seven or eight now and had grown up here. Sky flicked his overgrown blond fringe and grinned, showing a missing tooth. Timmy, with red curls and a solemn expression, patted the back of his bike.

'Who is it?' Timmy whispered through the dusk.

'I think it's Kade,' said Sky, lisping.

'Howdy Stranger,' said Timmy. 'Did you see many Injuns?'

Kade laughed. 'Not the kind you mean, cowboy.'

'Hey. Do you like my new watch?' asked Sky, thrusting his wrist at Kade. These kids, like him, spent so much time in trees and rivers that any piece of technology was a sparkling jewel to them.

'It's great,' said Kade, more at Sky's enthusiasm than at the new watch. Then without a goodbye the kids tore away up the hill behind him. Kade realised he had not looked at the time. He hurried on downhill, knowing the kids would come careering down the drive at full horsepower.

There was no news about his mum, or they would have said.

When he arrived at the courtyard, he was surprised to see so many cars parked there, under the firs. He looked up at the sky. Of course, it was full moon tomorrow night. Midsummer. People were here for a party. He saw a large white thousand cc overland motorbike and felt his anticipation reach a peak. Stirling was here.

The side door to the Lodge was open and he heard voices from the communal kitchen. He could see Ursula and some others drinking wine at the long table. He felt almost at home as he walked in. 'Hi everyone,' he said.

'Kade! Wow you're so tanned,' said everyone.

That night he was fed some stodgy bland food that he really enjoyed, and, thankfully, he was not asked too many questions. They could see that he was exhausted. When he closed the wooden door of the yurt he was glad to be left alone. Amid familiar people he felt lonely and he missed his mother. He turned his thoughts to his dive. He'd need some food – waterproof food: fruit, vegetables and maybe some fresh fish. Also a powerful torch. No, two. Three *and* waxed matches. Maybe a medical kit – those rocks could be sharp. What else? The Ganges' stones and a knife.

It was nearly a year since his mum had gone. If he found some answers to the questions that had troubled him, he would be free to give his love to Brooke.

# Iceberg

Brooke woke at three-sixteen am, as she had every night since Varanasi. Three-sixteen am. Question time. She played a game with herself – naming fruit and vegetables in alphabetical order. Usually she found its lulling boringness stemmed the flow of worries and bored her to sleep.

A for apple

B for banana

C for carrot ...

Anger? No, she hadn't felt it. 'What a wanker,' she'd thought, 'what a tosser.' But her heart hadn't been in those thoughts. She just hoped Kade was okay. Was he okay? *Was* he okay? Was he *okay*? Perhaps worrying if he was okay stopped her feeling too angry. You couldn't be angry at the dead, or the wounded, or the completely screwed up, could you? Well, actually, yeah you could. She was angry at a friend's boyfriend for overdosing on heroin and *he* was dead.

Three-twenty am. Again. But tonight she was not going to feel sorry for herself. Instead, anger shook free from its inhibitions. Yes, Kade was completely screwed up – but did he have to take it out on her? She had been perfectly happy with her rose-tinted glasses. They had suited her. Why did he have to rip them off? Was she to blame for coming from a happy family, with a mum and dad and sisters? Was it her fault that no great disasters had befallen her, that her parents and grandparents were alive, that she had grown up somewhere normal? No, it was not, although he had certainly seemed to try and make her feel guilty. But someone can't *make* someone else feel guilty. They

131

can make the situation conducive to it, but ... you can lead a horse to water, but ... She must have chosen to feel guilty. Brooke became even angrier at herself for being angry at herself. She tossed and turned.

D for ... D for ... D for damsons

E for eggplant

F for fig ... fennel.

Why was it always about her? Were all the events in the world designed for her to learn about herself? Was everyone else, the whole universe, a figment of her imagination? Was she the centre of everything? Was Kade just a person-shaped experience designed to help her grow? And when would she be fully-grown? When could she put all she'd learned into action? Three thirty-five. A red light on the clock ...

G for Grapes.

H for ... H for haricot beans

I for ... ? I for ... ?

At ten past four, Brooke concluded that there were no fruits or vegetables beginning with 'I'. She concluded that everyone was the centre of the universe, without that getting in the way of everyone else being the centre of the universe. And she concluded that, yes, she was marginally angry with Kade. Then she slept.

The first thing she thought of when she woke was iceberg lettuce. Then she noticed the killer hangover. Nausea, headache, jetlag and hunger mixed with happiness and relief to be home, well, and at Sam's. She massaged her temples. She hadn't been drunk for months. Smoked dope, sure, but no alcohol. She was cheap to take out drinking now. She'd only had three spritzers! Water. Must drink water. In the kitchen she poured a glass. Good old city tap water. Its gritty feel was the best thing for exfoliating the sticky throat of hangovers.

She put the kettle on. It was glass and she watched the water boil. Where had the water in the kettle been? Through seven people already? That *was* pretty disgusting. Drank and pissed and bled and sweated by seven people. Or was it actually rather lovely? Did the water really hold their feelings? Had Kade really been able to Taste what she felt while he kissed her? It had certainly seemed so.

Kade was always in her thoughts, whenever she turned on a tap, or drank, or washed. She wished she had a 'Kade off,' button, so her trains of thought did not always lead to him.

She took a cup of tea to Sam, and told her of Kade's dark glossy hair and bright light-green eyes, a colour she'd not seen before or since.

'You told me all this last night honey,' said Sam, so Brooke described how Kade had changed the way she looked at the world, how now, everything seemed connected and things that were just stories before, seemed possible. But she made light of his claims.

'I thought you went for blond men,' said Sam, leaning back on the pillows.

'So did I,' said Brooke. 'But I don't anymore.' She no longer went for *men*, she went for Kade.

'What about that bloke you used to see – James?' asked Sam. 'Wasn't he your type? I remember you came home one day all excited, saying you were in love. Nice car he had.'

Brooke's hand was clasped to her mouth. She had completely forgotten about James. She remembered she had told James she loved him, because she had thought that was what people were supposed to do. But *that* had not been love. Kade, she would love forever, even if she never saw him again.

The way he smiled after he kissed her. His hands. The backs of his hands. His fingertips on her lips. The way she felt as she lay next to him, her body filled to the edges with love, as if she could hold him so close she would somehow be inside him, look through the same eyes, join their heartbeats. At first she had thought that she would be comfortable *being* him. But that feeling had changed. She would not want his life, but she hoped he was okay. Tenderness beat in her heart.

'Sam,' she said dreamily. 'I don't know if Kade and I were souls who were meant to meet, teach each other something and then part, like tourists in each others lives, or if we were supposed to join and grow? Or were we two people, full of ideas, full of love, but with too much past and too much craziness ... '

Sam looked at Brooke and said gently, 'Listen honey, I think, for the moment, you just need to come down to earth. Go home, see mum and dad and Charlotte, see your friends. Relax. Whatever will be will be.'

'Yeah. Maybe you're right,' said Brooke.


All the way back to Euston 'Que Sera, Sera' played in Brooke's head and she found it fairly effective at blocking Kade out. By the time she boarded the train she had just about tricked herself into feeling optimistic about going home.

The train sped through the suburbs and out into the fields and Brooke saw the first shimmer of the canal that had rippled its way through her childhood. The train slowed for her station. Her eyes glazed over, her autopilot set for home. She tried to shake herself out of it. Sure, it would be fun to see everyone at first, but then what would happen? Same as ever. Friendly. Boring. 'In the end, I stopped going back,' said Tree, in her memory.

As the train braked Brooke heard a loud crack from the platform. A man, fallen to the ground, clutched a can of cider upright, despite being in the process of defending himself from the half-hearted kicks of another man, also successfully hanging on to his can. The crack of the cider drinker's head sharpened Brooke up. Her eyes unglazed. 'I don't want to step onto that platform,' she thought. 'Sod Rayton, I'll stay on the train. Sod the hundred pound fine. Actually *sod* the hundred pound fine. I'm not going to pay that.'

The train pulled away, and she stood, feeling refreshed, and went to see the conductor. With assertiveness well honed by bargaining with rickshaw drivers, she convinced him to let her just pay the ticket and not the fine.

'Where do you want to go then love?' he asked.

'Stirling,' replied Brooke, controls fully wrestled back from her auto pilot.

She returned to her seat elated that she had been so well received, and feeling a hundred pounds richer. Scotland. The highlands. The end of the line. Just for a while she could find a time in which to unwind, or perhaps to wind up and gear up before returning south. She would go to the softness of the countryside, where nothing was squared off at the edges. She would find the Sight.

# Cheers

Dawn light pushed past the canvas and through Kade's eyelids. He woke disoriented, thinking he was in an Indian tent at the Kumbh Mela, until the fresh and smoky scent of the air found him.

He stood and stretched, well rested. He dressed and then rummaged through his bag for the metal bottle, found it, and left the yurt. Striding downhill through the other homes, the tipis, Mongolian yurts, Bedouin tents, caravans, and the bright coloured tents of those on camping holidays, he headed for the treehouse. Stirling might be there.

The treehouse circled an old oak by the river. Kade had helped build it and it was splendid, with proper floorboards, glazed windows, a potbelly stove, a double bed, a door carved with the rune for 'tree' and a veranda all the way round. Sure enough, there was Stirling on the veranda, feet up, shirt off, smoking.

'I've never seen you in the summer,' Kade shouted up at him, through the branches.

'Kade!' said Stirling with pleasure. 'Wow, you're tanned. Come on up.' Kade climbed the uneven but strong spiral staircase. Stirling was waiting at the top to embrace him: a big bear hug, to squeeze out shyness.

'Here,' said Kade, as they stepped apart. He presented the bottle of Ganges water to Stirling.

'Brilliant, you remembered!' said Stirling. 'Thank you.' He reached into the room and withdrew a near-spherical glass decanter. 'Here's the rest. Let's mix in the Ganges.' He motioned for Kade to do so. Kade picked the wax seal off, undid the stopper, paused to say, 'It's from upriver. It won't make anyone sick,' then carefully emptied his water into the decanter.

Stirling held the mix up to the sky. Morning sunlight passed through it, casting a watery shadow on the tree trunk. 'From Kittim and Mecca, from Jerusalem and the Vatican, the Nile and the Amazon, Victoria and Niagara falls, Iguaçu and Alice Springs, the Ganges, the Thames and the Tay. Stored at four degrees – water's favourite temperature. Beautiful!' He took a couple of shot glasses and filled them. 'Here,' he said and placed one in Kade's hand.

Kade looked closely at the water in the decanter. Sometimes water was diseased. People said water *carried* illnesses. For Kade, water that spread illness was ill itself, not a carrier but a sufferer. Was this water capable of spreading health? Happiness? Sacredness?

'Cheers!' said Stirling, knocking back his shot.

'Cheers,' said Kade and did the same.

As the water slipped over his tongue he felt ... he felt? Nothing. Nothing more than water. His mouth was confused, expecting to be Tasting emotions, feeling as though it had misheard, but nothing came. The only feelings he had were his own. The water made him happy. It did not force him to feel second-hand happiness. It made him happy because it quenched his thirst. It was just water, plain and simple.

Excitement grew in Kade. He was transformed into an ordinary man drinking water in a treehouse with a friend. He looked at the trees and the river and the loch beyond, noticing how they simply *were*. Nothing more, nothing less. But beautiful. Kade laughed out loud. 'That really hits the spot,' he said.

Stirling looked closely into Kade's eyes, reading him. 'That's genuinely done something for you, hasn't it?' he said. 'I'm saving the rest for the party.' He put the stopper back in the bottle and clapped his hands together. 'How was India?'

'Amazing. How was the rest of the world?' asked Kade.

'Pretty amazing. Amazingly pretty.'

'I met a beautiful girl,' said Kade, briefly feeling the need to confide, then unable to say more.

'Maybe you'll see her again,' said Stirling after a pause.

Kade suddenly felt disorientated. The landscape increased in intensity, especially the river. Kade felt a pull, as though the river was a magnet. It was the same pull that had brought him here, instead of searching for Brooke. He excused himself from Stirling with a 'Back in time for the party!' and ran to his yurt. In a trance, he packed the things he needed, then heeded the pull to the willow pool.

# Immersion

Brooke stepped out onto the stillness of the platform, crossed the tracks and hailed a taxi from the tiny rank, feeling mildly embarrassed about her southern accent.

The driver gossiped all the way out of town and on into the mountains. The campsite had changed he told her. It used to be alright, but years ago the owner had experienced a life crisis and now favoured a different kind of camper. As they drove down the steep driveway, Brooke saw what he meant. The field between the road and the loch was coloured by, not only normal tents, but also wigwams and large round pale tents, with walls made of wooden lattice, and marquees like those at the Kumbh Mela. Campfires smoked. So this was where Kade had grown up.

The driver dropped her off in a courtyard by a large stone house and drove away up the hill. Brooke passed a group of parked vehicles: some old, some new, some kitted out for living in. Ducking as the wind pulled the fir trees forward to stroke her, she approached a big grey wooden door at the side of the building. Warm light peeked through the slats. Ivy grew over half the wall, and on her left was an old fashioned well with a bucket. Birds sang and a fat white duck wandered about. There was She could hear drumming, and smell garlic and smoke in the air.

Finally, Brooke knocked on the door and it was opened by a middle-aged woman with a kindly, pretty, been-there-done-that-and-survived face. Behind the woman was a plump collection of raincoats, scarves, and hats, and above them, on a shelf, was a tangle of spider plants with a statue of Bacchus peeking out.

'Hello. Um, I'm hoping to camp here,' said Brooke. 'But I don't have a tent.'

In a posh Scottish accent the woman said, 'Well, we're pretty busy because of the solstice, but I 'spect we can squeeze you in.' She smiled and introduced herself as Ursula.

'Means bear doesn't it?' said Brooke, liking the woman.

'Yes,' said Ursula. A pause. 'Hang on a sec.' She reached behind the open door and, with a magician's finesse, extracted a tent. 'Easy to put up this one.'

As Brooke walked down towards the loch, through the site – the Sight – it dawned on her that Kade must have felt quite at home at the Kumbh Mela. She looked at the glowing-cheeked people moving around the field. Most looked too old to have skin that good, although one or two had deep wrinkles as though a giant had left his thumbprint on their faces. A few had dreadlocks, which Brooke thought looked much more appropriate here against the backdrop of heather and bracken than they ever did in cities, against concrete and glass. Some pretty young women were dressed a bit like fairies, in delicate dresses and negligees with muddy edges. Dogs ran around, and kids too. Brooke could still hear drumming and birdsong and she could smell something delicious cooking. She could not see Kade.


There it was: the pool. It seemed slightly smaller than the last time he had seen it, but it spoke as loud, inviting him in, like the eye of the storm, like the centre of the universe. He sat beside the water and watched it throw itself over the black bones of rock to pound the pool, showering out sound and scent as it changed from white to green to red-brown, and then white again as it reached the edges. Kade could see the tunnel entrance, but only because he knew it was there.

He waited until the sun's tilt had disguised the tunnel completely, then he stood, threw his backpack in, raised his hands, touched his palms together above his head, looked at the sun, flexed his spine, and dived. He swam hard until he reached the pool floor. Among the fish, rocks and waterweeds, he flipped over with arms outreached and looked at the wet sun, swaying in his ripples.

He breathed out hard. He breathed out his fear of finding his mother's body, and his 'what ifs?' about Brooke. This was the right thing for him to be doing. He knew. His expression softened and his air bubbles streamed upwards to join the sky, carrying anxiety away with them. Nothing to fear, he told himself, nothing to regret. He pictured his lungs, his tiny alveoli like water sponges, no need for air. Telling his heart to prepare for a different style of oxygen, he breathed in.

It came easy. As the water entered him he felt pleasure, wonder, satisfaction and relief, and those emotions were his own. With lungs full of water he felt whole. No argument between liquid and air. Very relaxed. His organs, blood, skin, hair, face, all water. 'Why me?' he thought. 'Why can I breathe water?' It felt strange but also normal and good.

He picked up his pack entered the tunnel and began to breathe darker water. He swam a few metres, then realising he did not need to make his life harder, he switched on the beam of his headtorch and swam on.

So close to the rock he felt vulnerable but his pace was confident as he made for the cave where he last heard his mum's voice all those months before. *'We are inside the mountain.'* He'd been so young, he realised.

He swam through water that could have been anywhere, could have been anything. Perhaps it had been drunk by him, or been sap in the willow above. It would go on to be anywhere, anything, maybe drunk by Brooke, passed around the world, and sweated out at a ceilidh a thousand years from now.

When he arrived beside the first cave and looked up into its entrance, he was hit by an image of his mother's decaying body – on the floor in the cave, or worse, floating in the water near him. Moving. The shock made him thrash, trying to fight the water that had taken her. The water turned loud. His throat tightened. He drank some water and released some. He heard his own voice say 'Kade!' and began to breathe again, knowing a fight with the water would kill him.

He decided against entering the cave. If by any chance she had survived, and was there, she would have heard him. He waited, quiet, then swam on, further into the tunnel, the corridor. Gradually he realised that there were more phosphorescent caves. Then the more he saw, the more he could see, appearing from nowhere, becoming visible because he was looking. Each cave felt like a thought, happening only because he was in the process of thinking. It felt like he was swimming in his own mind.

He swam on and on until he forgot he was breathing water, until he forgot he had ever been anywhere else. His brain synapsed at light speed: he could physically feel new pathways forming in his head, mapping this world: a world that only he knew about and only he could explore. No divers could make it through. It was too cold, too far and too dangerous. But for him it felt as easy as floating. Then the tunnel came to an end.

On his left was a submerged cave, large and beckoning. To the right was another. Choosing the left he swam in, feeling the sudden hugeness of the water. There was no light here except his beam. He swam on, feeling the freedom of not having a safety line or a diving buddy, then shuddered, aware that breathing water did not mean he was unable to become lost, swimming deeper and deeper into the planet, until he was at the centre.

Being in the caves felt like dreaming, and he did not want to wake, but he tried to liven himself up, to make sure some part of him remembered the route.

Kade saw a light and swam towards it, thinking of the light at the end of the tunnel? Not death, though, but the sun through clouds of ripples. To the surface.

His head broke through the roof of water his mind was still inside the tunnel. Then he saw the Sight's beach about two hundred metres away. There were people putting lights in the trees. Behind him was a continent of loch, the grey green surface blowing towards him, grey currents pulling him further away from the beach making him feel uneasy, isolated. He turned off his torch and, wary, began to swim underwater towards the shore.

Brooke watched as rigs, decks, wires and fairy lights unravelled from vehicle boots. Speakers were stacked up like Stonehenge and lights placed like fireflies in the trees. The smoky campsite murmured with conversation. The river, a huge insistent rush, sounded like traffic or a thunderstorm approaching. Following the sound, she walked across the field towards the edge where birch trees grew, and, holding a silver-white branch to ensure she did not pitch down the steep bank, she saw the river. White water became flat glassy water patterned by reflections. She saw a willow tree by a pool. Was that Kade's pool? Was he here?

She followed the water with her eyes, moving her gaze with the speed of its flow. At first fast, then gentle as it neared the loch, becoming a stream running through a green-carpeted wood of silver birches, then crossing the beach and entering the loch as through it were breathing out.

In the wood a young couple talked, bathed in sunset, and stroked flowers to distract their hands. She turned her gaze back to the gorge. Dusk had reached its crevices before settling on the field. So this was where Kade was from, this funny, beautiful place.

With a crack of electricity the field was flooded with beats. The water's sound was submerged, and Brooke turned around. People were gathering round fires. A few began to dance. Brooke approached a fire.

'Hello, like some tea?' asked a woman with long blonde dreads, holding a mug towards her. Brooke smiled and accepted, settling down by the fire. The flames veiled her body and steam veiled her face. The tea tasted muddy, earthy. Her tongue began to tingle. Tea with something. She was glad of the steam veil. She felt shy here, unsure quite how to behave. This wasn't home and it wasn't India. She knew no one. Sadness was creeping in. Kade was not there. He should be there, but, for all she knew, he was still in India. She stood and turned to the stranger on her left. A tall black man, looking into the fire.

'Do you know someone called Kade?'

The stranger turned to face her. The tribal scars on his cheeks were unexpected. 'Yeah,' said the man, with an African accent. 'Who's asking?' He was wary, but not challenging.

Half of Brooke wanted to say 'Sarah Brooke. His lover,' but Kade had left her. She was not his lover.

'I met him in India,' she said. 'He recommended this campsite,'

'Oh, right,' said the man. 'Well, I'm Stirling. A friend of Kade's.'

Stirling seemed to notice Brooke's quizzical look. 'When she was pregnant, my mother saw a British stamp with a picture of Stirling castle on it,' he said.

Brooke smiled.

'And you are?'

'Sarah.'

'Pleased to meet you,' said Stirling. Instead of shaking hands he passed her a joint, which she accepted.

'Is Kade around?' she asked, as casually as she could, before realising that she should have said 'pleased to meet you too.'

'He was here earlier ... ' said Stirling.

Brooke's heart leapt. He was here!

' ... but he ran off on some kind of mission. I don't know what. He's a bit of a strange one, isn't he? Do you know him well?'

There was tenderness in the man's voice. Taking a deep drag of the joint, she flicked the ash to the ground and sent the smoke to the sky.

'Yes, I'd say so.' *When* is he back?

'He said he'd be back for the party.'

'Oh,' said Brooke, and took another drag. But, it didn't feel like he would be back. She sipped more tea. The tingling she had felt on her tongue continued down her throat and into her stomach.

'He *did say* he'd met a beautiful girl in India.' Stirling looked Brooke in the eye then changed the subject. 'It's set to be an excellent party. Clear skies, happy people. If in doubt – *dance*, my mother always told me.'

Brooke smiled at Stirling and turned towards the dancers.


Something brushed his leg. Waterweed. A fish. Pike! Relax, he told himself. It has no interest in me. He quickened his pace. Then something solid and warm grabbed his ankle. He cried out, and instinct made him kick as hard as he could, but the grip tightened, pinching his skin. Holding. Not a pike. A hand. A person. He felt a flash of relief at not feeling pike's teeth, then panic and terror as he was pulled deeper and the sun and sky disappeared. A murderer? Was there a murderer in the loch? Had his mother been murdered?

He saw her looking at her frogman killer, desperate for help as she took her last breath. Her vulnerability made him ache with love. Then he saw her defiant, knowing that she would die, looking at her killer calmly as the moment came. Softening his resistance he knew he could not drown even if he wanted to. He decided to play dead, let himself go limp. He felt vengeful. A life for a life. He could terrify this killer by being alive. Pull their mask off. This murderer had picked the wrong victim. They weren't like him – they needed an aqualung.

Down. Part of his journey through life, taken through this water, pulled by this hand through layers of darkness, fathoms nearer to when he would finally stop being 'Kade.' The hand kept on pulling and, frightened, his heart missed a beat. In the silence, his thoughts and feelings blossomed into a pattern he could understand: it was too deep and too fast for any diver by now. His mum's voice flickered in his memory, saying 'You don't get it from my side of the family, must be through your father.' Waves of realisation ran through him. 'It's not a murderer's hand. It's someone like me!'

Kade's fingers spread, as though, now he was being pulled down through the water at this lightening rate, he could finally relax. Then, just as the buzzing heat reached the outer edges of his body, the pull changed direction and his blood ran cold. The depth and the dark were real. The pain of the hand's grip was real. Suddenly, he felt lucid. Even if it were magical, the hand was somehow pulling him down to earth. If this person was like him, then why were they pulling him? Could a waterbreather be a murderer?

Kade swooped both his hands down to his ankle. At the same moment he found himself flung into a cave. The force sent him backwards, blinking in the phosphorescence. The figure followed. No tank. It came closer, fast, towards him. Kade flinched anticipating a blow. Instead, the man put his hands right up to Kade's face. The hands spoke angrily.

'Never go to the surface!'

Webbed fingers talking. What was going on? What were they talking about? The hands dropped and were replaced by a man's face. Kade could see every vein. The man looked him closely in the eye. For a second, Kade questioned whether he was dreaming, but his senses were too strong. He recognised the man. He had not imagined this man all those months ago, not been crazy. Kade felt overwhelming happiness.

But the man was staring at him, showing him his anger and so not seeing Kade, or his happiness. The hands were moving so much they were shouting and stuttering. Then something caught the man's eye: Kade's headtorch. The man pulled away. Noticing the pack straps on Kade's shoulder, his expression became confused, then despondent. His hands began to move, shaking a little, talking to himself. At first Kade could not make out what the man was saying, but he kept repeating it. 'No! I was *sure* he was a Waterman. I could Taste it.' The man looked so sad.

Kade lifted his hands and signed 'Hello.'

Startled, the man looked at Kade's face, finally seeing him. 'I'm like you!' thought Kade. With large pale eyes, ringed blue with veins, the man stared deep into his eyes as if asking him a question. His skin was smooth, but he seemed old. He stared until Kade was unafraid. Then he spoke again. 'I thought you were a Waterperson, but you're not a Waterperson. You look like a Landman, but you're here, breathing water. You are neither. What are you?' asked the man. Landman? Waterman?' 'I am like you,' thought Kade. But he was also not like this man, with webbed fingers and visible veins.

A grey beam shone into the cave. The man fell into silhouette. Kade was dazzled. The beam came towards him, immersing him. His eyes adjusted and he saw that it was a headtorch. Aurora's torch. His mother's headtorch.

But it was not her. The woman's white-blonde hair was plaited and the veins around her eyes gave her a tabby-cat like appearance. She, like the man, was not wrinkled, but not young. As she straightened up, Kade saw she wore a swimming costume, leopard print, inside out, M&S label showing. On her fingers were rings, gold, worth a fortune. And on her head was the headtorch.

'WHERE IS MY MOTHER,' he shouted, but the water stopped the words.

'Who is he?' the man asked the woman.

The woman smiled reassuringly at Kade, then began to examine him with her hands. She started with his hair, but quickly moved to his eyebrows. She had none. There would be no point in trying to keep water out of eyes here, he realised. She stroked and pulled Kade's brows and looked closely at his eyes. Kade saw that the woman had the same colour eyes as him. But her corneas seemed thicker, coarser; perhaps providing protection from the water. She looked closely at Kade's stubble, and ran the back of her webbed hand along his cheek. The touch was inquisitive, not affectionate, but its gentleness poured calm into his bloodstream. Kade could see the woman's heart beating. Moving to his neck, she felt his jugular beneath his skin, and then ran her hands down the side of his body until she reached his feet. Here she smiled.

Kade began to sign 'Who are you? What am I? Where is Aurora?'

The woman took his hands in hers, felt between his fingers and touched each nail. She turned to his palms and looked there carefully. Then she released her grip and said to the man, 'Styx. He's her son.' As she said the words, her hands rippled the water and Kade felt the ripples on his skin. His heart leapt. Mum! His mother was here. The woman turning to Kade signed, 'My name

147

is Severn,' and embraced him. She signed just like Aurora, in the same accent.

'That's her headtorch,' said Kade.

'Yes,' said Severn. 'She gave it to me, and said she would not need it anymore.'

'Where is she?' asked Kade.

The woman beckoned and began to swim away. Kade followed, terrified and excited. They swam down and down. They passed through a narrow tunnel into a cave, darker than the others. She was here? Was she? No. She couldn't be. It was underwater. His abilities didn't come from his mother. She was human. Was?

On through the cave. The floor was covered in white coral. It grew like hands, stroking the water. A strange Scottish coral that needed no sunlight. Severn would lead him through here and out into a dry cave where he would find Aurora shaken, but alive. Severn stopped and moved the torch beam around the floor, looking for something. A twinkle came from below, like a bright star in the milky-way. Kade's eyes focused. His stomach turned. The coral were hands, skeleton hands.

'She's here,' signed Severn, and smiled.

Kade felt sick and tried to wake himself up, to pull himself out of that reality. But instead he was drawn deeper, closer, until he was right by the hands that wore the ring.

For a moment he was absorbed in the physicality of bones strung together with what looked like fishing line, anchored in, swaying in the current, waving. All the hands waved. But these were his mother's hands. They wore the diamond ring he had known since he was a baby. The ring that had sparkled over his bed, become caught as she brushed his hair, become wet as she lifted him out of a bath, shone in the sunlight as they laughed together. The ring his father had given her.

Kade's tears were invisible underwater, but his grief was not. It grabbed him like a hurricane. He closed his eyes, wanting to die, to become a wave on this macabre sea of hands. Then he realised he couldn't deny it anymore. He understood. The last moment of a life where he could hope his mother was alive, was over.


The dancefloor encircled a giant oak. As Brooke approached she had a flashing image of the tree as a whole, roots beneath reaching as far under the dancers as the branches did over. For a few seconds she felt dizzy. Which way was up? She paused, waiting for balance to return. When it did, it was accompanied by a desire to dance.

At the edge of the dancefloor her hips began to move to the beat, taking her forwards until she was captured by the party.

Danced with her whole body, her whole mind, as if for her life, she spiralled round the tree. This was Yggdrasil, the tree of life, the pathway from the sky to the ground, from the heavens to the underworld. It was her escape from the flood of Kade-emotion that threatened to engulf her. The trunk, the roots, the branches, the dancers all teemed with water, water made shape by meeting solid matter. Energy flew round her, through her, then she, the other dancers, the tree trunk, the leaves, the branches, the roots and the soil became one ball of movement. Beauty, thought Brooke, sheer beauty. Like looking into the sun.

Night fell. Brooke forgot she had no job, no money to speak of, no plans and no Kade. She danced until every part of her relaxed and she felt still inside. With her feet she stamped out the last of the anger she felt towards Kade for leaving her. Clenching and unclenching her fists she halted the *what-ifs?* and the *buts*. With her hips she shook herself free from anxiety, from pitiful hopes, from regrets. With her whole body she made new patterns for herself, new routes for her thoughts and emotions to flow through.


'How?' asked Kade. 'How did she die? How did she live her last days?'

'I found your mother,' said Severn. 'Drowning. I took her to the nearest dry cave and revived her, but then she was trapped, because she wasn't a waterbreather and it was too far for her to swim to land.' Guilt and self-forgiveness fought a familiar battle in Kade's head. 'Styx found you in a different place, and took you to another dry cave. By the time Styx found me and told me about you, you had gone. We cared for Aurora until she died. She wasn't able to withstand the cold damp of Underwater. She told us about you. She told us a lot about everything.'

Kade began a choked underwater sobbing. Drowning in enormity, in bittersweet futility. 'I could have saved her.' If only he'd gone back in. If only he'd told the authorities about the caves. If only he'd acted quickly. If only he hadn't wanted to protect the caves. If only he'd gone against his instinct.

'If you could have saved her, you would have,' said Severn as Kade's tears merged with the surrounding water.


Brooke watched the full moon rise, pulling the dancers as it did the tides. This was where Kade had grown up. This was his land and his people. No wonder he was strange. *They* were strange. But she felt so comfortable, dancing as if swimming, feeling that she wouldn't mind if she died right here and now, the fairylit tree her last sight. She wouldn't die though. She was alive and safe here with these strange people she didn't know.

She continued to dance and the moon continued to rise, and the moon's aura seemed to reach down and encompass the tree, the dancers, her spirit, the loch. The moonlight, just for the night, was powered by the dancers' energy. The music sounded like falling water. She was dancing to the rhythm of water. All night she surfed waves, was pulled by currents of sound, floated on lakes and was taken up in the spiral vortices of cloud and rained down again.

Kade would come and find her soon. She was ready, cleansed and happy to merge with him once more, now that she had found herself again.

Severn led Kade away from the graveyard cave and into a rounded cave with smooth walls that glowed with chalky green light. 'Our people –' she signed '– *your* people – the Waterpeople, were once Landpeople. We breathed air. We stood on the surface. We hunted, fished and gathered. Back then *all* people spoke silently, using their hands. That way we didn't scare the animals we hunted, or disturb the quiet of the forest. We put nothing into the air except song. When your mother came here and spoke land-language we thought that she was singing, but she explained to us that that was how Landpeople always speak.' Severn looked up and seemed to laugh, although it made no sound. 'She told us that we couldn't just call ourselves 'the People,' as we did then. She said we were 'Waterpeople.' We liked that. And she gave us names, because she couldn't pronounce ours. Her fingers were not dextrous enough. She named us after rivers.'

Kade imagined Aurora speaking to the Waterpeople, explaining the world. That made him happy. He had so many questions. Had she told them about planes and trains and computers and cities? Had she left any messages? But Kade could not sign as fast as he thought, so he said nothing. Severn continued, her hands moving rhythmically, repeating a tale she had clearly told many times. 'We, the people, lived up there, outside this loch. We were Landpeople. Then the Big Rain came. The waterfalls on the mountains widened. Every part of the mountains became white with moving water. The loch rose. We could hardly see to sign because of the rain that fell. It fell until it closed us in, making our mountain an island, forcing us higher and higher up the slopes.'

The flood! All those things Brooke told him in India!

'We had enough to survive for many years after the rain stopped. Our mountaintop offered food and shelter, but all the others had been washed to rock or buried by water, and we saw no other people. Slowly we noticed the wildlife changing. The butterflies grew weak, having nowhere else to fly to. The mammals grew weak, having no new blood to breed with. No

151

birds came from across the water. Many trees died and our land became barren.

'We could not spare the trees to build boats, and there was nowhere to sail to. We became expert swimmers. Underwater gave us relief. Many of us yearned for our ancestral places, now submerged, so we learned to swim deep and long so we could visit those places.

'One day a child went missing. She could not be seen on land or water. It was feared that she had drowned, but after three days she returned, fell to her knees and poured a torrent of water from her mouth. Immediately a willow tree sprang up. A willow tree has grown there ever since.

'The child had met spirits that taught her to breathe underwater. She began to teach the other children.' Severn's hands moved with hypnotic rhythm and her feet tapped the side of the cave causing subtle currents that ran at the rate of a heartbeat. The rhythm touched Kade's skin as the myth entered him. He was not expected to respond; he felt lulled.

'The old generation of air-breathers taught the new generation of water-breathers all they knew and then were gone. We continued our lives underwater, living on our ancestral lands, now waters. We adapted. Our eyesight became more sensitive, so we could see better to talk, fish and gather. Our fingers and toes became webbed. We became impervious to the cold. We lost our protection from the sun ...

Unexpectedly, Severn reached out and stroked a lock of Kade's hair, breaking his trance. 'And we lost our ability to breathe air.'


Brooke was thirsty. The air had become cold, enough for her to see her breath. The moon was gone and the crisp brightness of dawn swept through the field, highlighting the dancers. Children, signals of morning, began emerging from their beds to walk in the dewy grass, wearing pyjamas and wellies. Then sunshine arrived, spilling onto the field and chasing clouds from the sky.

Brooke left the dance floor in a loping way, feeling the sun's rays melt against her back.

The fires gave out an occasional lick of green or blue as people threw coloured powder on. One fire was alone, beyond the others. She walked over. Oh how gorgeous. Someone had laid fresh flowers on a round stone. In the centre was a ring of small glasses, each filled with water, each delicate enough for a fairy. How thoughtful of someone to think of the thirsty dancers. She drank a glassful. It was cool and metallic, like gold or silver. She drank another, then anoth –

'Hey. What the hell are you doing?'

Brooke jumped at the African voice, and spun round. 'Stirling,' she said, smiling sheepishly, feeling embarrassed, but not yet knowing why. 'It is Stirling isn't it?' Stirling did not look as angry as he had sounded. He looked amused.

'What *have* I done?'

Stirling took a stride forward and took the glass from her hand, laughing. 'You, my dear, have just drunk more than your fair quota of sacred water.'

'Oh. Is it very precious? Why are you laughing then?'

'I don't know,' said Stirling, as if he *did* know. He shrugged his shoulders. 'I spend the last six months gathering water from sacred places in one hundred countries, then you come along and give it no more reverence than tap water!' Reaching into a bag he produced a Highland Spring bottle. 'I'm laughing because perhaps it doesn't need any more reverence than tap water. But, *hey*, drink this instead.' Stirling swung the bottle over to her, along with a smile.

'To your good health,' said Brooke, and glugged away, guilt free. It did not taste as good as the other water though. What a brilliant thing, to gather water from all over the world. Why hadn't she thought of that?

A woman was passing between the fires, handing out watermelon. Brooke thought of India. So much was similar here. The clothes, the expressions, the way people seemed to feel at ease. The forest ... the forest was like the one where she'd looked through Kade's bag. Another wave of embarrassment washed through her. She remembered the bottle of Ganga river water she'd found. Had she drunk a drop of that in Stirling's mix? She was dying to ask Stirling about Kade but held back. Kade *had* told Stirling he had met a beautiful girl, but Brooke couldn't be sure he had meant her. Almost sure, yeah, but ... but she wasn't sure if she could conduct a proper conversation anyway.

The watermelon woman reached their fire. She had long straight black hair, wore suede trousers and a bikini top, and carried a machete.

'Hi,' she said. 'Watch carefully. I'm going to show you something never before seen by human eyes.' She placed a whole watermelon on the ground and brought the machete down. The fruit fell into two pink ovals. 'There,' the woman said with a smile. She carved it and gave pieces out.

The watermelon juice entered Brooke, and its earthiness brought her down a little. As the sun rose the party's mood became jubilant, verging on ecstatic. Faster and faster the music went and faster and faster the dancers followed. Brooke felt blinded by sound. Disappointment was beginning to encroach.

'Seen any sign of Kade yet?' she asked Stirling.

'No, but I'm sure he'll be back soon,' said Stirling in a confident tone that fell slightly at the end of his sentence.

'I hope so,' said Brooke, looking up at the driveway expectantly, feeling like a dog looking for its master. She had danced all night, fuelled by excitement at seeing Kade. Now the excitement was dissolving. The mood of the party no longer echoed her inner mood, so she retreated.


'Then the water retreated,' continued Severn, 'and our Waters became bordered by land. We found ourselves isolated in the loch. Later, the Landpeople arrived. We tried to make contact with them, but they caught one of us and killed her so we hid – no longer swimming to the surface. We have lived in these caves for longer than anyone can remember, longer than we can remember our ancestors' remembering. And now you're here.

You are something new,' said Severn. 'Aurora said you could breathe air *and* water, but that you didn't know it.'

Then he realised. His father was a Waterman. 'My father. Is he here?' he nearly asked. Instead he said, 'There are more of you,' and was answered with a wide grin.

He followed Severn and Styx through shadow and light until they reached a huge cave. Above was air, below, where he was, was water. The phosphorescence was strong, almost day lit. Kade's eyes focussed. His heart began to pound. There *were* more of them. Of course there were. His heart leapt. There were about a hundred Waterpeople – men, women, children, and babies, above him, below him, surrounding him. Kade's mouth softened into a grin. It was a village. No buildings, no *stuff*, but definitely a village. Severn turned round and smiled at him, obviously proud of her people. She beckoned him on past curious faces with pale eyes seemed to warm to him.

Brooke Brooke Brooke. She had to see this! The alternative survivors of the flood. Were these her watersprites?

A group of children approached, less shy than the adults, and looking quite different to the adults. The kids had the translucent skin and webbed hands and feet that all the adults had, but some had tendrilly ears like sea dragon's ruffles, others were covered in patterns formed by pigment running across their skin. They swam around him, tickling him with hair as soft as rose petals, and startling him with acute curiosity.

'He's one of them. He's a Dry,' said one.

A *Dry*?

'Is he one of them?' they asked Severn. 'Are you one of them?' they asked Kade. 'Have the Drys learned to breathe water?'

'No,' replied Kade. 'But I can.'

Then all the Waterpeople were next to him, around him, looking at him. His mind searched for some equivalency, some category. He and the Waterpeople were as strange as each other, but Kade was the visitor. He felt like he had in India, surrounded by people unashamed by their interest. A tiny baby swam past, freer than any baby on land. It pulsed with green lights. Kade was entranced. The baby's mother gathered it in, drawing it to her breast and there it fed, gravity-free, occasional swirls of milk escaping into the water. As it fell asleep its lights gradually dimmed. Kade blinked. The blink lasted a long time. Inside the darkness he saw the Waterpeople, the whole village. They grew small and began a spiralling procession. Starting with the baby, they entered his chest, filling his heart.

Brooke walked down to the loch and stood on the stony beach in front of the cage-like exposed roots of a huge grey tree. She looked for Kade over the water, as though he would miraculously swim towards her, but he did not, so she left the loch and began to walk up alongside the river. Wild grasses tickled her legs. All that time together, all that love they had created, and for what? She kicked a stone into the river. He wasn't here, wasn't playing along with her fairy-tale. She had come all this way, but the dreaming was over. Of course, because she hadn't *told* him she was coming, she could hardly expect him to be waiting. And she didn't know if he wanted her. Maybe it would be best to give in, to enjoy the love that had been. Perfect? Short-lived.

But her life was still intertwined with his. Indirectly, he had brought her to this beautiful place, showed her a wonderful time. A lovely party, flavoured with anticipation of him. Meeting him had brought her here, to this river, now turning wilder as she walked uphill.

The path ended, and the sides of the river formed a gully. There seemed to be no way on unless she crossed a pool to climb up through a waterfall. She sat down and caught her breath, then found herself smiling as a path made itself visible. Stepping-stones took her on a waterborne route, and overhanging branches provided safety from wobbling stones. After a deep breath, she continued, carefully climbing up the side of a fifteen foot fall, gripping ferns and rocks for balance.

The air was fresh – fresh as the Himalayas. Had this water ever been there? The waterfall sound mingled with the music from the party ricocheting through the valley. Tu-ke-tuh tuk-eh-ta

Tu-ke-tuh tuk-eh-ta. Hesitant at first, she told herself to trust the river, and its tiers of waterfalls. Each time she encountered rock faces ahead she half expected to turn back, but there was always a way. A stone would appear for her foot, a grip for her hand. The waterfalls seemed to understand the rhythm and size of her body. She slipped into a confident trusting pace and, in return, the water and rocks revealed the way to her, inviting her up and on and allowing her to remain dry. Soon she could climb the cliffs without hesitancy and was leaping and bending and practically flying up the falls. She laughed out loud. She felt like a watersprite. All those dry myths she had studied, but this was it! This was the real thing. This was the feeling those myths were trying to capture. The joy. Feeling mischievous and wild, loving this new path, she began to climb the highest cliff yet.

As she pulled herself up, Brooke knew she was at the pool she had seen from above: the willow pool. Just as Kade had described, a weeping willow grew on an island in the centre of a large pool. The pool had been formed by the wide heavy torrent of water that poured over the wall of black rock at the back of the space. The willow's trunk grew at an angle. Brooke crossed over, using more stepping-stones, and parted the willow's boughs. Inside was like a room in a dream, green lit and calm, despite the roar of the water. She sank her feet into the damp ground. It held her steadily. She sat down with her back against the trunk, feeling she was playing house. Here was a den. She could set up home under the willow.

She was on the edges of something. Something water and something air and something else. Buzzing filled her chest and sent pleasant chills up and down her body. What could she do? Leave the city forever? She could not live on landscape alone. Live here, with these people? On this site? She felt she would be welcome. But would it be enough for her to bathe in the waterfall and breathe fresh air everyday? Perhaps she could stay, a while at least.

She noticed algae and moss on a large stone, growing on many levels, like a tiny green city, sprouting piazzas and arenas and parks and trees, most vibrant in the centre where little white

157

flowers grew tall. Towards the edges suburbs unfurled. Brooke wanted to become tiny and live in the moss metropolis.

The reflected foliage filled the pool with pattern, like cell multiplication, like blossoming, like microbes generating. She felt compelled to wash away the sweat, the clammy cousin of fresh water that clung to her skin, and to feel mountain water pouring across her back – to stand in a waterfall and become part of its route, her body as solid as the old rocks, hydraulic power forcing away the fog that wandered through her thoughts. And she wanted Kade.

Brooke took off her clothes. She watched her heartbeat moving and felt more naked than ever before. She jumped into the pool. The coldness made her gasp, puckering her senses but opening something up. She put her head under and immediately felt warmer, then swam over to the waterfall, enjoying the tree's reflections rippling over her shoulders. Sitting on a smooth stone seat, she let the water flow over her back and head. After a few minutes it felt as though water was pouring through her body as well as over it. The cold of her flesh emphasised the warmth of her heart. All alone. Very happy. Not thinking about past and future, not even trying not to think. Just feeling. Just right. Waterfall fixed. Travel slough running away. Hydro-exfoliating the crud and the dust and the sticky fumes of bad moods and feuds. Oxygen caressed her lungs and her whole body and mind answered with approving animal instincts. Right here. All right here. Where was Kade? Was he okay?

Brooke closed her eyes and leaned back into the waterfall. What if Kade was not a nutter? What if his stories were true? Tears crept up on her, and she shed them into the water, and imagined her feelings, her longing and love and unhappiness spreading into the pool, and she wondered; how could his story be true? It was not true.

The sky darkened, and Brooke felt keenly that she was intruding, too deep in the gully. All her bad habits, resentments and doubts had nowhere to go, nowhere to dissipate. They were reflected and magnified by the water. The wind picked up. She clenched her jaw and shivered. Not safe here.

As she began to move, she felt as though the rocks were changing angle, consciously trying to throw her off. She reached out, lost her balance, fell into the pool and caught her thumb against a jagged stone. Her blood turned transparent pink as it joined the bubbles of the fall. The stinging turned to pain and then to panic.

She swam to the island and got out using one arm. Using her knickers, she tried to stem the blood and was reminded of when she'd cut herself on the bus window. That cut had only just healed and now she had another. She felt exposed. Something supposed to stay inside was leaking out.

She threw on her clothes and clambered downhill, finding it much harder to descend the rock faces than to ascend. Flushed and dirty, she arriving at the loch. Uphill, Stirling stood near a fire. She ran towards him.

'Brooke!' he said, not seeming to notice that she was cut. 'Have you seen Kade?'

'Is he here?' Brooke's heart pounded.

'No.'

'You ... you sound worried,' Stirling seemed more boy than man.

'Nah – Well, a bit.'

'What?' said Brooke forcefully.

'Timmy – one of the kids – has just got up. He says he saw Kade swimming in the loch yesterday at about seven. No one's seen him since.'

His words set Brooke's thoughts at each other. Seven? That was when she had arrived. Was Kade avoiding her? Did he know she was here? But what was Stirling saying? Had Kade drowned? No. If Kade could breathe water he could not drown. No. That was just a story. But if he was crazy and tried, then ... *he went off on some kind of mission...* Stirling had said –

'And the police have just been here. They mentioned they found a drowned body in the loch yesterday evening. You didn't see anything did you?' The blood drained from Brooke's face. Stirling tried to reassure her. 'I'm sure it's not him. I think they said it was a woman.'

Unsure what to say, Brooke concentrated on the pain pulsing in her thumb. The party was still going on. No one seemed worried. Eventually she asked, 'Is there a doctor here?'

'You've hurt yourself?'

She began to sob. All the 'If onlys' she had sent away with dancing were back. Stirling put his large arm around her shoulder. 'Go and see Ursula up in the Lodge. She's a trained doctor.'

Brooke looked uphill. The sky was greying. The Sight did not look so pretty anymore. Fairyland was now muddy. Dogs attacked rusty cans. The music sounded scratchy. There was litter in the long grass. A newspaper. A picture of a topless girl, thrown away, discarded, a huge muddy boot print on her chest.

Brooke ran up the hill and knocked on the door of the Lodge. Ursula answered in a cerise silk dressing gown, with a cup of coffee in her hand, just woken up. Maybe she had been to enough parties in her life. Brooke held up her wound. 'Stirling said you'd be able to help me.'

'That looks bad. How d'you do that?'

'I scraped it in that pool where the willow tree is.'

'Well, at least it'll be clean. I'm sure it's not as bad as it looks. Come on into the bathroom.' She led Brooke to the back of the house, where the windows looked out over the mountains. In a dark corridor Brooke stopped, arrested by a picture of Kade as a boy next to a woman so like him she could have been a copy. Brooke wanted to stay watching, as though Kade and his mother might have something to say to her if she waited long enough, but Ursula was calling. Brooke followed her into a room of carved wood panels, shining and multi-hued, covering the walls and curving round the sides of a raised bath tub big enough for several people. The room was the work of a craftsman. Pressing Brooke gently on the shoulders, Ursula indicated she should sit down. Brooke felt the knots of wood look at her.

Ursula began to clean Brooke's wound. 'Don't worry,' she said. 'I used to be a doctor.'

'Used to be?' asked Brooke.

'Yes. I figured I'd do more for people's health providing a place like this.'

She might be right, Brooke thought. But it was a strange place, with such indefinable undercurrents. One minute it was heaven, the next Brooke wanted to get away. She had felt so comfortable, and so nervous. And now they'd found a body.

'You picked a pretty part of the Sight to hurt yourself.' Ursula held Brooke's hand gently at the wrist. 'You're a friend of Kade's, Stirling says.'

'Yes,' said Brooke. Why wasn't Ursula saying anything about the body?

'Such a shame about Aurora.' Ursula began to wrap a bandage round.

Brooke wanted to ask who Aurora was, but felt sure that Ursula had endowed her with more knowledge than she actually had, and that was why she had allowed her in this room – the bathroom felt like an inner sanctum – so she remained silent. Then she remembered Kade's birth certificate that she had spied on in the woods in Manali.

'I remember when she first came here. So young, so feisty. Insistent on staying off the grid. Only sixteen. Your arriving here reminded me of her. She arrived just in time for a party too. Mayday, it was. We were having a maypole dance – a good old-fashioned fertility ritual. She was so beautiful with her black hair and rosy cheeks. She seemed so ripe. All the boys wanted her. I took her under my wing, not knowing how much I was taking on.'

Ursula pushed her fringe out of her eyes. 'She was pregnant you see. Either when she arrived, or just after. Wouldn't say who the father was. Seemed to be more interested in the willow pool than in men. It was as if it were her lover. She went there everyday. Wanted to have the baby there.' Ursula finished winding the bandage, but held onto Brooke's wrist. Brooke wondered if Ursula was absent minded or keeping hold of her on purpose.

'In the end I persuaded her to have the baby here.' Ursula said, then lowered her voice an octave. 'Kade was born in that tub right behind you.'

Brooke turned to glance at the bath, shook off Ursula's hand and moved forward slightly, as if avoiding the ghost of the afterbirth.

'Like all human babies his soft little body was ninety-seven percent water. He had a crown of hair which, like all humans', grew in spiral formation. His little toes, like some human babies, were slightly webbed. The look in his eyes, as he opened them to see his mother, was, according to her, more special than any baby ever born, human or not.'

Why was Ursula telling her this, in this way?

'He came out all clean and immediately started feeding at Aurora's breast. Time seemed to stop. I left them together and watched the moon from the window in the corridor. Then the placenta started to come and Aurora became uncomfortable. She stood up in pain. Then we realised that all the time he had been feeding, Kade had been underwater. All that time! Newborn babies don't need to breathe straight away, the placenta still gives them oxygen, but the cord had stopped pulsing. He must have been under there for twenty minutes.'

Ursula looked directly at her, but Brooke could not work out what was going on, or what the look meant. She waited for Ursula to laugh. Was this a joke, a bullshit story to test her gullibility? Ursula looked completely serious. 'We never told him about his breathing water.' She sighed. 'We didn't want him to try it again and drown.'

'Ursula, why are you telling me?' asked Brooke.

'I'm not sure,' said Ursula. 'Maybe you're a good listener, or maybe you turning up seems significant.'

'Kade is missing, you know?'

'I'm sure he's fine,' said Ursula, much more confident than Stirling had been. She stood up. 'Pink or blue safety pin?'

'Either,' said Brooke. What was going on? Had she been brought here, encouraged to dance, given tea *with something*,

162

made to think Kade could be dead, and then told he wasn't? Brooke felt jumpy, raw.

Ursula put the safety pin in. 'I remember the last time I saw Aurora. She and Kade were walking down the hill. I was in the kitchen. They were wearing their wetsuits. I could tell from the back that they were both excited about something. The memory is clear, like a movie.'

But not to Brooke. That was not her memory. She had not known Kade then, or even been aware that he existed. Did she know him now? What had happened to the understanding, the relaxed feeling they had shared? What had happened to the Kade she first met?

She did not know Aurora, and never would. Never first hand. And she did not know the mythology of this place. She did not want to get caught up in the Sight, not knowing who or what to believe. Was there some kind of plan between Kade and these people to mess with her mind?

'There,' said Ursula, with a shake of her grey-blonde mane.

Brooke noticed she'd used a blue safety pin.

'Thank you,' said Brooke.

'Pleasure.'

'Ursula?'

'Mmmm?'

'Have you got a pen and paper?'

Brooke wanted to catch the wave of determination that rushed towards her. She'd unstick herself from this social mud and go and see her family, where things were clean-cut and she knew where she stood.

'Sure,' said Ursula, 'I'll go and get one.' She left the room.

Brooke looked around at the wood-panelling. Little eyes, everywhere.

'Would you like to have a bath?' called Ursula.

There was nothing Brooke would have liked more. But not here, not now. Least of all in this bath, where Kade had been born. That would be too much.

'No,' she called to Ursula, more abruptly than she had intended. 'Thanks.'

Ursula returned with pen and paper. Brooke wrote down her name, address and number. Another waterfall. Another note. She did not write anything else. She handed it to Ursula unfolded. 'Please can you give this to Kade when he comes back?' Ursula looked disappointed. Brooke took a breath and asked, 'Now how much do I owe you for last night's camping?'

# Blueprints

Kade suddenly felt edgy and tired. 'Can I see where she lived, please?' he asked. Styx, understanding, led him to the dry cave. Kade climbed out of the pool in its centre and coughed up all the water from his lungs. The air was damp, but dry in comparison. Styx remained in the pool, breathing water.

'Aurora called this the Dry Stores,' said Styx, holding his hands above the surface.

Kade looked around. It was another phosphorescent cave, but piled high with *stuff* – bits and pieces, rubbish, all sorts of land things, the debris of human culture. Landpeople seemed to know nothing about the Waterpeople, give or take a few mermaid and kelpie myths, but judging by the Dry Stores, the Waterpeople knew a great deal about the Landpeople. Cans, bottles, knives, fishing equipment, clothing, toys, bits of boats', heaps of jewellery and a box of dynamite were gathered in the cave like some crazy car-boot sale. One corner was laden with books, newspapers and magazines. The papers, like everything else in the cave, had been wet once, and formed crumpled yellowing layers, like a clamshell, or an old man's toenail. The library ranged from children's books to trashy novels to ancient leather-bound volumes. Most abundant were fishing manuals and nature guides.

'So cool to have a written language,' said Styx, reaching up.

'Where did you get all these things?' asked Kade.

'We found them in the loch,' replied Styx, as he held his breath to look out of the water at Kade. 'Of course.'

There was a bed – a mattress, and two sleeping bags. Kade touched it. Damp; damp that never properly dried. Was this where Aurora slept? No wonder she had not survived long here.

'Your mother taught us so much. She said that there are so many Landpeople that some of you have the same name. She said that some people speak different languages and don't understand each other. She said there were billions of Landpeople, but we didn't understand her. She said we have no concept of numbers.'

Kade smiled.

'Severn showed Aurora her name when she arrived, but Aurora couldn't say it. She said she named Severn Severn because the sign for her name was made with seven fingers. Then – and I remember her smile – she decided to name us all after rivers.'

Kade wondered what had happened to the rest of his mother's body. He didn't want to know. 'Can I be alone for a while?' he asked. Styx left without a word, but happily.

Kade needed to rest. But more than he needed to rest, he needed to think. He ploughed his face into the bedcovers and discovered that even more than he needed to think, he needed to feel. Sitting up again he looked around the cave and noticed a book on top of a pile of others. Déjà vu visited for a moment, leaving anticipation in its wake. The book was a pink Five Year Diary. Teenage handwriting declared it the property of Hayley Anderson. As he opened it the pen fell out of the spine, see-through, pink, out of ink and strawberry scented. Trembling, he began to read.

January First. *Dear diary. Got you for Xmas from Dad. Cos you've got a lock I can say I got drunk 4 first time last night.*

He shuffled through. Most of the words were destroyed by water and Hayley had stopped writing by mid-January. When he saw the handwriting change from Hayley's to Aurora's, his hands trembled. There were only a few entries, along with some drawings of Waterpeople and one of him.

*Man says Kade ok but gone. So happy is ok.*

*Man understands 'name' but I cannot say his. Will call him Styx. Seems to be some kind of Shaman. Saved my life.*

*The one I knew is not here. I can only wait.*

*Now understand:*

*The sperm hadn't known she was different. It left his body for hers when his body was hers. Only once inside the egg did the sperm know he was different, she was different. They were different.*

*The egg was surprised at the possibilities that had entered her world. 'What shall we do with these blueprints?' she asked.*

*While egg and sperm were just two cells, one inside the other, they made a pact. The baby would have his father's senses and abilities, and the appearance of its mother. The baby grew inside his mother, a layer of water cushioning each other.*

*Strange life*

*Too much coughing. Too cold.*

*But I am lucky, to have had Kade. To have seen this.*

*Need new pen.*

The word *pen* was scratched into the paper, inkless.

# Food

Kade lay down and was sucked into sleep, dreaming of water appearing in places it should not: bubbling over desert sand; splashing onto microchips; working its way to a duck's skin; soaking his mother's lungs.

When he woke, his flesh felt like mud and he was ravenous. He took an apple out of his bag, heard a splash, and turned around to see Severn beckoning. He joined her in the pool and filled his lungs with water. The feeling of mud turned to silt and then into flesh and blood. Severn's eyes widened. 'Landfood!' she said. He handed her the apple.

'I had one of these when I was a child,' she said. 'Many of them fell from a boat. Back then I wasn't scared of being seen. I reached up, plucked an apple, and took a bite. I had never tasted anything so delicious and sweet before.' She took a bite of the apple in her hand and the crunch travelled at a rate of knots. She savoured her mouthful. Then she passed the apple on to the other Waterpeople, who had been drawn to the sound. 'It's safe,' she indicated.

'We have to test landfood carefully,' she said to Kade. 'It's a slow process. First we touch it with a finger, followed hours later by a touch on the lips, then a small taste, which we spit out, then a tiny swallow. If that is okay we eat a small piece each day, and finally we can declare it safe.' Severn's eyes lit up. 'Are you hungry?' she asked. 'There's your food there.' She pointed to the cans. 'Or do you want some of our food?'

'I'd love some,' replied Kade, bringing smiles to the faces of those who had watched their conversation.

Severn led him back to the village-cave, to a feast that would not have looked out of place in a Tokyo restaurant. A Waterperson handed him a long delicate branch of seaweed, or rather lochweed, each of its fronds parcelling pieces of trout, salmon and shellfish. He bit the parcels as they swayed in the current. Kade made the sign for delicious. It seemed that the effort Landpeople would reserve for cooking, the Waterpeople put into presentation. Gravity, or the lack of it, did not allow for bowls of mussels, or plates piled high, instead dinner swayed like an animate forest. To eat while submerged was a delicious wonderful multi-levelled experience, and he was glad of the distraction.

'Is it true,' asked Severn, 'that there are places in the world where the water runs hot?'

'Yes,' said Kade, thinking of Iceland and New Zealand. Then thinking, just up there, outside the loch, the taps run hot.

'I don't even know what hot feels like,' said Severn. 'Aurora tried to tell me about it.'

Of course, thought Kade. No chance to feel hot here. Not ever. Once he'd tried to explain music to Lila. A mostly fruitless task, except that she understood rhythm. A smile swept over Kade's face. He had a box of waterproof matches in his pack.

'Wait here,' he said. 'I'll show you heat.'

He fetched the matches and swam up to the air-filled upper half of the vast cave. 'Come and look,' he said.

'You can see heat?' asked Severn.

'Sometimes. Sort of.'

The whole village swam upwards. Kade trod water, head in the air. A hundred heads followed, expecting something, holding their breath. The matches were bigger than normal matches, and bright green. He struck one. The sound came first, echoing around the chamber, and then the flame appeared, turning the water gold.

Half the people disappeared underwater. Some were brave. Severn and Styx and several others reached forward to touch the fire, but drew back quickly when they felt the heat.

'It can burn,' said Kade. 'It can hurt you.'

For a reason he was not quite sure of, he pressed the burning match to his palm. He smelt his flesh burning. He was awake now, for definite. The match went out, with a fizz.

'Fire is sharp,' said Styx, as he encouraged Kade to come back beneath the surface.

# Necklace

It was a long journey home. Finally Brooke rang the bell of her parent's house in Rayton.

Samantha answered. 'Brooke you crazy bitch,' she chastised with a voice full of relief. 'Why didn't you let us know where you were? You look a state. Are you alright?'

'Yeah,' said Brooke. 'I'm okay. I did say I was going away again for a couple of days.'

Brooke frowned. She had worried so much about Kade's safety that she hadn't considered that people would worry about her. She had a family, a network, *responsibilities*.

'I don't remember you saying anything,' replied Sam, understated.

Their mum and dad appeared in the corridor. Brooke ran forward to hug them.

'Oh it's so good to see you,' said her mum, pouring her perfumed scent into Brooke's heart. She held Brooke at arm's length and looked at her. 'Well, you've got a lovely tan.'

Brooke's dad kissed her on the cheek. 'You shouldn't worry your mum so,' he said, simultaneously sounding straightforward and ironic, and typically pretending he was not the one who worried. 'Sam said you met some weird man. We were afraid he'd carried you off to his lair.'

Brooke was about to say 'I'm not a child anymore, I can look after myself,' but she wasn't sure if it was true today.

'You could do with a wash,' said her mum. 'Did you not have a bath *all* the time you were away?' Only in mountain pools, thought Brooke.

'No. But plenty of showers.'

'Have a cuppa first though, eh?' said her dad.

Over insipid tea Brooke gave her parents a heavily edited run-down of her trip, leaving out her excursion to Scotland, and then she escaped to the bathroom.

Soaking in hot water, Brooke was grateful to be alone. Everyone had questions, but they had not been there, did not understand. So much had changed, and so little.

The tap dripped once, loudly. She kicked the enamel. Every drop of water in the bloody world reminded her of Kade.

After her bath she went to her pale green room. It was so clean, so ordinary. She began to unpack, looking at all her hibiscus things. So stupid: a dress with a strip of Hawaiian hibiscus print running across the chest; a hat with the same print; a hairclip with one big white flower; shorts; t-shirts; even pencils – everything laden with fucking hibiscus. It looked ridiculous. She had taken it so seriously.

In a decisive swoop she bagged it all up to take to charity, throwing in a box of hibiscus tea for good measure. As she tied the bag she caught a glimpse of herself in the mirror, looking all flustered, wearing the carved hibiscus-wood necklace. It seemed almost part of her body. She stroked the flower. The necklace wasn't cheap rubbish. It was the nucleus of her hibiscus watersprite craze, the first hibiscus thing she'd bought, just after she'd read about the Andaman islanders using hibiscus to protect themselves from straying watersprites. Did she really need protection? Maybe. She took it off and put it on the windowsill where it stayed, still and quiet in the sun, as though holding a secret in its flower.

Brooke was tempted back to the rucksack. She sat in the middle of the floor, reached into a bulging side pocket, drew out a packet of hibiscus-scented incense and laughed out loud. Then she became serious again. Kade had not liked incense, claiming it irritated his lungs. Then how had he coped in India at all? She put it down, reached back in to the pocket, and extracted her medical kit and her notebook. She had bought the kit at Heathrow, to calm her nerves at suddenly being alone. It was complete with intravenous needles, so that should some disaster befall her, or some exuberant medic insist on immunising everyone on a bus, she would not have to share any that had been inside other people's arms. It seemed silly now. India was not that backwards. She – the Brooke that she had been – seemed silly.

Brooke felt as she had when she'd looked through Kade's things in Manali, only this time she was spying on her past self. She felt sorry for her recent self, now being scrutinised and remembered patronisingly by the self she was now.

Casting aside the medical kit, thankful that she'd not needed it, she shoved the half emptied rucksack under the bed. Landing on the covers with a bounce, she began to read her notebook. Again she felt she was spying on herself, but as she turned the pages, she noticed her younger self had frequently been more, not less, capable and intelligent than she was now. At least back then she had bothered to write down her thoughts, her understandings – her *research* – unlike 'After She Met Kade.' What was she going to do about her studies? Pretty much all her research had halted when she'd met him, thinking that simply by *being* at the Kumbh Mela she would absorb all she needed to know about myths. But that had been a ruse for herself, so she could concentrate on being with Kade. Now it felt like a mistake.

But just because she had stopped, did not mean she could not start again. She chewed her fountain pen. 'I'm not afraid,' she said to herself. 'Not of watersprites.' What exactly was it that made people think they needed hibiscus to protect them from watersprites or to be tied to a mast so as not be drawn to mermaids? What were they really afraid of? Her theory was that humanity was still in shock from the great flood, and all myths to do with water, at their depths, referred back to it. Now she realised that her theory did not come near to explaining all the imaginings humans had with water. Each drank water. Each observed it. Each made routes and forms for water to flow. The water *was* each of them.

Brooke slowly pushed a lock of hair behind her ear, touched her fingertips to her cheek and smiled in a puzzled way at the spooky idea that everything – people plants and animals – was under the control of water. 'We *are* water,' she said aloud. Just water bound to a few other molecules. A quiet thought said 'speak then,' and she began to write.

*I have always been part of the process, in the shaping of flat stones carved with letters, and the shaping of ceramics and hide and papyrus and paper. I team with pigment and make ink. My messages get across.*

She watched the ink dry.

*I will:*
*Know your innermost thoughts, but rarely threaten you.*
*Carry you before you are born.*
*Nourish you and all things that you eat, and quench your thirst. Bathe you and keep you healthy. Carry you to new places.*
*And you can give me new shapes and new colours, new flavours, new potencies.*

*I will:*
*Dramatise your nights, making lightening with my cousin electricity.*
*Bring colour to your days by raining into the sunlight.*
*And double the beauty of the world with my reflections.*

*In the skies, I will unfurl my language in pictures, and you can try and interpret my meaning.*
*I will be found in the most surprising places.*

Brooke put down the pen. Water was talking to her, *through* her. But riding on the back of water, present in each drop of ink, was Kade and the things *he* said about water. Kade and his stories were a waterborne virus she could not shake. Would never ever shake. Did not want to shake. Tears fell down her cheeks; wet, salty and powerful. The book dropped to the floor.

174

# Cells

He did not know what day it was, or if it even was day. He did not know which way was up. Without lungs full of air he no longer floated upward by default. To reach the surface was now a conscious effort. But he felt normal, even.

After the next meal Kade asked Severn about the kid's birthmark constellations, tendril ears, and glowing lights. Severn looked at Kade and said 'You don't know do you? Your mother didn't choose your eye colour, or your shape or anything?'

'I don't think so,' said Kade. 'But I do look very much like my mum, so maybe she had some power over it.'

'Maybe,' said Severn. 'Watch. I'll explain it to you. Waterpeople have a lot of control over our DNA, as Aurora called it. That's how we got these.' She held up her webbed fingers, then drew them back to continue talking. 'Well, we think that's how. It happened so long ago. But to tell you the whole story: the planet is roundish, we know. With an axis joining the poles like this.' She manoeuvred an invisible planet between her hands, a palm on each pole, then let go to talk. 'When the planet's axis is unstable, as it has been for the past few thousand years, the boundaries that divide species become less defined. It's not that whole new species evolve, just that the boundaries get fluid.'

Kade was becoming familiar with Severn's indirect way of reaching the point. He had stopped feeling hurried, but a sense of urgency was emerging again. He wanted to tell them so much, to teach them as Aurora had.

175

'Like humans,' he said. 'I mean, Landhumans, have produced carrots with jellyfish genes. The carrots' leaves glow when they need water. And scientists added a spider gene to a goat. Then they made this super strong flexible material from the goat's milk that can go through the atmosphere, into space.'

'Ah. Space. That's another discussion I want to have with you. And what's a goat? Anyway, that's not quite what we do. We don't mix genes from different species. We just guide our DNA closer to our wishes.'

'How?'

'When a child is being made, the parents decide what they want it to look like, what qualities they want it to have. Over the last generation our technologies have advanced a lot.'

Technologies? 'Do you have a laboratory, where you make children?' asked Kade, thinking how incongruous a lab would be.

'No!' said Severn in amusement. 'We make them the same way your people do, but with less heaviness.' She tapped her body. 'The technology is *in* us, embodied in our shapes and abilities. Now we're getting playful. That's why those kids have those birthmarks and tendril ears. The tendrils were inspired by sea dragons. We saw a picture in a book.'

'Cool. But how do you do it? Did you mix their genes with sea dragons?'

'No. As I said, we don't mix our genes with other species. Where would we find a sea dragon anyway?'

'But what about her?' asked Kade, pointing to the baby. 'How can she have those lights if she is not part jellyfish?'

'She's amazing isn't she? Her mother went into trances and traced back through evolution until she found the point before humans and jellyfish became differentiated. She appealed to that part of her cells to make itself manifest in her child and the baby was born with lights.'

The possibilities were endless and yet most Waterpeople looked similar to each other. There was only the occasional person with amazingly beautiful hair, or huge hands that made them the swiftest swimmers. There were a few who were ugly to his eyes but maybe beautiful to the Waterpeople because they were unusual. The Waterpeople were mostly good-looking to him, or would be if their veins were not visible. How strange it must be to grow up knowing your parents had chosen your DNA pattern, your looks and abilities.

Kade thought of the things Stirling had told him, about how dark skin was great in the sun, and melanin useful for keeping tropical diseases at bay, about pale skin with its ability to absorb vitamin D, good in cloudy climes, and Inuit chubbiness, useful in the cold, and Andean lungs –large enough to cope with high altitude. Had any of it been a conscious choice, rather than a gradual adaptation to climate?

People chose their partners consciously at least. But was that even true? Weren't people guided by scent to choose someone with a complimentary immune system? A person with a weak heart and strong stomach would be chosen by someone with a strong heart and weak stomach. Was that all it was, his attraction to Brooke? No. Surely – definitely – there was something more to it than just finding someone biologically suited to have kids with.

If he wanted, he could choose someone as physically different as possible to himself and have a child who looked different to him. That would be sudden change in one generation. The idea that there were billions of women he *could* choose from gave him a sense of freedom, even though he only wanted Brooke. The Waterpeople had not had such chances. They had to choose one of their own kind, someone they had known since they were born. How was it living here, in such a small community, with no chance to move away? Entrancing to him, but boring to them? Perhaps the Waterpeople were making children with tendril ears and flashing lights because they were bored!

Kade chewed on a piece of trout, thoughtful. Things like this, like meeting the Waterpeople, did not happen to ordinary people in ordinary life. Kade's brain was having trouble understanding that it was real. It kept trying to tell him that he was dreaming, or bewitched. Yet another part of him was happy to accept all this, the extra-ordinary encompassed inside the ordinary, because these people were, in their own way, normal.

With all the absorbing, compiling, ascribing and describing, feeling and dealing and reeling, the muscle of his mind had to become more flexible and capable than even it realised it could be. But he still could not get his head round the idea that his father was a Waterman.

Subtly, but full of intent, he looked at the dozen men who he guessed would be his father's age and could be his father. There was no point in looking for a resemblance. The veins were distracting, all the Waterpeople had aquamarine eyes like him, and anyway he was so much like his mother he was practically a male copy. His focus rested on one man, whose longish hair moved in the underwater breeze. As the man chewed he seemed content, strong. As he looked up at Kade his gaze was gentle, too gentle to be the look a father gives his long-lost son.

After dinner, people came to talk to Kade. Mostly they told him about their relationship with Aurora: 'She taught us new signs.' 'Told us that we are still secret.' 'Bloody hell, you look like her!'

A particularly vibrant girl approached, causing Styx to look worried. Many faces watched the conversation. 'We thought we were all alone. The only Waterpeople. But because of you, *apparently* we know we are not,' she said and gave Styx an anti-authoritarian glance.

'What do you mean?' asked Kade.

'She didn't worry about you drowning because your dad is a Waterman. Not that any of these men will admit ... '

'No, Seine' said Styx to the girl, insistently. 'Kade's dad was not one of us here. We are not-the-only-ones.' This seemed very important to Styx. He turned to Kade. 'We were angry at first, when Aurora told us. Not with her of course, but we wanted to know who – who was your father – because whichever man it was broke the rule not to contact Landpeople. We introduced your mother to all the Watermen that had been alive when you were conceived. Aurora said that your father was none of them, but another. Another Waterman.' Styx smiled. 'You are the proof that we are not the only ones.'

Seine broke in, her voice challenging. 'We always thought there must be other Waterpeople, but we never *knew*. Not until her. Not until you. But it must be. It must be true, mustn't it Styx? About the loch beneath?'

# Trent

The next day seemed more normal. Charlotte told Brooke she was mad to have gone to India when she could go to America or the Balearics or somewhere nice and clean. And as far as 'this bloke' Kade was concerned, Charlotte only wanted to know if he was good-looking.

'Yes, absolutely gorgeous,' said Brooke. 'From his black hair and aquamarine eyes right down to his webbed feet.'

'Yuk. You're a freak,' said Charlotte making 'puugh' noises as if she had something disgusting in her mouth. She left the room to 'go and do something more interesting.'

'So what about Kade?' asked Sam.

'Oh, Sam,' said Brooke.

That night she picked up her pen, but soon stopped writing, and just listened to the voice, which rushed over her, too fast to record.

> *Streaming down from Scotland, through the forlorn industry of Lancashire, fallen chimneys altering my path, moving past traces of chemicals and long-dead cotton mills, which used to run on my energy. Meandering through Manchester, held down by canals for miles. Winding up in breweries, not knowing where I'll be when someone opens my can. Boddingtons in Bangkok. People in pubs near Strangeways, drinking water in their beer, that was their beer before.*

*On down to Lincolnshire, a level place of no great excitement but plenty of birds. I watch the windmills, milling the air. I miss being milled, watching the direct effect of my power.*

*Further south, spreading out, bogging down. Leaving the waterfall energy behind. Inclined for the Thames, to meet and greet and run free to the sea. Or on a plane to Bahrain, drunk by a guy who finds a new appreciation for me in a hot country. Or to climb inside trees, look down from the leaves, and sway in the breeze. The river, myself, mirroring my ease.*

*Many ways to go to London. Many ways to be abandoned. A hundred years soaking the bricks of a sewer. Caught up in hospital, staying sterile so I can mix with injections to fight infections; trapped in a body deep underwater, unable to free myself from being somebody's daughter; held in a decanter by a host who never has guests; trapped in the pipe of a forgotten home, waiting for someone to enter forbidden territory so they can partake in me – practicality not gluttony. Or arriving twice inside a hippy practicing auto-urine therapy. He drinks his own pee.*

'Don't we all, ultimately,' thought Brooke, smiling.

*Many places to end up unexpectedly – in the coffee and tea and booze that make them want more of me. Swept up in a can of ice tea. Gulped down in Sydney. Sipped by a lecturer, then spat across the room as he becomes animated about his subject. Sipped by a pregnant woman, and becoming her baby.*

*Never-ending routes: Wherever I have travelled before I can travel once more, flowing through billions of brains, soaking through terrains, meeting lands through soil and sand.*

The water talk spurred her, and the next day, Brooke booked herself back in at university for the autumn term. It did seem less important now, though. She tried to look forward to going back. Meanwhile she had to do something, so she found a job as a waitress in a café with beautiful lighting. She also returned to her old weekend job as a lifesaver. The money mounted up and she took driving lessons and started saving for a car (not an Audi though).

Waitressing, lifesaving and driving all held a feeling of floating. Driving was like controlled freefall, protected from rain and wind. As a lifesaver she sat hovering over the deep-end, a dive into the water always on her mind. Waitressing was always like floating near to chaos.

She felt in limbo. Kade, India and Scotland behind her, and nothing much in the present.

She briefly considered renting some bleak cottage to contemplate her life – be a bit Buddhist. She wouldn't *actually* do it, she knew, but a part of her was already sitting in that cottage, in the dusk and the rain. Most of her, though, was in Rayton, and home felt okay. She immersed herself in activity and fun and meaningless dead-end chats.

She missed Kade.

One day, she decided to go to London. She skipped off the train and wandered through sunny Russell Square to the British Museum. Happy to be out of Rayton, she looked at the blue sky through the glass triangles of the domed roof, and thought of how she had tried to interest her friends and family in water. She had really tried. Because of the strength of her feelings, plus the floods and the melting ice-caps and the desperate need to clean all the water in the world, she had thought they would be receptive.

'Why d'you buy mineral water,' she would ask. 'In plastic?'
'Cos the tap water tastes like shit.'
'But it doesn't.'

'Well, that's your opinion Brooke.'

'Why are you pouring that paint down the sink?'
'Well, where else would I put it?'
'In the recycling centre?'
'But I'd have to drive there, and I don't want to spill paint in the Audi.'

'Charlotte, don't you think it's amazing that water—
'Oh Brooke, shut up. Please.'

'Hey don't throw your fag butts in the river!' she'd said to a group of teenagers.
'Fuck off ya ginge.'

'But mum, this stuff actually says it harms the aquatic environment. Why're you putting it down the loo?
'Mmmm, I s'pose you're right darling, but it gets it so clean.'

'You know water is the only liquid that expands when it freezes. Isn't that amazing?'
Completely blank looks.

Of course she could turn to the Internet for acknowledgement, but it did not offer anything much in the way of real understanding. So she'd jumped on a train. Research! London!

Satyrs, hands on hips, leaned forward obstinately, their legs becoming lion's feet, supporting a giant vase. Behind, in a glass cabinet, a tiny chubby boy rode a fish next to a nautilus shell whose spiralling core was carved into a visored helmet, and whose outside was etched with galleons. Three miniature babies, carved as triplets in the womb. Small ivory skulls crawling with snakes and frogs, and hornbill skulls with beaks intact, but foreheads depicting incredibly detailed Japanese scenes of bridges, trees and crowds. Crazy amateur engravings on mother-of-pearl reminded her of the art on the cover of a punk album.

Then a merman! Dry and dark like a mummy, no taller than a baby, little hands held up to its ears as though writhing in pain. She should pick him up and drop him in a pond. Then he would be okay, rescued, re-saturated. His expression was so desperate, his glass cage so definite. He did not at all seem to be the half-monkey half-fish con piece that he probably was.

'Looks real, doesn't he?' said a voice at her shoulder.

'Yes. Trapped,' said Brooke as she turned to the stranger. He was pale, like the stone of the courtyard, with long white hair, and too old to be trying to chat her up. She liked him, and she said, as they peered at the small merman, 'I'm looking for watersprites.'

'Aye?'

'Yeah.'

'There's a good one in the South American room.'

'I've never seen that room!'

'It's tucked away. I was just on ma way there. I'll chum you if you like.'

' 'kay.'

It was good to hear a Scots accent, she thought as she followed the man past sumptuous sexy naked marble men (one being beautifully sketched by a black teenage boy in full sportswear), and past stone age axes; giant seashells; mastodon jaws; a collection of greenstone Tiki men that made her smile; and through the doors into the face of the Aztec fire serpent, Xinhcoatl.

'Here,' said the man, beckoning. 'Here he is.' He pointed at a sombre stone figure, wearing a splendid stone head-dress. 'Tlaloc, meet ... '

'Brooke.'

'Brooke meet Tlaloc, the Aztec rain god.'

Tlaloc looked pleased to meet Brooke.

'An' this is the Aztec goddess o' lakes, streams an' childbirth,' said the man.

'Who, me?' asked Brooke.

'Nah. Her – Chalchiuhtlicue. That sculpture. Her world was flooded. Well, she flooded it. An' the people turned intae fish.'

'Interesting.'

'An' ah'm Trent,' said the man.

'Hi.'

Trent seemed very pale against a display case of scary turquoise mosaic masks. He was not so old, she realised. His hair was more albino than white.

'I wonder if there are any sculptures of Oannes. I might go and ask at the information desk,' said Brooke.

'Oannes?'

'Just some dead bloke from the middle east.'

A beat.

'See you then,' said Brooke. She left Trent in front of four carved-stone women, each holding their hands to their bellies in individual, specific ways.

'Bye.'

The courtyard was full of foreign teenagers. Brooke wanted to retreat back to the dimly lit calm of the South American room. When the French woman on the information desk looked up from her computer search and stated 'No, nothing on Oannes.' Let down, she turned away and saw Trent. 'Cuppa?' he indicated.

'Okay then,' said Brooke, planning one anyway.

They sat on one of the long tables outside the gift shop, and began a conversation that started with Trent saying 'Blimey, ma feet are aching. So who's this Oannes then?' and ended with Trent saying 'You keep talking about the element o' water, but water's no an *element*. No really. Chemically it's a *compound*. Hydrogen an' oxygen. Aitch two oh.'

Brooke smiled at Trent, then downed the last of her tea, said Bye, and wandered off, tickled by this fact. She had known it before, but it suddenly held new significance: it was romantic. Two kinds of atoms, each happy to explode given half the chance, coming together to give the planet life. Aitch Two Oh Yes, she thought.

# The loch beneath

Kade badly wanted to find the loch beneath. He set off into the body of the loch, alone.

But as he swam further down, the water would not let him pass. The sediment thickened, and his lungs couldn't take it. Frustrated, he tried again, but had to retreat upwards to the clearer water. It felt like surfacing. He shone the beam of Aurora's headtorch down to where he wanted to go, to the murky water. It was futile without diving equipment and he had none.

A loud sound, like a giant wasp, pulled at his ears. The water began to move in nauseating waves. Above, a speedboat made a dark shape against the sky. Following it was a rainbow, a mesmerising trail. Oil on a puddle.

Pain ripped through him as he struggled to force out the thick, smoky, oily water. Then hands pulled him away. Clear water washed through him, and he could breathe again.

'Styx! You're always pulling me!'

'You can't breathe the coloured water. You can't. No one can. Come. Come here.' Styx pulled him towards the large boulders at the loch's inside edge. 'What were you doing! Do you want us all found?'

'No!' No. 'I was looking for the loch beneath.'

'What, up there?' asked Styx, smiling and pointing to the surface.

'No, below, but the water's too murky.' He paused, struck by the smallness of the Waterpeople's world. 'You are so isolated.'

'Yes.'

'But if you found the loch below – '

'Kade, I've searched for it all my life.' Styx's expression was troubled. A man who cannot find what is lost. 'It's a myth.'

'But Styx, if you stay here ... if the Waterpeople stay here, you will be found. Humans...Landhumans have all this new technology. They can scan – '

Kade did not have the words, the signs, and he lost the will to explain. The Waterpeople had enough concerns. And who would go scanning Loch Tay anyway? All eyes were on Loch Ness.

'Come on,' said Styx. 'Let's get back to the caves.'

Kade wanted to go back to the Village cave, to safety. Right here he felt trapped between discovery by people and death by sediment. They began to swim.

'Come in here,' said Styx, leading Kade into a new cave. It was noisy and turbulent, but Kade felt like he was in an office. The settled expression on his face said that this was Styx's place.

'This is your room?'

'Yeah, look up there,' said Styx, suddenly boyish.

Kade swam to the surface and looked up. His ears hurt with torrential sound. Water poured down the walls. It was lovely. Something bright travelled down with the flow, and Kade reached out to catch it. His hand was repelled as he realised it was a chocolate wrapper and he wanted to shake it away, but instead he pocketed it, protecting the water.

He ducked back below the surface and breathed deep. He felt Styx's hand on his arm. Kade felt intimidated, and looked Styx in the eye, until Styx began to speak. 'I found you,' said Styx. 'I thought you were a Landman and I took you to a dry cave. I saved your life. Then you left. Other people saved your mother and I got to know her well. We all wished you had not gone, all of us, especially your mother.'

Kade stared at Styx, emotions burning. Styx looked into Kade's eyes. 'Your mother told me something about you. She said that you taste the emotions in water. It's true, isn't it?'

He believes it, thought Kade. He really does believe it. The first person.

'Yes,' said Kade. Then he frowned heavily, stunned and puzzled. His hand lifted, open, trying to catch a thought.

Something huge had happened and he had not even noticed: he could not Taste the Waterpeople. He had forgotten about the Tasting – for the first time *ever*. Wow.

He drank some water, consciously trying to Taste. He could perceive *something*, but it was like trying to understand a foreign language.

'I can taste emotions too,' announced Styx, cupping Kade's shoulder with his hand. 'But we are the only ones here who can,' said Styx. 'You and me.' Styx hung in the water next to him, with his head down. Another Taster. Then Styx straightened himself. 'Sometimes it is a burden, isn't it?'

'Yes,' said Kade, smiling.

'Perhaps ... you are my successor,' said Styx.

'What?'

'I am not a family man,' said Styx. 'My role here is the Taster. I look after people. Aurora said I was this ... ' Styx spelled out the word Shaman. 'Or this ... ' Doctor.

'How?'

'I can tell the mood of the people by the water that's been inside them. I pay attention. I am the one who understands the people as a whole. I know if something's wrong and I seek to make it right. But I'm becoming weak.'

*Was* he a Waterman? Not culturally. Kade suddenly wanted Brooke there to witness what was going on – to witness him. Now he understood how she must have felt when he had told her about the Tasting – amazed, lost. He pictured her with him in the Tay, wearing a wetsuit of hibiscus flowers.

'Kade, can you stay? I think I have found my successor. You are like me. But amphibious. Better,' said Styx.

Kade felt dizzy in the water. No other species breathed air and water. Was he the only one? Could he really do it for so long? What had happened to the Tasting?

'Think about it,' said Styx. 'Then agree.'

# Fishing

Kade could not sleep underwater. As soon as he drifted off, he choked. His sleeping self seemed unable to breathe water. Maybe his body feared he would drown, or float around and bang himself awake on the cave walls. The Waterpeople slept in alcoves made by the bubbles of whatever had rippled through the mountain and created the caves. They never seemed to bang themselves on the walls of their train-bunk size rooms. Maybe they had dreaming echo-location. He had tried to sleep in one of the alcoves, but his body wanted the confines and relative dryness of the Dry stores.

Lying down on the sleeping bag he became aware of his sleep-self emerging. He longed to meet that sleep-self and ask him what he did in his other life. He knew what he got up to in the dreams he remembered, but what about the other dreams or all those hours when he was asleep but not dreaming? He could not tell himself. His sleep-self was a stranger.

He is out in the loch, quite deep, others at his flanks, but cannot see them. Something sparkles in the corner of his eye. His hands reach out, wrap round a big trout, hold tight.

He woke grappling with the fish.

Breakfast that day (he thought it was breakfast, he thought it was day), consisted of lochweed and some chunks of chocolate that had been recovered from an overboard picnic hamper. He wondered why there was no fish, then remembered his dream and described it to Severn and Styx and the other people present. Most Waterpeople did not quite understand him as well as Severn and Styx did. They had not had prolonged contact with Aurora,

189

but basic words like fish and dream were understood. Everyone looked interested. A young man confirmed. 'You dreamed you caught a fish?'

'Yes.'

The man smiled. Severn leaned to Kade and said 'He wants to take you fishing. Right now. We fish only when one of us dreams of fishing and as soon as possible on waking. Sometimes it takes a long time for someone to dream fishing.' Some other Waterpeople came near. 'They'll show you how.'

Kade was pretty sure he knew already.

They swam out and asked Kade to tell them when to stop. Kade reached a place where it felt right, like his dream, and then several of them formed a line, indicating that Kade should be in the middle. It felt good to be flanked by Waterpeople. The people not in the line swam away, out of sight. Then Kade heard them swimming fast towards him, herding silver sparkles. He reached out and grabbed a fish. It tried to swim on, through his fingers, using the fast-moving slippery skill of scales. Instinctually he tethered it with his teeth. Others also had fish in hands or mouths.

They swam back to the caves like otters and went through the main cave to a place where the rest of the Waterpeople were waiting to help gut and clean and rip-apart and make the fish beautiful again, a place where the water would carry the leftovers away from where the Waterpeople lived.

Kade was very proud of his catch and of his people. He was a successful fisher. This felt like acceptance. But no one made the fuss he expected. When he tried to draw attention to his catch they started talking about a small boy who, on his first ever fishing trip, caught a fish twice his own size and killed it too. They smiled teasingly at Kade as they spoke, then they all tucked into the trout. It tasted wonderful.

Kade was enjoying the company of the younger Waterpeople. It was a relief to be away from Severn and Styx, just for a while. 'Do you really only fish when one of you dreams it?' he asked.

'Of course,' said the man, Tyne. Then after a pause he added, 'And we never ever pretend we've dreamed of fishing.' He moved his hand in a shimmy that expressed laughter. 'Do we Seine?'

'Never!'

After they had eaten, Tyne asked Kade if he would take them to the Dry stores. Seine and he used to go there with Aurora, he said. She would look through the pile of things and tell them about the Landworld. Aurora had named them, by telling them the names of dozens of rivers and getting them to choose.

The three of them swam to the Dry stores pool. Kade got out. As he went through his coughing-retching routine he felt embarrassed, watched. But embarrassment began to dissipate with his first few air-breaths and it left completely when he saw the impressed looks on their faces.

As he stood up he noticed a mineral water bottle. Full. Unopened.

'It's new,' explained Seine. 'We don't know what it is.'

Kade picked up the bottle and looked at the familiar snowy alpine mountains on the label. 'What do you think it is?' he asked. He waved it at them. Tyne flinched.

'Tell him,' Seine said to Tyne.

'Freezing liquid,' said Tyne.

'Turns water into ice,' added Seine.

Kade laughed. Where had they got that idea? Where had the idea to have that idea come from? The idea of some kind of threat? Tyne signed under the water, saying something to Seine that looked like *Dry*. Lots of *Dry*. *Drys*. That word the children had used. It seemed derogatory.

'No,' said Kade. 'It's water. This is a picture of where it comes from.'

He wondered how much they knew. Could he ever learn the grammar of their culture. The Waterpeople were human, and these two recognised the symbol of snowy mountains, but the way they interpreted the world was so different from his people.

*His people?* Even among his people there were so many interpretations. Each person lived in a different world. Even he and Brooke interpreted things totally differently - too differently. No. Not *too* differently.

'It's water from a long way away, across the sea. They put it in a bottle to take it to other places.' People like Stirling.

He glanced at the huge pile of books and artefacts, unable to imagine going through these things with the Waterpeople, telling them of the significance of each. That felt too tiring. Having to think about everything. *Everything, and* be the expert.

Kade turned the lid and clicked the bottle open. 'Do you want to try it?'

They looked reluctant. Kade took a sip to show them it was safe.

And experienced the Tasting for the first time in weeks. His Taste buds exploded into life. The emotions were ancient. He detected struggle, futility, and imagined a man struggling with a copper smelt. He tasted a happier note, satisfaction, and imagined the man had succeeded in his task. But he could not be sure of the truth of that image. He could only be sure of the emotion not its cause. He licked his lips.

'I'll try,' said Seine.

Kade passed her the bottle. She took a sip.

'It tastes still,' she said and passed the bottle to Tyne.

Still? For a second Kade fooled himself into thinking that they knew the difference between sparkling and still. 'It is still,' he said. You can get sparkling water too, with bubbles in it.'

'Bubbles?'

'You know. Tiny balls of air.' He made a tiny Jacuzzi in the water by Seine and Tyne.

Tyne put the bottle to his lips and sipped. 'Yes. This tastes still, not moving. Like it's asleep.'

'Can you try pouring it to us from high up?' asked Seine.

Kade stood and poured a spiralling stream of water into their mouths.

'Better,' said Tyne. 'Tastes like water now.'

'Tastes alive,' added Seine.

Seeing how little there was left Kade replaced the lid.

'That's cruel,' said Tyne. 'Why don't you pour it in with the rest? It's not good for it not to be joined.'

'Reminds me of home.'

He took a sip every day, to remind himself of the Tasting, until it was finished.

# Tequila

Brooke had not enjoyed her birthdays since she was little, and she had been feeling touchy lately anyway.

'Well, it is the anniversary of one of the most traumatic days of your life, no wonder you look miserable,' said her dad, over breakfast, on Brooke's twentieth. 'They didn't exactly take you out, hold you upside down and slap you, but it was close.'

'Yes yes, I know the story. I had little marks on my head for months from the forceps.' Brooke glared at her dad then turned to look at her mum. Surely she would chip in at this point. 'Why you didn't leave it to gravity I just don't know.'

'That was just what you did in that hospital love. You gave birth on your back and the baby got presented to you all clean. I didn't know any better.'

'Okay, okay. Can we change the subject,' said Brooke. 'I'm trying to enjoy my breakfast.' She was about to snap.

Charlotte appeared. 'Happy birthday Brooke! Wow. Twenty. Shouldn't you have a mortgage and a car and a proper job by now?'

Brooke stormed out of the room, went upstairs, grabbed her bikini and MP3, put them on, went to the end of the garden and lay down.

It was a beautiful bright late-July day. White clouds moved evenly above. She felt wound up. It was not just her family. It was everything. In the world. She pushed *play* with her thumb and meditation music began trying to calm her down. Seconds later she turned it off, irritated. She put on a Bollywood track and watched the shapes in the sky. There were the usual rabbits and cats, great folds of condensation becoming fur, then dragons, then crones on rocking chairs, which edged their way forward, becoming the faces of medieval countrymen, then smiling movie-stars, then mushrooms. It was like the voice had said – the water molecules were arranging themselves into the shapes they had been in before. People, animals, plants and mountainsides.

Brooke clicked the music off. Clouds were water dreaming! Water could remember what it had been. Water had a memory, and Kade had the key to reading it.

But why?

Brooke felt tears, squeezed from every part of her body by the relief of being allowed to believe him. She stood.

Her mum was walking towards her with a parcel. 'Can we start again?' asked Jane, adjusting her glasses.

'Yeah,' said Brooke. Her mum's blonde roots were showing. It was a rare sight, brown hair with light roots. The brown dye job was all part of her mum's lifelong plan to become more normal. Brooke had seen photos of her before she was married. With her glasses she had looked like a Valkyrie librarian – achingly beautiful, with waist-length waves. But the long blonde hair had got in the way, claimed Jane, not only physically, but also when she wanted to be taken seriously. Strangers had constantly been staring at her and giving her unwanted attention, so she'd cut it short and dyed it darker.

'Here,' said Jane, handing Brooke the pink-wrapped parcel.

Brooke unwrapped it, smiling. When she saw the hibiscus pattern she tried to keep smiling. Damn. Her mum had obviously thought about it carefully, but got it wrong. Brooke pulled out a beautiful expensive-looking bra and knickers set, embroidered with red. It was lovely, but her mum had not noticed that she had discarded her hibiscus? 'They're great,' she said. 'Thank you.' A birthday lie. A year ago she would have been delighted.

There were other presents too: a photo frame from Charlotte and some driving lessons from her dad. When Sam arrived she announced that she was taking the family out that night, no expense spared. Brooke felt happier.

After ordering the seafood special Brooke admired the arrangement of purple fuchsias. Did the colour clash with Charlotte's hair or go? Sam's hair was chestnut, Brooke's auburn, and Charlotte was totally flame-haired. *We gradually ran out of brown genes* her dad would joke when people commented on it. Very funny.

Her dad, Cliff, looked sophisticated this evening in a dark blue suit. She liked his tightly curled salt and pepper hair. In old photos he had wild long hair, like a spare member of the Jimi Hendrix Experience. She thought she remembered him with hair like that, but she was not sure.

Cliff was a businessman, high up in sugar. Until university Brooke had thought sugar was a relatively benign business: sweet, like her dad. But lectures at university had drummed into her that, not only did sugar cause gut and tooth rot, it was also the backbone of slavery. She had never mentioned to her peers that sugar was paying for her course and she had not mentioned to her dad that sugar was the root, or the cane, of all evil. Especially considering that, if not for sugar she might not be at university at all, in more ways than one: some of her dad's ancestors, *her* ancestors, were kidnapped and sold in Africa, brought by trade winds to the Caribbean and then invited to England when the country had decided to all be middle-class but realised there would be no bus conductors or cleaners. Perhaps Cliff had *sugar* and pepper hair.

Cliff was examining the rough edged tawny-coloured sugar lumps the restaurant provided. He was so straight. Once she'd told him a story she'd heard at university. An anthropologist gave some South American Indians their first taste of sugar. Before that their only experience of sugar was their annual honey-hunt. After four spoonfuls of white stuff they were up for two days! It was like speed! When she told him this story her dad had made it clear that he did not like the drug reference.

Weren't girls supposed to go for men who were like their fathers? Or was that just the case since Freud said so? Anyway, Kade was not like Cliff, except he was not keen on drugs either. Perhaps it was being surrounded by them on that camp, the Sight, that had put him off. Or, more likely, he had enough going on in his head.

Their food arrived and Brooke tucked in, washing it down with plenty of champagne.

'Twenty!' said Cliff. 'I can't believe it. It seems only yesterday that you were knee-high to a grasshopper!'

'What age,' asked Charlotte 'is it that you suddenly have to start speaking in clichés? 'Cos I'm going to kill myself before then.'

Their parents nearly took the bait, but Charlotte gave a sweet smile to show she was teasing. Sam picked up her glass. 'When I was sixteen I said I was going to kill myself when I was thirty.'

'Only a coupla years to go then, eh?' said Charlotte. 'But don't Sam, please.'

'I hear drowning is the nicest way to go,' said Sam.

Brooke's heart jumped. 'How would people know that?'

'Oh, I know,' said Jane. 'When I was young ... '

'YounGER' interrupted Cliff.

'When I was young*er*, there was a man who was pulled under in the weir. They threw in a ring and he had the chance to take it but he didn't. The person that eventually jumped in to save him had to fight with him to pull him to the surface. Later the man said he was glad he'd been saved, but he had been enjoying drowning. Very relaxing, after the pain subsided, he said.'

There was silence for a moment.

'Do you think it's possible to breathe water?' asked Brooke, giving Sam a nervous glance.

'Well, yes!' said Cliff.

'Really?'

'If you are a fish!' He shook with laughter.

Brooke decided to venture no further into the conversation topic. Sam looked relieved. Protective of their parents, she did not like them worried. Brooke had mentioned Kade to them, but not in any detail.

'Dessert?' asked Sam.

When the waiter came to take the order Charlotte bleated out that it was Brooke's birthday. Brooke was embarrassed, but she got a free tiramisu, complete with sparkler.

After dessert, the sisters went to the pub. Cliff did not like drugs, but he thought underage drinking was alright for Charlotte as long as she was with her sisters. The pub had been the Barleymow then had gone through various name changes until it had emerged limply as 'The Pike and Coriander'.

Brooke went in first. It was crowded and noisy. Lovely. She turned to Sam and Charlotte, 'Three tequilas?'

'Three tequilas!' they confirmed.

'Three tequilas. Salt and lemon,' said Brooke to the barmaid.

'Make that four. I'll pay,' said the man next to her.

Brooke clenched, and turned her head slowly. James.

'Hi, um, how are you?' she asked. God his hair was so *greased*. He stank like the toiletries aisle of a supermarket.

'Good thanks. *You* look great.'

Brooke blushed, but was unsure why.

James managed to procure them a table by doing a good impression of a vulture besides a couple nearing the end of their drinks.

'Okay, lick here,' he said and licked the dip where his thumb met his forefinger.

'What? I'm not licking your hand,' said Brooke.

'No. Stupid. Your own hand, for the salt.' He leaned towards Brooke, put his hand on her knee and whispered, 'You've licked a lot more of me than that before.'

Brooke winced.

'Right,' said James, once their hands were salted. 'You lick the salt and swish it round your mouth with the spit – '

'We *do* know how to do tequila,' interrupted Charlotte.

They licked, they said bottoms up, they swished the succulent alcohol round with their tongues and as they swallowed they each shoved a lemon quarter into their mouths. Brooke's went down smooth, but Charlotte got the timing wrong and spluttered. James hit her more than heartily on her back.

'Why did the Mexican push his wife off the cliff?' he asked, when Charlotte had recovered.

'I don't know,' said Brooke. She'd forgotten about his awful jokes.

'Ta-keela,' said James in a Mexican accent.

It took Brooke a few seconds to get, and then she could not help laughing.

'What do Mexican carpet layers say?' asked James.

'How many square feet do you need?' offered Charlotte dryly.

James ignored her. 'Underlay, Underlay,' he said, guffawing.

Sam stood up. 'I'll get the drinks in,' she announced, then whispered, 'I think he's on a roll,' to Brooke.

James continued his stand-up routine until he asked 'What's the difference between a pigeon?' and the sisters realised they hadn't said a word to each other for ten minutes and told him to shut up.

'One of its legs is both the same,' said James and laughed until he was red in the face.

'It's Brooke's birthday today,' said Charlotte.

Brooke shot her a glare. James turned to Brooke and embraced her, pulling her into a kiss on the lips, which lasted an embarrassingly long time. But actually felt quite good. His hand wound round her waist. Brooke knew she was very drunk, with blurred judgement, but James did have a good body and he did make her laugh.

'I think I'm gunna throw up,' said Charlotte. One look at her told them she was not being metaphorical. Sam escorted her to the toilet.

'Hey. Come to a party with me, Brooke,' said James. 'It's just round the corner.'

'Maybe.'

When her sisters returned Sam said she was taking Charlotte home. Brooke did not feel like going home. She felt lively. 'I'm going to a party,' she said.

'Suit yourself,' said Sam, with a drunken attempt at a knowing look, then left, guiding Charlotte through the door with her.

The party was hosted by a guy Brooke had never had anything to say to at sixth-form and who was now eating a bowl of vodka jelly on his own. It was one of those parties where most of the girls have left, or not arrived yet, or were never coming in the first place. It smelled like a brewery in a marijuana field and Brooke's feet stuck to the floor as she walked down the corridor into the kitchen. There the party's only two girls were having a water fight. They were both losing, to the delight of the boys watching.

Brooke saw a bonfire in the garden and walked outside. James followed. A few teenage boys were sharing a joint.

'Last kiss?' one boy asked Brooke.

'What?' They boy passed her the joint, which had about a drag and a half left. It was strong though, she noticed as she inhaled. 'Thanks,' she said.

Exploded melted glass bottles and burnt cans formed the majority of fire-fuel. She threw the butt in, lost her balance slightly and was caught by James, who then did not let go. He nibbled her ear. The wind licked at her wet earlobe. He turned her head and kissed her, sticking his tongue in her mouth. Brooke sat there, open-eyed. Could she do this? Did she want to? Her body told her she did. She wanted some physical comfort.

'I missed you,' mumbled James as his hand attempted to reach into her waistband. 'I'd forgotten what a great snatch you have.'

*Snatch?* Brooke jumped up. 'I think I'm going to be sick,' she said, more to herself than him.

'I'll be here when you get back, babe,' said James.

She staggered home, lay fully clothed on her bed and resolved to think of Kade. She fell asleep seconds later.

During the several times she woke in the night to gulp down glasses of water, Brooke praised herself for leaving the party. No, she couldn't sleep with anyone else, not at the moment, even if they were a lot nicer than James.

# Animals

'When I was a little girl,' Severn said to Kade. I watched a group of horses swimming across a river. Hiding from the riders, I saw a wonderful slow storm of white legs and muscled stomachs. I wanted to reach and touch them. Another time I saw a dead cow, which I did not want to touch. It was all bloated.' She looked down, then seemed excited. 'It's strange when you first see a four-legged animal. Such a grip on the land they must have with four legs.'

Thinking about animals made Kade miss land, especially the sun's undiluted brightness, rain, wind, the moon's reflection.

He told the children about birds, which he translated as 'Skyfish'. Apart from otters, who would come into the Village cave sometimes, birds were the most familiar of all the air-breathing creatures. Mostly the children knew them as dark shapes that flew above them, moving like ultra-fast fish, or as kingfishers that dived right into the water and out again just as fast, at home in air, water and trees. A couple of children had seen birds sitting in trees, but seemed reticent to talk about them. To see the kingfishers they must have broken the taboo against going near the surface. Kade had noticed a few feathers adorning the Waterpeople. Maybe they were decoration, or maybe they had some other meaning. Styx was particularly fond of feathers.

'Where do birds come from?' asked the children.

'Okay,' said Kade, choosing to take the long way round, and avoid chicken and egg arguments. 'You know newts? On land we have newts, but because their skin is dry they look more like tiny crocodiles.' The children swam backward as Kade swept forward in a two-arm impression of a hungry crocodile. Land children would have laughed and squealed. These just looked excited at their play-fear.

'We call the land-newts lizards. Some of them decided to live in trees. Then the lizards in the trees thought it would be safer to leap from tree to tree rather than walk between them. Lots of animals eat lizards you see, so the less they are on the ground the better. After a while some of these lizards developed flaps of skin, which helped them glide.' Kade looked at the children's webbed fingers and his own webbed toes and wondered if that was the same process. 'A while after that, the skin became wings. The lizards grew feathers and then they became birds.'

'How old are lizards when they become birds?' asked a child.

'Oh, sorry, it doesn't happen in one lifetime. The species of lizard evolved slowly over a long time. It's not like butterflies.'

'What are butterflies?'

Kade explained the butterfly's cycle and they all joined their thumbs and fluttered their fingers like butterfly's wings. Then, tired from watching him talk, the children began to play.

'I'll be the bird and there's the land. Now I'm in the air and you are in the water. You are a fish,' said one child.

'But I want to be a bird.'

'You can be a bird next time. But this time I'm gunna eat you. Look, I'm flying.' Folding her pretend wings, she dived towards the little fish-girl. Then they all began to join in and Kade was encircled by children swimming round and round above him, like a stingray disco.

What did they really know about the land or about Landpeople? They knew about pollution. Waterpeople could not breathe polluted water. But crucially they did not know that pollution was caused by Landpeople, by Drys. After all, people had been around for ages, and pollution was new. Obviously Aurora had said nothing. He wondered why, but followed suit and said nothing himself. Kade felt ashamed of Landpeople.

The Waterpeople worried that water was becoming sick. Maybe it was. Kade was concerned that *he* was becoming sick, as Aurora had. The damp was getting to him and he coughed a lot whenever he was breathing air. The transitions he had to make to sleep were becoming too much for him, for his body. The cave where he slept felt like a half-way place. Not wet, never truly dry. He did not like sleeping where Aurora had lived on her way to death. He did not like sleeping on her bed, but he had no other, and anyway if he moved it to another dry cave it would be soaked by the transition and never be as close-to-dry as it was now. He missed fire.

Styx put no direct pressure on him to choose, to take his role, to become a Waterman doctor. He had asked Kade the question once and left him to answer in his own time, but Styx did tell Kade his own power was becoming weak – dilute. All the Waterpeople were becoming weak. They had been isolated so long that their immunity was suffering.

The brain is like a muscle, Styx said. The more it is exercised, the more flexible and the stronger it becomes. Immunity is similar. Without fresh exposure to disease and illness, the body loses the tools to build up immunity. This was a problem for the Scots Waterpeople. They were hermetically sealed in their loch and caves, isolated from others, and from disease. Like a mind with no fresh ideas, no stimulation, their immunity was in danger of becoming feeble.

Styx said he was feeling old. They needed one of them to have the Tasting for all of them to be healthy, and no Tasters had been born in the loch. Kade understood why no parent would willingly wish the Tasting on their child.

But Kade was not sure if Styx was revealing everything. Kade, among the Waterpeople, was a celebrity, albeit one they left in peace most of the time. His arrival, in Aurora's wake, had fuelled their imaginations. As he watched the children playing birds, he wondered what changes he had made to the Waterpeople already. Would knowing him increase their resilience to Landhumans culture if they were ever discovered?

Or make them more vulnerable? They were so interested in the Land.

Then again, the Waterpeople had successfully stayed out of the way of Landpeople for thousands of years. They wouldn't want to start making contact now. 'Fuck!' he wanted to say out loud. 'What a secret.'

The Waterpeople looked healthy enough. Why was Styx so desperate for him to stay? 'Because I represent a fresh slice of DNA?' Kade asked himself, because he had no one else to talk things through with. He had noticed some of the Waterwomen eyeing him up. They found him attractive he guessed. But how thoroughly could attraction be separated from the need to breed? Especially when that might help the immunity of the Waterpeople.

Anyway, the Tasting had changed. He could not taste the Waterpeople, could not decipher their emotional language. But how could he tell Styx this? Was he only welcome as long as he had the Tasting?

The funny thing was Kade was relieved. He loved it, or rather, he loved *not* having it.

# Chlorine sprite

After the James incident, Brooke was ill. Good and ill. Telly in the bedroom ill. Longing for sleep ill. For a while in its life, some of the world's water became part of Brooke's white blood cells, and some her red. It played with the illness, teasing it slowly from her body.

It was like being little. Safe, warm, sick as a dog, but knowing that you'll be okay; that people cared.

As Brooke snuggled up to her pillows a memory snuck out from its hiding place: chlorine, running showers, white tiles, shampoo, sodden swimwear, her own little big tummy. She had been only just tall enough to reach the push-tap at the pool showers. She was alone there – her mother and sister elsewhere. Then she imagined him. He was tiny. No taller than a tile. He smiled at her. A mischievous smile.

'This is the *girls'* changing room. You're not allowed in here,' she had pretended saying to him.

'I can go anywhere I like,' he had replied with a tinkling voice, seeming very proud of himself.

They played together: he persuaded her to turn on all the showers and they danced under the water until she could hardly see him through the steam. He was sliding across the wet floor, falling on his bum and laughing.

Then her mum came in and told her off for wasting water. The tiny person waved goodbye, swam across the footbath and dived into the main pool.

'I just saw a fairy,' Brooke had announced to her mum, unsure whether she was making it up or not.

'A fairy? At the swimming pool? No, darling. It can't have been a fairy. It must have been a watersprite.'

Little Brooke was confused. She had never realised she could make things up and people would believe her, but her mum believed her.

She had thought so at the time anyway. Now, face in pillows, she felt tenderness for her mum and the sweet way she had been that day in the pool changing room. *That* was the start of the hibiscus thing. The true nucleus of her interest in water myths. It had all started with a lie, but not in a bad way. She thought of Kade. His lies were certainly better, nicer, and gentler than James' truths. That is, if they were lies. She was still unconvinced by the claims, but the longer she was apart from Kade the less she minded whether the water breathing and water Tasting stories were true or not.

# Kissing the surface

One day, Seine pulled him aside. Using her body to shield her speech from the others, she said 'I want to show you something, follow me.'

They swam through dark caves, him following the sound of her body. They turned a corner and Kade's eyes had to adjust to the light. The end of the dark tunnel was another entrance to the loch. He swam on, thinking of the loch beneath.

As he emerged from the tunnel Kade stopped thinking. He was astonished by the colours. Generous blocks of sunlight shone through the calm waters. Waterweed rose up, swaying like green cat-tails. The stones were a family of red, pink and buff. A small golden brown pike swam under him, made visible by the sunlight on its back.

Seine's feet moved rhythmically up and down, her hands visible at her sides. Her calves had a beautiful curve. He swam higher, watching the way she used her legs, buttocks, the small of her back, her shoulders, to move with the least resistance. He dropped down again, behind her, watching as her legs moved up and down, closing and parting, catching the light. Then she stopped and turned to face him. He felt shy, despite where he had just been looking.

'What did you want to show me?' he asked.

'I want us to kiss.'

'To kiss?'

'I want to try kissing a Dry.'

His senses told him she was not coming on to him. There was nothing she was doing that he recognised as flirting. But she had asked for a kiss and it felt like a secret.

'I want to see what it's like,' said Seine.

To see, to feel. He was interesting to her, exotic, desirable. The sunlight had made its way into the edges of her body, showing the pink in her hands, her ears, her nipples. How opaque he was compared to her. Was she wondering what went on inside him? She could not see his every heartbeat as he could hers. Her heart was fluttering.

'Okay,' he said.

She kissed him on the lips, tickling the inside of his mouth with the tip of her tongue. She began to drift away with the current and he reached for her hip, but just brushed her skin.

It was very strange. He could not Taste anything. Seine was the only girl he had ever kissed who did not immediately reveal her emotions through her saliva. He could see, though, where Seine's blood flowed. She was aroused, but she could see that he was not. Without the Tasting, kissing did nothing for him. Pulling away completely, she looked him up and down.

'Not so Dry, And not so hard.' She raised her face, seeming embarrassed. 'Let's have a look outside.'

'The surface?' He glanced up. 'But it's day.' But Seine had swum off. Kade overtook her. For all they knew they could emerge next to a boat, or be spotted from the shore.

'I think we're near those round houses they built over the water.'

'The crannogs?'

'Let's go and have a look.'

He held her arm. 'No. Not in the day. Anybody could see us, even here.' They were three or four strokes from the surface. 'We can't. Waterpeople don't. Styx *said*.'

'We don't all do as Styx says.'

She continued swimming upwards, appearing more and more delicate the closer she swam to the sun. Kade pushed to catch up with her. 'This is near enough' he said.

'Well, I'm going up.'

He was desperate to stop her. 'What about your people? Don't you care if you get seen? Get found?'

'Kade. Don't worry. I know I won't be seen. I can feel it. I wouldn't go if there was any doubt.'

Was this true? Did she have some special intuition, or was she bluffing? Confusion grabbed him, chasing him away from the surface, edging him away from Seine.

Seine looked at him. 'What if we *were* found? I might meet a Landman whose blood did respond to me and I could have a child like you. Would that be so bad?'

'I don't know,' he replied, no time to think about her question. 'Look Seine. You might be sure you won't be seen, but I am not. I would have loved to see the sun, still and un-flickering, but ... ' He swam away without looking back.

As he made his way through the dark tunnel he realised Seine's offer of sexual intimacy was the first opportunity he had turned down in a long time. He had taken the opportunity to go to the caves the first time, to go to India, to speak to Brooke by the waterfall, to not get back on the bus, to discover the Waterpeople, but he could not take this opportunity. Brooke was the only one who Tasted right.

In the village cave a group of people were encircling each other, like dancing whales, to keep sight of each other. One was telling a story about a shipwreck his grandfather had seen. Kade joined them and learned how the Waterpeople had taken the dead to the depths and taken the living unconscious to the surface, and how the Waterpeople were nearly seen, and how they got drunk on the wine from the wreck. 'The Landpeople have red water that actually makes you want more water,' said the storyteller.

Behind this man's hands Kade noticed Seine saying something that only he could see; an underwater whisper.

'You have a woman-love already,' she said and smiled.

But he didn't. He did not have Brooke. He missed her. Kade shook himself back to the story. 'Have you only ever drunk water?' he asked the group.

'Of course,' said the storyteller. There was no way to contain flavours, and stop them mixing with the loch. 'Well, water and fish blood.'

So Kade invited them to the Dry stores and made them tea with a box of cellophane wrapped teabags he had squeezed into cold water. The Scot in him knew he would love a cup of hot tea. With milk. Now.

The group become quite raucous. They had never had caffeine before, although Kade had already seen them behave like that and was pretty sure they had some sub-aqua psychedelics or something similar.

Later on Seine approached him. 'What did you do with the presents we gave you?' she asked, slightly challenging.

'Presents?'

'The stone and the bone. Do you have them?'

'No,' he said. He hadn't thought of them. 'The stone I gave to my woman-love.'

Seine smiled, seeming to enjoy the romance of that. 'And the bone? Our carving?'

'I sold it.'

'Sold?'

'I exchanged it for food and travel.' He briefly wondered if he had done an offensive or impolite thing, but Seine's face said he had not, so he continued. 'You know the birds that fly the highest?' he asked, because this was how the Waterpeople described aeroplanes. Seine nodded. 'I went in one to a place far away, a place it would take years to get to otherwise.' He looked around and saw a child of about two. 'It would take as long to get to as the time it will take for that child to grow old.'

'The world above is huge,' said Seine.

'Yeah,' Kade agreed. Bigger and more complicated than Seine could ever imagine.

'Why did you go?'

'To see a festival where they gather to enjoy water.' That was the simplest way he could put it. 'There were millions of people there.'

211

'Millions?'

'As many people as all the Waterpeople who have ever lived, and more still.' Seine's eyes widened. If she didn't have all her veins and arteries showing he would find her very pretty. Aurora must have had fewer prejudices than him.

'I want to go,' she said. 'I want to see the land.'

'But you can't breathe air,' he said.

Seine looked at him accusingly, as though he had criticised her. 'No,' she said. 'But perhaps my children will be able to.' She seemed upset, but defiant.

Kade reached for her hand. 'Seine,' he said. 'Your children would not be you.'

'You're right. It's too late for me. My parents were afraid, but I am not.'

'What were they afraid of?'

'Making an air-breather.'

Kade's thoughts fell into place: the drop that breaks the dam had finally fallen. The Waterpeople, with their 'technologies' must be able to change from water-breathers to air-breathers in one generation. His DNA was not necessarily needed.

'Has anyone ever tried?' he asked.

'No,' said Seine. 'No parent wants a child that would leave them.' She paused. 'Or possibly drown at birth.'

'Oh.'

'And Styx forbids it.'

Kade asked Styx why it was forbidden to try and make an air-breather. Styx explained that the Waterpeople wanted to hold on to their cultural identity, to reinvent it everyday. They did not want to become air-breathers and have to *preserve* their culture and tell stories to their children of how they had once breathed water. Their cultural identity was the child of their biological identity and they were proud to be water-breathers.

Styx gave the impression that they did not want to breathe air, any more than Lila had wanted to hear. Kade could tell that Styx had picked up a few opinions from Aurora.

'Also we are not confident that we could make a *both*, like you are,' Styx added, in a confessional way. 'If the baby could only breathe air it would die, or we would have to leave it up there.' He indicated towards the surface.

The Waterpeople might be discovered, thought Kade, and was filled with dread.

At dinner, Seine ignored him until they had finished eating, then she said. 'You have no parents to worry about you. You can leave.'

He could not decipher her tone.

# Rayton

In Rayton the voices continued:

*Chilling through Chelsea, hanging out in the plants of someone studying botany, or in the Thames, surrounding a boat owned by a woman who really wanted a castle and moat. At a dinner party, inside the eyes of those who gloat, the remote, the choked, the coked. In a puddle reflecting a Porsche, in the cocktails of a launch, in a ring of sweat around a builder's paunch.*

*Injected with chlorine, and mixed with taurine at a festival, never boring. Dancing in a stomach, then retched out into a misty light. Trodden into tents by the intense, the tense, those on the defence zipping up their tents, and those without pretence, those making amends, and chilling with friends. They like me. They are me. Playing water pistols, shot by a caress of wet, tagged by what was once someone's sweat.*

*Tumbling through India, loved, ploughed, praised aloud. Caught up in bottles of Limca, the favourite of the sugar drinker. Highly rated, appreciated, flavoured and savoured and salivated. Sometimes lifesaving, sating desert cravings. Melted in the north by a monk for his tea in the snow; sweated by a Goa beach girl with something to show.*

*Down through the Ganges, silver beaches, plenty of leeches. Former snow becoming slow, warm and mellow. Around corpses of the drowned and the poor. Past swimming teams and onto toothbrushes and into yogis in the dawn of Varanasi. And gradually, into the plumbing of the city, for you to drink me.*

'The connection between Kade and me is more than just lovers,' Brooke thought, and relaxed.

# Rain

Kade lay in bed with the sleeping bag pulled up to his chin. Dry? That's what the children called him: a Dry. But Kade was neither dry nor wet. He could not shake the lack of definition; the feeling of spongy dampness. His teeth felt soft in their gums, as if they were made of flesh, not enamel. His body and mind felt like mushroom gills, snails' feet, moss, the pages of a dampened book, the spongy pith of plants.

He *wanted* to immerse himself in the Water world, but he could not sleep there. The transitions from breathing water to air to water again were now totally exhausting. He desperately wanted to belong to one world. But unless he could sleep underwater, and unless he could Taste the Waterpeople, he could not be properly part of their world *and* be himself. He could not fulfil the role Styx expected of him, and until he had a role, he would be a guest, an exotic oddity, *not one of them.*

If he stayed, without the Tasting, he *could* be a family man, father children, add his DNA to the pool. But something inside him balked at this thought. He was too young to be a father, and he did not want a normal isolated life underwater any more than he wanted such a life above. He felt, acutely, the Waterpeople's isolation, and he understood their loneliness. Yet he still did not truly *know* how they felt. Without the Tasting, he knew them less well than he was used to knowing people.

He shook off the damp bedding, suddenly and hurriedly, and gave it a scornful look. He felt he would die if he slept in that bed even once more. He could slip away to the yurt, collect his mattress, shrink-wrap it so it was waterproof and drop it in the loch. After a few secret raids he could make the Dry stores quite cosy. He would fetch a rug, a few smooth-paged books; a lamp; some batteries. Maybe a laptop, or some games or music, to blow the Waterpeople's minds. Some food. A stove! At the Sight he could have a quick word with people. Tell them he was off to India again. Then return to the caves, and stay. But everything would soon become damp again.

On his front on the cold floor he stroked the cave's pool, feeling it was a *confidante* to his thoughts. Drawing some to his lips he willed himself to Taste the Waterpeople. Their Taste should be everywhere, spreading from the water they breathed and drank, from their blood and milk and more. Maybe he was not listening hard enough to Taste them, so to speak. But, nothing. Perhaps it was because water was everywhere that the emotions were undetectable, like background noise. He tried again.

At that moment, her blood reached him. Brooke. Real, earthy and strong. Happiness and sadness, anxiety and calm. It was definitely Brooke. It tasted delicious, nourishing and beautiful. It *Tasted*.

Brooke. His Brooke. Where had she been? Where was she now? How soon could he see her?

He slipped into the water and swam to the large cave, where the Waterpeople slept. It seemed that they all breathed in and out simultaneously as he swam past. They were above him, below him, in the rock bubbles all around. It felt like swimming through a forest.

He swam quietly, trying not to wake anyone. His instinct told him to leave without saying anything in case they thought their safety jeopardised. *He* was not sure he could keep this secret so how could they be sure he would not give them away? A part of him feared they might want to keep him here because of his Tasting ability. He had still not admitted to Styx that he could not Taste Waterpeople; if he left, he would not have to admit it. He still wanted the Waterpeople to see him as one of them.

Once he reached the centre of the loch he swam upwards, flooded by memories of sunshine and Brooke. He missed her desperately and had to show her all this. The Waterpeople would want to meet her, wouldn't they, when he came back? Urgency to be with her propelled him upwards. She must be near. Her Taste was so strong.

It did not seem to be getting lighter. He questioned whether he was really swimming to the surface. Or sideways? Or down? What was that sound? Something approaching?

Suddenly his head and chest thrust into the air. He emerged so fast that he fell straight back under the water. This could not be the loch surface. Too dark. He put his head out again. Something whispered around him.

Night. Rain. How could he have forgotten about rain? He smiled, invigorated.

It was three or four in the morning, he guessed. As he swam for the shore with his face underwater he thought of *her*: in the waterfall when they met; in the field with the fireflies; in the guest house; in bed.

He imagined her underwater, with the Waterpeople, swimming free, hair moving in the current, naked, eyes bright, so happy to have met these people. She'd help him understand them.

But ... she could not breathe water. She would have to wear a mask, an aqualung, a wetsuit.

No. Not even that. The village cave was most likely too far for a Dry to reach before the cold crept into their blood.

But he could bring the Waterpeople to meet her! He and Brooke could live in a cottage by the shore and they could spend summer days swimming with the Waterpeople.

No again.

Within himself he knew he simply wanted to see her, to be close to her, to be in her company, to hear her laugh. He had not *heard* anyone laugh since going underwater.

The clouds parted and a full moon shone through, indicating that he must have been away at least a month. He had slept whenever he was tired, never knowing how long for. He had always been warm enough, and had eaten frequently. But he had had frequent cravings for fresh fruit and, especially, fire. He wanted to be truly dry – as dry as a man could be, being mostly water. Dry by a fire with Brooke. The shore was nearing and he quickened his pace, pumping the water in and out of his lungs.

He arrived at the edge, crawled out and coughed all the water up. Each convulsion made him grip the shingle harder. The wind whistled. He paused. His hands were so pale, the blue of his veins visible in the moonlight. He felt his nakedness. Shorts had made him shy underwater so he had discarded them. But now?

'Fuck,' he said. He was naked in the middle of the night in the howling wind, in the middle of nowhere. Air hurtled into his lungs, painfully. A sheep baa'd. The sound was rough and loud. He made out the shape of the mountains behind the Sight and set off towards them along the beach. His walking muscles woke up reluctantly and his chest hurt. At a barbed wire fence he stopped, gripping the post, breathing hard. He could see his breath. Once again he was surprised at how pale his hands were.

The fence reached into the water to prevent sheep changing fields. Dozens of these fences divided the land leading to the Sight, so Kade waded to where the loch was undivided and swam the rest of the way home with his head above water. Home? Home.

At dawn he reached the Sight's beach. He crawled across the shingle and collapsed into the long grass, confused. What had happened? He had chosen to be a Waterman. Why was he here? He nuzzled the grass with his face, smelling the earth and listening to the birds.

The next thing he heard was a child's voice.

'You're nudey!'

Timmy! The child glowed, red curls bouncing against rosy opaque cheeks.

'They found a body,' said Timmy. 'It was your mum.'

'I'm sure she's okay,' said Kade, the first words he had said aloud.

'Not really,' said Timmy, glancing at his feet. 'And a pretty girl came looking for you. Sarah.'

Sarah Brooke.

Timmy ran off, returning with Stirling who helped Kade to his feet, gave him his shirt and said, 'You know, I'm worried about that water collection of mine. It makes people do crazy things.'

# Waterpeople

Brooke was standing on a chair feeding the tropical fish in the kitchen when the phone rang in the hallway. There seemed to be constant ringing everywhere, people shouted into phones, televisions blared, car horns hooted, machinery bleeped, lifts talked. So much noise. She swore she saw the fish wince at the high-pitched ringing.

'Charlotte!' she yelled. 'Get that will you. I'm feeding the fish!'

The ringing stopped. 'Brooke!' yelled Charlotte, standing right next to her with the handset. 'It's for you!' Brooke turned to grab the phone before Charlotte said something embarrassing.

'It's some bloke,' said Charlotte, loudly. 'Sounds a bit Scottish.'

Brooke wrestled the handset from her sister. 'Hello!' she said, speaking down the phone, but directing her annoyed tone at Charlotte, shooing her out of the room.

'Brooke?'

Brooke's heart pounded. She felt weak at the knees and very aware of herself, standing alone in the middle of the room. Was it really him?

'Kade?'

'Yes.'

His rich voice warmed her.

'How are you?' she asked, trembling.

'I'm fine. How are you?'

'Fine. How are you?' she said, then winced. 'Where are you?' she asked quickly, trying to cover up her nervousness. India? Scotland? *At the end of her street?*

'I'm in Scotland. At the Sight.' A pause. 'I miss you Brooke.' Brooke was about to say that she missed him too, but Kade continued talking. She stepped down from the chair. He spoke quietly and fast, clearly as nervous as her. 'I went to the caves.'

'What caves are they?' asked Brooke, immediately hating herself for her patronising tone.

'The underwater caves.'

Brooke could feel it. His presence, that feeling of them together, the love, the confusion. 'I thought you might have died,' said Brooke.

'I'm sorry. Everyone thought that.' He sounded very far away.

'Brooke,' he said, voice cracking. 'I found ... '

'You found what?' she interrupted. It was so good to hear his voice. She was so happy he was alive (although she had never really felt him to be dead). Did he want to come and see her, meet her family, her friends? Would he fit in?

Why could she only hear silence? Why wasn't she with him, near him? What? What had he found?

Oh god. Maybe he had found his mum's body. More gently, she asked, 'What did you find?'

'Waterpeople. I found Waterpeople.'

Brooke's heart sank.

'Oh no,' she said and took a couple of steps backwards.

Oh no, she had said it aloud.

Oh no. Not more craziness.

Brooke ripped herself away from herself. 'Kade. I miss you too. But I've got to go.' She pressed the button. The phone clicked off. 'Enjoy *your* waterpeople.'

She ran upstairs, buried her face in the bedcovers and burst into tears. How dare he? How *dare* he be crazy?

222

Kade stroked Brooke's handwriting, then screwed up the address and number. He placed the receiver back on the kitchen wall and just hung there. 'She doesn't want me,' he called.

Stirling and Ursula, who had left him in private, came back in. Ursula poured wine. 'Why not?' she asked, as if Kade not being wanted was impossible.

'She thinks I'm *crazy*.'

'Oh Kade. She was clearly crazy about you,' said Ursula, exchanging a glance with Stirling.

'No,' said Kade. 'She doesn't want to know.'

'Try and think how *she* feels,' said Stirling. 'She meets you in India, falls totally in love, and then you desert her. She turns up here, desperate for you, but not knowing if you wanted her. That's pretty brave.' He downed his wine and began gesticulating with the glass. 'Then you disappear the moment she arrives – not telling anyone where you've gone.' He put the glass down suddenly but quietly. 'Or now, where you've been.'

'But ... '

Ursula took over, sympathetic. 'I know. You did not know she was here. But *Brooke didn't* know that. She might have thought you were avoiding her. Then you ring her out of the blue, just as she's probably getting over you.'

'Ouch,' thought Kade. He had once thought he wanted Brooke to get over him, but hearing those words he realised he did not ever, ever want her to *get over* him.

'No,' he said. 'She thought I'd drowned and she left. She didn't care.' He spoke without conviction, knowing Brooke cared.

Ursula poured some more wine. 'She clearly cared a lot. It was all too much for her. I mean, if you are never told someone is dead, are they really dead to you? You know that better than anyone. She couldn't face the possibility that you might be dead, because she loved you so much.'

'Call her back,' said Stirling.

'No.' That wouldn't work. No phone-line was wide enough to carry his feelings to her. He'd deserted Brooke, his mother and now the Waterpeople.

He *had* to see Brooke, even if it was just for a proper goodbye. He had chased her in Manali and she had come seeking him in Scotland. He loved her and she loved him, but she might not wait forever. Perhaps she was scared, perhaps she thought him crazy. But now he could prove –

'Kade. You're just scared,' said Stirling.

'It's more complicated than that,' said Kade. He looked at Ursula, rolling a cigarette with fingers filled with worry, and at Stirling, holding his chin in his hand, elbow propped up on the table. These people were caught up in his drama, interested in his life. They cared about him. Ursula had known him forever. He trusted her completely. Stirling had appeared in his life less than a year ago and Kade had trusted him on sight. He loved them. But he could not talk to them like he could Brooke. Ursula was too maternal, too proud, and Stirling – Kade had the feeling that when they talked he and Stirling were having a deeper conversation than their words revealed, and it felt strange.

Brooke, though, was straight up. She told him how she felt and asked how he felt and did not really offer advice, which was a good thing. Most importantly when he kissed her, he *knew* how she felt. She had liked him kissing her. He longed to see her face. Yes, she *might* have believed he drowned, but maybe she believed he could breathe water. He had told her as much.

'Stirling?' asked Kade.

'Yes?'

'Can you give me a lift to the station? I could catch the overnight train.'

Stirling smiled. 'She's worth it. I knew when I saw her that she was perfect for you.'

'She'd be welcome here,' added Ursula.

# Under the bed

After the call Brooke felt seasick. Lying on the bed (a twelfth-birthday present), she became aware of the paraphernalia beneath. She had not yet unpacked properly. She swung herself onto the floor and slid her India rucksack out from under the bed.

She pulled out a cream silk dress, tracing its gold embroidery with her fingertips. It was crumpled but pearly, soft and luxurious, too glamorous and exotic to wear around Rayton. Would she ever find the circumstances where it was appropriate? Did it fit? How did it feel? Brooke pulled off her tracksuit and tried it on. Perfect. She tied the sash and sat down, the fabric's fluidity inviting her to move in a more elegant manner.

Next she unpacked a collection of trinkets. Each had seemed so important when it had been bought in a market or found on a riverbank, but none had become the talking points she had anticipated. There was the crystal, given to her as protection by a Californian woman on a train. Maybe its best place was under the bed. There were a dozen other stones, each carefully chosen as a memento of a waterfall or river. At the time, Brooke had been sure she would remember where she had found each one and the occasion it represented. The stones were in a camel-leather bag. She poured them out onto her lap and tried to remember the origin of each. She examined their texture, weathering, colour, shine, taste, weight, and aspects with no name. There was sandstone, slate, dusty pink river stone, yellow river stone and quartz. It felt good to make clear categories for them, to name them. Of course, she could not remember which came from where, but it did not matter, somehow they were all from the same place: the place inside Brooke when she had nothing else to do but look for pretty stones, before Kade's craziness pushed to the surface. She decided to keep them all, but not to bother doing a show-and-tell for her family. The stones were wonderful jewels because they kindled her memories, not because they were remarkable on their own.

She fetched a bowl, filled it with bathroom water and placed the stones inside. They looked shiny and delicious. Brooke put them on the windowsill beside the bed.

Next was a pile of garish holographic stickers of gods: Lakshmi sitting on her lotus; Parvati riding her tiger; Shiva meditating with a fountain of water emerging from his head; and baby blue Krishna playing his flute with chubby fingers. All were rendered just the right side of kitsch. She had bought them more for the fun of the transaction than their beauty.

There were bus tickets, train tickets, hotel receipts. To keep or to throw away? Did she want to sit looking at these again in a few years, retracing those routes? Leafing through, she found the Delhi-Manali ticket, the route on which Kade had deserted her. She threw them all in the bin. How dare he leave her and then phone?

Then she pulled out a memory card. That meant pictures. Brooke's heart jumped as she thought of what she had captured. Must have been from the beginning of the trip, because she had lost her camera. She did not remember actually losing it, just it no longer being around. She could not wait to see the pictures. She could get them done in an hour in town.

Brooke checked the bottom of the bag. Just grains of sand. Then she checked the side pocket. There were some sticking plasters and what felt like a ring. She pulled it out. It did not look very Indian. She did not remember buying it. It looked Art Nouveau, or Celtic, the stone rhinestone or diamond. She pushed the sand off with a silk sleeve, then dipped the ring in the water on the windowsill and held it up to the sunlight. Beautiful. Really looked like a diamond. She put it back in the bag and shoved the bag under the bed, almost guiltily.

She caught the bus into town, dropped the card off in Whoppaprint and went to the café next door to sit out the hour. It was her favourite, a brightly lit builders'n'students café with a difference. With the aid of papier-mâché, it looked like a yellow cave. In the middle was an artificial fountain and waterfall. The pump was visible and the flowers were plastic, but it was flowing and alive nonetheless. She ordered hot chocolate.

Brooke flickered with excitement. Had Kade put the ring there? Was she supposed to keep it, wear it, sell it? She had not even tried it on. She swirled her spoon in the chocolate froth.

A group of boys came through the door. The after-school crowd. As they passed, she heard one of them say 'Hello beautiful. Nice dress.' Brooke glanced down, realised she had forgotten to change, and smiled. The compliment sounded sweet to her ears, even though it was mainly intended to amuse his mates.

'So,' thought Brooke, 'life has been relatively normal for a while; now things seem to be getting interesting again.' She had not really talked about Kade much, but he had entered her thoughts everyday. Over time, though, she occasionally made it to evening without thinking of him. She'd even woken up one morning realising she hadn't thought about him at all the day before. That was pretty good going, considering that, for months, he'd jumped into her mind every time she turned on a tap, had a drink of water, or bathed. But recently she'd managed to loosen the association between Kade and water. His presence no longer flowed through every drop. She'd even been able to drink without thinking of him. Then he had phoned, quickening the hold that had never really gone away. She missed him.

Half an hour to wait before she would see whether there were photos of him. One photo she always carried in her mind; a perfectly captured moment of Kade surrounded by turquoise sunlit water, smiling.

Four pm. The photos must be ready. Brooke paid for the hot chocolate and then went to Whoppaprint and paid an outrageous amount in return for a shiny yellow pack. Delaying the desire to

227

look at the pictures, she returned to the café, and ordered another hot chocolate, waiting for it to arrive before she indulged herself.

The first shot was of the tangled and gnarled wiring of an Indian telegraph pole: the urban equivalent of a jungle tree laden with lianas, taken to show her friends back home and say, '*Look how they do things in India.*' The next was the customary beautiful sunset over Delhi. Amazingly the photo had managed to capture, rather than edit, its beauty. Then the photos went north, to the Kumbh Mela – to the sadhus carrying tridents like Neptune, to the naga and aghori babas crossing a bridge, and walking through town in their hundreds, revered and feared and covered in ashes. These shots were also intended for friends, to illustrate India's uniqueness, but the photos did the Mela no justice; most just showed a sea of grey, taken from too far away.

Gradually the photos became less show-and-tell, more for her. Feeling less homesick, she had started enjoying thinking of no one but herself. There were no people in these shots, just plants and animals, beautiful colours and a sense of freshness. Then she saw him, hiding between rocks, seen from a bridge. Urgently, she leafed on. The shots climbed a hill, past flowers and springs, until she reached the pink-rock waterfall in Laxman Jhula. That was the last photo she had taken before Kade came into her life. She had recorded the waterfall, then sat and written in her book, occasionally glancing around, pretending to herself that she was checking for visiting watersprites. She had felt a presence, and looked up to see Kade smiling from the turquoise water. She remembered falling in love at that instant. Or had she initially tensed up and tried to ignore him?

Brooke's hands shook slightly as she reached the next photograph. She held it gently, feeling the relief of being able to stare at him now as she had always wanted to, without making him feel uncomfortable. He stood in front of a Banyan tree, providing scale to the hanging root system. He looked so young! Handsome and dark and young. How could someone she felt she had known for an eternity look so young? Had she looked that young? It really was not long ago. She missed him.

The last photo on the film was Brooke holding a firefly. Kade had taken it. Brooke could see that she was smiling, but her face was blurred. She put down the photos, remembering the love and forgetting the fear and craziness.

'You finished with that, love?' asked the waitress. Brooke looked up from the photo and back to the café. The cup was empty.

'With the cup? Yes. But not with him,' said Brooke, and showed the picture of Kade to the waitress.

'Mmmm handsome,' said the girl.

# Fast

Kade was leathered up and sailing over the hills, stomach at a slightly different rhythm to the rest of him. He loved the way the road blurred and the fields rushed by, yet the distant mountains, less responsive to speed, changed perspective very gradually, and the sky remained still as ever.

He was moving forwards in his life, flanked by hills and water, towards Brooke.

Fast. Could the Waterpeople ever imagine anything as fast as Stirling's motorbike? He had hardly told them anything about modern things. He had felt as though it could contaminate them. Was he right? What would Brooke think?

Just past the pub he caught a glimpse of red and white safety tape and a crowd of people up on the hill. The bike was going too fast for him to focus on what was going on, but it was obvious that they weren't police or mountain rescue. There was something different about their texture. The bike passed a line of parked cars.

'Can you stop by the pub?' yelled Kade

They pulled into the forecourt a few minutes later. Kade's butterflies threatened to become nausea.

'Stirling,' he said. 'There's something going on.'

Kade looked over the rapids. The red lights from the pub touched the tips of the waves. The rapids were Kittim's swimming pool, playground, courting ground, tourist attraction and for some, church. Half his childhood was spent swimming into the whirlpools with the Taste of happy water on his tongue.

More innocent times for sure. Could the caves be accessed from here?

Stirling looked at him through wind so pervasive it seemed to catch the light. 'I don't like pubs much. I'll stay out here.'

'Okay,' said Kade, and opened the door of The Bridge. It was packed. Warm air filled his lungs and relaxed his posture as he navigated to the bar. There were tourists and locals, families and dates, and in the corner sat a group of oldish men he had never seen before.

'Looks like all the village and all the tourists are here tonight,' he said to the landlady, who was too busy to recognise him. Kids from the Sight did not come into the pub much. Generally they preferred to drink in the treehouse.

'Yeah,' she said. 'It's this cave thing.'

Kade felt a rush. 'Oh?'

'You musta heard? They discovered an underground cave; reckon the whole mountainside is full of caves, like honeycomb. This place is going to change, I tell you.'

'Good business for you, then?' said Kade, trying to remain calm.

'Yes,' she said, as though she were trying to summon up the enthusiasm for change. 'What can I get you?'

'Scotch please. No ice.'

The whiskey was deep caramel. The pub seemed to glow, people's excitement pushing into the air. Next to him was a family of locals, mum, dad, and two tracksuited teenage sons, out for a Saturday Night. The more Kade heard the more dread he felt.

'Dad, you've got to come and see it soon,' implored the eldest. 'There are all these men there with machines.'

'There's some women, too,' said the younger. For this he received a 'don't be cheeky' look from his mum.

'There's some of the boffins over there,' said the elder boy, gesturing toward the men in the corner. They wore tweed and were poring over some papers. They looked like Kade's grandfather had; white haired and delicate. As Kade moved away from the bar he heard the younger son whisper to his brother, 'And those girls at that hippy camp are really something else.'

As Kade made his way over to eavesdrop on the boffins, The Skye Boat Song came on the jukebox (especially for American tourists who had arrived in Kittim keen to trace their Scottish roots).

He looked at the group of men. Were they foes? Would they stand on the shore, or would they dare follow the route he had been, into the caves? How could he protect the Waterpeople? There was no way he could let them die or be captured. They had to be free.

The Scotch distilling his decisiveness, he worked his way to where the four men sat. On maps marked with red pen, the men seemed to be playing a boffin's version of pin the tail on the donkey. Kade eavesdropped.

'I think there has to be another entrance here,' said the one who wore gold-rimmed glasses.

'Yes. That makes sense, I suppose,' said another with a splendid but nicotine-stained moustache.

How had they found out? He had only told one person about the caves – Brooke. Would she have told anyone? He drank the thought down and it burned through his cells.

'Excuse me,' said Kade. The four men looked up, startled. Feeling like he had disturbed children at play, he said 'Mind if I ask what you're doing?'

The one with the nicotine moustache responded. 'We were wondering how far the caves reach.'

'What do you reckon?'

'We think it's feasible that they continue for some way into the mountain, don't we gentlemen?' The other men nodded and mumbled affirmatives into their drinks.

'Can you find out for sure?' he asked. Did they have some kind of scanner, a Loch X-rayer? Maybe they were looking for helpers.

'The team are working on it now,' said the one with gold glasses, in a way that suggested the matter was not to be discussed now, or possibly ever.

'There'll be an information stall on the bridge tomorrow,' offered the one with the nicotine 'tash.

They gave him a look of dismissal and Kade moved away. He almost turned back to say 'No, don't. Don't fuck it all up.' But he heard one elderly voice say:

'It is beautiful, isn't it?' He could hear the smiles in the murmurs of the others as they agreed. It *was* beautiful. Then the voice said, 'Tomorrow we dive.'

Kade returned to the bar. He liked whiskey because it had a low enough percentage of water-per-alcohol to transmit few emotions, so he knew how *he* felt: determination. 'Another please,' he said. 'Do you know how the caves were discovered?' he asked, as the barmaid pushed the optic.

'Aye. They found the tunnel a few weeks ago when they were pulling a body from one of the burns. It was that woman that disappeared from the Sight.'

Kade heard a noise escape from his mouth.

Still holding the glass to the optic the barmaid turned her head. Her hand reached to cover her mouth. Now she recognised him. 'It was your mother, wasn't it?' she said kindly, as she pushed the optic again, and then once more. She passed him the glass. 'Here. On the house. I'm so sorry for your loss.'

The pub felt like it was squeezing him. He joined Stirling on the low wall that edged the rapids. 'They found some caves,' he said, trying not to show his worry. 'Beneath the loch. I've got to get back to the Sight.' He took a gulp of Scotch.

'Really?' asked Stirling, suddenly charged up with enthusiasm. 'Caves?' Then he looked down again. 'But what about Brooke?'

Kade did not answer. The drink trickled down his throat, bringing with it the sensuality and pain of being with Brooke and then not being with her. He wanted to be close to her, as close as they were in India. The scents came back to him. The fresh air of Kittim became hibiscus, vanilla, heather, rose, the electrical aroma of a storm, her body, their conversations, the Taste of her happiness.

But she would have to wait.

'Gotta go Stirling,' said Kade slurring a little. 'Can you take me back to the Sight?' He stood, knocked back the rest of the whiskey, and lost his balance, nearly going over the short wall and into the water.

'Whoa,' said Stirling, catching him. Kade wandered toward the bike, then Stirling announced: 'Kade. We're walking home. I refuse to take such a drunkster on my bike.'

'Oh … kay.'

The road home was well lit – dusk only having a tender grip on the summer night. As the moon rose the loch became silver. Looking across the fields to it, Kade felt the water pull like a magnet. Several times he veered off the road, stumbling into fences and forests, but was pulled back and marched on by Stirling.

'But the Waterpeople. Their caves,' said Kade, but he had slipped into Sign language without realising, and when he did realise, he was filled with relief that Stirling could not have understood him.

Stirling began to talk of his recent travels. Kade recognised the tone: Stirling was talking him down. Kade was not high, nor angry, but the ordinariness of the chat took his mind off his desire to run to the loch, dive in and shout warnings to the Waterpeople. Shouts were useless anyway, he knew.

When they reached the Sight, Stirling frogmarched him downhill and sat him inside the yurt.

'I've never seen you like this,' he said. 'So full of fire.' Stirling held his palms up as though warming them on Kade, then became serious. 'Whatever it is that you have to do, it will be better done in the morning, sober.'

Kade sat sulkily in the dull light.

'Why?' asked Stirling. 'Why are you so desperate? You've just come back, after disappearing for *two months*. Not even telling anyone where you've been. And you want to go off again on your own. Relax, settle down. You're all over the place'

Stirling lit a fire and sat by the door. Kade tried to push out past him, but the look in Stirling's eye put him in his place.

'Kade, tell me why you are like this. What's happened to you? Where were you? Were you with the people across the loch? Where were you *really*?'

Kade choked down the secret, swallowed his desire to tell everyone about the Waterpeople. 'Stirling. I *can't* tell you. I just can't.' His voice cracked. The fire and the whiskey felt as though they had melted something physical in him, and tears dropped from his eyes.

'Okay,' said Stirling. 'Just relax. It's okay.'

Kade was exhausted. The fire was warm and the sheepskins soft.

# Water drinking

Brooke lay under the duvet, unable to sleep, her mind intent on replaying the telephone conversation. Waterpeople? What waterpeople? Was this a new level of insanity? If it was ... if he were insane, it was a beautiful kind of insanity. *He* was beautiful. His stories were brilliant – but his expectation for her to simply believe him confounded her.

Waterpeople? People who lived near the water? Perhaps he had found some people that could help her with her research about watersprites? Maybe he was not crazy? *Why* had she hung up? She had ruined it now. Whichever side of sanity he walked, he was not vicious; he was wonderful.

Inside her closed eyes, lights pulsed, pleasantly, like the halo of the moon. The pulsing extended through her body and would have been uncomfortable if she had not let it flow. She imagined a little silver fish, smaller and flatter than her palm, gliding under her skin, gently loosening all the remaining caught parts, then dissolving into her bloodstream.

She was slowly spinning, unwinding. She perceived the delicate redness of her blood, teeming with electricity and emotion, edged with light. It felt good, an intense purr that grew so pleasant she could not lie still anymore.

She reached over for a glass of water. As the water flowed into her, she felt it taking on the glow of her body. First arteries, veins, routes, then it went beyond the soft confines, into metal, pipes, concrete and brick. Then outside to a reservoir, filled with reflections of sailing boats, and collections of fish. Treated and heated, and before that, dribbled, by a baby, an emotional innocent. She felt its happiness.

The flickering stopped. The light became constant. Joy lit every pocket of Brooke's soul. She sat up straight and gasped. This was real. She expected to be sweating and shaking at such an intense experience, but she felt calm and physically relaxed. A tasting.

A Tasting.

Filled with energy, there was no doubt left in her. Naked, she reached into the pocket of her rucksack and took out the diamond ring. She paused, catching sight of herself in the full-length mirror. Slowly she put the ring on her ring finger. The ring was meant for her to wear, she knew that. She moved her hand to sparkle the diamond, and then kissed the stone. Such a traditional symbol of love – a silver circle, the never ending shape, with a diamond, coal made strong by pressure. Old, so old. The ring was antique, but the diamond much older, the coal it was made from once trees, where sap ran. Sap that may have once been blood, sweat or saliva.

Brooke shook herself. No time to get entranced. She had to tell Kade about the Tasting. *Her* Tasting. What she thought was a Tasting. She *had* always kind of believed it, thought it was feasible, that he could do it. But now –

Now it was all real.

Real love.

Not the kind of love that could be happy being transmitted through telephone wires and bounced off satellites, but a love that wanted physicality.

She started packing. Right. Clothes, waterproofs. River stones? Yes. Sleeping bag? Tent? No. She would stay with him. Notebook? For sure. Photos? Yes. Money, keys, toothbrush. Uh, huh. Hibiscus necklace? No. Passport? Yes, you never know.

Swimming costume!

Okay, packed.

She fastened the clasps.

She would tell him about the Tasting. He was the one person who would believe her, although maybe these waterpeople would too. She slipped on the silk dress and white wool coat, scribbled a note explaining that she had gone to Scotland and would be fine, and rushed out the door, nearly tripping on the morning paper. She walked, and then ran to the train station, not wanting to miss the morning train north. She just made it.

Breathless she sat back in her seat and admired the diamond ring.

But if he had intended for her to find the ring then why had he left her on the bus? Her thoughts refracted, searching for the right answer. Was it because he did not really love her?

No.

Because there was someone on the bus that he wanted to get away from, someone who wanted to put him back 'on the grid'?

Maybe.

No.

Because he had licked her wound and tasted fear?

Probably.

Yes.

And if he had not Tasted the fear, he had seen it in her eyes. She had betrayed him by not trusting him, and by fearing him. She was desperate to show she did trust him now. Once she had felt she was not really good enough for him, too ordinary. At the same time she had felt that she was better, saner, than him. She had been Sarah the suburban student, not Brooke the fearless. He must have seen that in her, that ordinariness, and tried to protect her. She felt tender at that thought.

Instinctively her hand reached for her hibiscus necklace, momentarily forgetting that she had shed that person already. She touched the diamond instead. Now she was both; sensible Sarah who would filter the more crazy side of Kade, and Brooke, who would love him for it, whenever, wherever.

# Danger

Sweat soaks his dream. Out of the pool Brooke emerges swiftly and sleekly, her naked form shimmers with a film of water, skin opaque gold against the green. She looks him in the eye and says 'I know.'

A tunnel of panic led him awake. Why? Why had he told her about the caves, the Tasting, the water breathing?

He tried to calm himself. Of course he had had to tell. A secret was not a secret otherwise, and he had wanted Brooke to be interested in him, to enchant her, to make her fall in love with him, all of him – water breathing, Tasting and caves included. But now, with the discovery, worlds were overlapping. The Waterpeople had always been discrete as a dream. Now their caves were to be explored, exposed. Their lives were in danger. His secrets were no longer watertight.

Poignantly and suddenly, he realised that *he* was a danger to the Waterpeople: his existence could give the Waterpeople away. Since his conception, the Waterpeople had no longer been a secret to all but themselves.

As Kade crossed over into full wakefulness a new idea followed him. Maybe his job, his role, was not to hide the Waterpeople away in his head, but to reveal them to the Drys. To unite. But he felt unsure and he desperately missed Brooke. He wanted her support.

In the doorway, Stirling still slept. Kade got up, as quietly as he could, but woke him anyway.

'Where you going?' asked Stirling.

'Up to the lodge, to make myself breakfast,' answered Kade and stepped over him. He had planned to go straight to the pool, but with Stirling's eyes on him, he would have to go to the lodge.

'Whatever this thing is that you've got to do, I'll go with you. I'll help you.'

'Thanks Stirling, but it's something I've got to do on my own.' But how, he wondered.

At the lodge he made coffee and porridge, and pulled Ursula's daily paper towards him.

It was just a small article:

### EXPERTS TO EXPLORE SECRET TAY CAVES

*Today divers will chart a newly discovered cave network at Tayside. Believed to reach deep inside the mountainside, the caves were discovered by divers searching for a body near the village of Kittim.*

*Cave diving is incredibly dangerous. Sheer cold prohibits dives exceeding twenty minutes. Exploration may be made easier by the discovery of a possible second entrance though a dry cave, found by walkers on the trail of a local legend about a sacred spring leading to an underwater passageway.*

What if the Waterpeople had already been found but the papers were not mentioning it? Kade shuddered. He clunked his spoon into his mug in what was supposed to be a dramatic and decisive gesture, but the sound was leaden. Outside, a plane flew high in the sky. How many people in it, three hundred? All those people moving round the planet. How many secrets? How many secrets as big as his? He looked at his coffee and thought of the milk, the dairies, all the people who worked there, the water and the thousands of people it had passed through, and the coffee beans and the farmers that had tended the beans and the children who had danced through the crops playing hide and seek.

People were all seekers weren't they? If the secret got out, they would all want to see the Waterpeople. At least he hoped they would. If the 'general public' were not interested in the Waterpeople he did not have much hope for Drykind.

Even worse would be if the Waterpeople had been discovered but the authorities were keeping them secret, as people said they do about aliens. If the authorities knew, then everyone should know. All those people, in all those planes cruising round the world like blood cells in an animal, should know.

Pollution, not people, was the real threat to the Waterpeople. Maybe if everyone knew about them, people would clean up their act. No. He *had* to hide the Waterpeople. Then, with Brooke, he could find others, other Waterpeople.

But would Brooke want to see him? He had deserted her after all.

There was no time to dwell on it. He had to reveal to them that they may be revealed. Kade raced to his yurt, his body quickening. He saw Stirling washing by the well. Stirling did not see him.

Kade grabbed the waterproof matches, his trunks and his pack, ran down to the willow pool, dived in and breathed.

But his lungs would not take it. He coughed like a drowning man. He clutched for the edge. In. Out. In. Out. Breathe the air. Breathe, breathe. He wanted them to be discovered, and he did not. He wanted to prove to Brooke he was not a liar. He had wanted more than anything for Brooke to meet the Waterpeople, and now he had to hide them. Brooke would never meet them; she would never believe him ... unless they found other Waterpeople.

He panted and then began to breathe more gently. To breathe water he had to be calm. It was so difficult. Why was his life so difficult?

Because it was. He swam down again and breathed out, trying to rid himself of anxiety. It would not be the worst thing in the world for the Waterpeople to be discovered. Que sera, sera. In

241

parallel, if he accepted that he may never see Brooke again ... No, he could not accept he would never see Brooke again. He *had* to see her. Finally, he found himself able to breathe in the water.

The tunnel was as familiar as home. He pictured the Waterpeople framed by the cave entrance: eating; chatting; going about their business; a line of kids playing chase; and Seine talking with Tyne. Then he pictured two divers watching them. Fuelled by urgency he burst into the cave.

But all was still. No one was there. He frowned into the green glow, wishing he could call out. Searching, he swam from edge to edge, looking into the dark crevices. Sometimes he worried about himself. Not that he would ever admit it, but when defending his ability to Taste, to Brooke, and, as a child, to anyone who would listen, he was not entirely confident that it was real. He could Taste the emotions, sure, but were they really there?

'Kade!' said his mind's voice as clear and unexpected as a stranger's. 'Stop doing this to yourself. You've *been* through this. But the Waterpeople: they're not here. There's every chance I imagined them. Kade! You're way down in the loch *breathing water*. What do you think? You're going to wake up in bed, having dreamed it all, except your feet are wet? Kade! Do you think you're in some mental hospital being spoon fed by a nurse while *believing* you are here?'

He shivered. Where were they? Had they really been here? He tried to conjure up the Waterpeople, as he had a few moments ago, but they would not come. The light dulled. Tears came.

Then Styx's hand grabbed his ankle, pulling him deeper to a level gaze. 'Kade! Where have you been?'

'Styx. Where are the Waterpeople?'

Styx gave no reply.

'I'm really sorry about leaving,' said Kade. 'But you cannot stay here.'

'We know that, Kade.'

'The caves have been discovered.'

'We know.' Styx gave Kade a stern look. 'Did you tell the Landpeople about us?'

'No.'

'Do the Landpeople know about us?' continued Styx, excited, not fearful; looking as though he would like the Landpeople to know.

'No, the Landpeople do not know about you, but they might soon. You must go. You *must* hide. You must leave this loch. Is there any way out? You said that my father was a Waterman, but not one that you knew. Could he have come through in a route you don't know of?'

'I don't think so. I think we know every part of the loch. I think he was a *both,* like you. I think he walked to the Willow Sky.'

'The Willow Sky?'

'Where your mother said she went everyday. Where you were conceived.'

'Maybe he was from the loch beneath the loch,' said Kade, desperately wishing he had been with them the previous night.

'Maybe.' Strange noises stalked through the water. Deep noises.

'Where are the Waterpeople?' asked Kade again.

Styx swam away through a corridor tunnel. Kade followed. At its apex Kade saw torchlight. His blood ran cold as he pictured the Waterpeople trapped under divers' beams. But as he approached he saw them passing stones to one another in a line. 'We are here,' said Styx. 'Opening up the way to the loch below.'

Kade's relief was quickly overtaken by anger. 'You knew! Styx. You knew where the loch beneath was. You lied!'

'Lied?'

'Did not say.'

'No, Kade, I did not lied.'

'But – '

'I searched for it. I looked and looked. All my life. Then I gave up. Then you wanted to find it and I began searching again. You went missing and I searched for you. I thought you must have been searching for the loch beneath and perhaps had been

243

harmed by the sediment. I didn't find you, but I think I've found the loch beneath.'

'Oh.' Kade was lost for words.

Styx looked mischievous. 'I Tasted it.'

Severn appeared. 'Hi Kade,' she said, releasing a slab of stone, and embracing him. 'Look this is where we think the ripple – Aurora called it an earthquake – collapsed the entrance to the loch below.'

'Well come on!' said Kade, suddenly full of life. 'Let's get through.' He swam forward to help. The Waterpeople looked at him, surprised, infected with his urgency.

They worked for an hour or more, pulling away at the dead end. Kade wrenched the stones with all his strength, spurred by the image of the Waterpeople caught in the tunnel like fish in a net.

The last of the loose stones came free. But Kade faced a giant wall of rock. 'No!' he yelled, nearly choking.

An image of dynamite flashed into his mind.

'Wait here,' said Kade and explained to Severn and Styx that he would go to the Dry stores, returning with fire that would let them travel further.

As he swam away, past Waterpeople talking about what had been said, he realised that he absolutely loved swimming underwater.

Hurriedly he worked his way through the stuff in the cave. Into the pool he threw his mother's deathbed. He threw in the books and magazines with all the secrets they kept from the Waterpeople, hidden in their tight little letters. He kept the journal his mum had written in. He threw away fishing equipment, bits of boat, and the worthless pieces of shipwreck. The clothes, toys, kitchen equipment, tin cans all went in. He came to the jewellery and paused. All the debris floating on the water, that was his world. He would have to live in that world. The gold, with its way of putting uranium into water to get itself made, he hated, but it would be useful. He knew what he wanted to do with Brooke and it did not involve work, not the money-earning kind anyway. He put all the jewels in his pack.

The diamond ring: Brooke's ring. Had she found it? No. She'd have said so on the phone. When he left it in her bag, he'd sworn to himself that if she found the ring they would be together. He'd imagined he was leaving things to fate. But that was just a stupid little rule he had made for himself. He felt free at realising he did not have to stick to it. They would be together whether she found the ring or not.

Kade blinked and shook himself. Using his headtorch, he surveyed the cave, checking that there was not one tiny thing for researchers to find and wonder how it got there. All that was left now was the dynamite. He picked it up and dived into the pool, through the debris that Landpeople would think was rubbish caught in a gyre. Pulling bits of paper off himself, he rejoined the Waterpeople.

'This makes fire,' he signed, round the bundle of explosives. 'I'll burn a way through to the loch beneath.'

He slotted the dynamite into the slab blocking the tunnel. He had never done anything like it before, but he felt calm. Maybe it wouldn't work, maybe he would be killed. He was not frightened for himself, only for the Waterpeople.

'If this doesn't work you must hide the best you can,' he said turning to the Waterpeople. 'Stay away from the divers.'

'No,' said Styx. 'I will not hide.'

Kade was startled. No? What did Styx mean, not hide? Were they crazy? Didn't they realise? He was hit by images of white tiled laboratories, of tanks, of contamination. Everyone would want to know about them, down to each cell. The Waterpeople would lose themselves.

He looked at Styx, trying to read him, but his gaze was drawn to the little silver dolphin Styx wore so proudly. An image came to him of a teenage schoolgirl, drunk, losing her necklace as she vomited off the edge of one of the loch's pleasure boats.

Styx was so wise here, but he knew next to nothing about the rest of the world. There was so much of it and so many bad things. Kade had Tasted it: unhappiness, desperation, craving, and the ache for the rarity of loveliness, freedom and kindness. He had Tasted it all in the water. What a Taste. He missed it like a city dweller misses carbon dioxide – despite himself. The world under water was so calm in comparison. The Waterpeople would not be able to cope with the Landpeople, whom he knew would not leave them alone.

Styx was glancing from one of Kade's eyes to the other. Could Styx tell what Kade was thinking? No, Styx didn't need to read his thoughts. Styx had the Tasting. But Styx did not seem to be Tasting Kade. He was looking at him with kindness and concentration, as though trying to transmit something.

These people were not some fantasy that Kade had to hide from prying eyes. They were living breathing people who could make their own decisions. Kade was not their chief, neither was Styx. They had no chief. They were stronger that way.

Neither were they some preserved people who he had the right to hide away from the modern world. The Waterpeople were here, in the present, in the same world. Not a parallel world, but this world. Now.

But sometimes secrets are necessary.

His desire to hide the Waterpeople from the world was as much for his sake as theirs, he realised. If they were discovered, he'd have to translate, to moderate. He would be expected to speak for the Waterpeople and for the Landpeople. But he could only speak for himself. And he didn't want any scientific experiments done on him or them.

'No. I will not hide,' repeated Styx, more gently this time. 'If you cannot burn a way through, I will meet your people.'

'If you can go, you must go. The Landpeople, whether they want to or not, will kill you,' said Kade.

Both Severn and Styx looked astonished. Kade tried to drum it in. 'Their illnesses will come on the back of their friendliness and you will be gone. Gone. Better you hide, for a few years more. Then you can be strong. Wait, until we are all ready for you.'

He saw that they trusted him, but doubted what he said about Landpeople. Aurora and he had been good to the Waterpeople, and had eroded their fear of strangers. Styx spoke: 'For so long all we had were our day to day lives, our hope of other Waterpeople, our myths and our theories about Landpeople. Then your mother arrived, and she and you brought us so much excitement. And you made Landpeople real to us. We can talk with each other. We can make children together. Landpeople are no longer shrouded in myth to us. Your people are as real as our people ... your other people. As real as you.'

'Okay,' said Kade, reeling with all the things he had kept from them about the land. 'But first we must try and find out more about your own people. Go deeper. I hope this works.'

He persuaded the Waterpeople to wait far away, then led the fuse to the nearest dry part of the caves. He lit it, and watched as the burn descended.

# Invisible

All knew the explosion heralded the arrival of something new, because the water changed. The change was invisible, but Tastable. Styx and Kade exchanged glances, each Tasting the new. Was it purer than the loch water? Probably, in the traditional sense, but it had a complexity far more refreshing than purity. Not a tumult of emotions, but a strong balanced Taste. Not happiness *instead* of sadness, or hate instead of love, or anxiety instead of calm, or any of what he thought of as opposites. The Taste melted the emotions together and they flowed through him, not grabbing or demanding, just happening. It felt wonderful against his taste buds, and quenched his thirst. It did not grab at him, claim him, alter him, or confuse him.

But, he had made his choice. He had chosen Brooke over the Waterpeople. He knew that. But a part of him wanted to go with them, to follow the Taste of that water, not to say goodbye. Maybe he could spend a few more hours here? He could tell them all about the Land.

No. No. His craving for Brooke was much stronger.

From his pack he took out the two Ganges stones. He gave one to Severn and one to Styx, 'For luck.' Then his tongue caught a Taste of something. There was no time for him to explain luck to them. He Tasted desire, interest, and a relentless thrusting need-to-know. He knew what it was: Wetsuits trap a layer of warm water next to the skin. The easiest way to warm that water is to urinate in the wetsuit. His lip curled at the emotions of the divers. They were close.

'Go! You must go,' he said, with exaggerated motion.

The Waterpeople sensed his urgency. Beginning with the mother and baby, they entered the door he had created, just as they had done when they spiralled into his heart.

Styx and Severn were left. Seine and Tyne lingered in the doorway, looking shocked and excited. 'Come on then, Kade,' said Severn.

'What?'

'Come on.'

'No – I ... I'm not coming.'

'What?'

Styx swam forward. 'Kade. You must come with us.'

'No. I'm a Landman.'

Styx laughed. 'No you're not! You are a Taster.'

Kade clenched his jaw, feeling the lack of truth, the lies, letting them go with his hands. 'I can't be the Taster,' he signed. 'Because I cannot taste the emotions of Waterpeople.' He could not look Styx in the eye.

When Styx spoke it was like a whisper. 'But we were sure that was why you came to us.'

'No,' said Kade.

Styx, Severn, Seine and Tyne looked upset. Then Styx recovered himself. 'You don't have to be The Taster. You could just live here with us. You could stay and be a family man.'

'I'll go back to my Landpeople,' said Kade, surprised by Styx's warmth, the lack of blame, the quick forgiveness. 'I can help you by finding more Waterpeople. I can cross lands and I can swim in waters far more polluted than you would ever be able to. My people can fly in the sky. I'll find more Waterpeople for you and I will try and unite you all. That's my role, I believe.'

'But how can you?' asked Severn. 'How would you know where to look? You told us that there are countless rivers in the world, countless lakes and underwater caves. It may be forever before you find any others. We may have all have died by then.'

'I *will* find more,' said Kade. 'Waterpeople are not totally unheard of. Landpeople have myths about Waterpeople. I know someone who knows the myths. We can follow the myths and we will find the realities. I know it.'

'Who knows the myths?' asked Styx.

'A woman called Brooke. A Landwoman.'

'She must be a very special Landwoman,' said Styx. 'To know them.'

'Many people know these myths. They are even in stories we tell to children. But yes, she is very special.'

'Is she your lover?' asked Severn.

'Yes.'

Romantic Severn smiled, content. Styx still seemed confused. 'Many people know myths about Waterpeople?' he asked.

'Yeah.'

'If they knew about us, why have the Drys never contacted us before?'

'The *Drys* aren't usually brought up to believe there is truth in myths.' Kade paused. 'They seem more interested in trying to find life on other planets.'

Styx seemed satisfied, unaware how close the possibility was of all the mermaid myths being blown apart by the discovery of the Waterpeople.

'Love is the best thing you can do,' said Severn dreamily. 'Love is the best match. Waterpeople are lucky if we fall in love. There are so few of us. We have to see what the best biological match is and go with that. There are so many of you.' She paused.

Kade could feel the approaching divers.

'But you have the opposite problem,' continued Severn. 'It must be difficult for Landpeople to find the one you love, with all the people in the world.'

'I had to go a long way to find it.'

'Love is the best match.'

Styx looked anxious. Kade looked at him and said, 'When I Taste her I know she loves me. If she ever stops loving me I will know and that will be our last kiss.'

'He is in love,' Styx said, both teasing and acknowledging. 'And his role is to find more Waterpeople. Why else would he have those air-breathing lungs but the heart of a Waterman?'

'I will see you again,' signed Kade. 'I love you all.' A sob escaped him as he felt his love for the Waterpeople pounding through his bloodstream.

'We love you too,' they replied and then turning swam through without a further goodbye, except for Styx, who stayed beside Kade like an unsure little boy. 'Oh just go Styx! Go and find some deep-loch folk! Find a route to the sea! Learn to breathe salt!'

'I wonder what it's like to be a Landman,' said Styx.

Kade put his arms round him, and would have whispered comforting words into his ear if he could. Styx pulled away, and then drew Kade into a manlier hug.

'Thank you,' said Styx as they drew apart. 'For all the excitement your mother and you brought us. He undid the dolphin necklace and pressed it into Kade's palm, so Kade could sign no more. Then, Styx signed 'See you,' and swam away to the loch below.

Kade felt utterly alone. Landpeople and Waterpeople would remain mysteries to each other, with him standing – swimming – in the middle, guarding the borders of those realities. The loch rang with their absence. It was no longer his place. Between losing the Waterpeople and finding Brooke, he was just a boy in a dark loch. He did not want to linger. He would not miss Brooke a third time.

Avoiding the risk of someone seeing him emerge from the willow pool, he swam for twenty minutes until he was at the place where the cave network met the loch. He could see sunlight at the end of the tunnel. The loch.

Then he saw the light from two head-torches. Frogmen. They swam towards him. He began to turn back, then smiled and decided to swim on. The Waterpeople were safe. They were now deeper and further than it was possible for a Landman to go.

In the light of their head-torches the frogmen noticed another diver. But as the figure passed between them they saw he had no tank and no mask. They saw he had the most amazing aquamarine eyes and gentle mischievous smile. They thought they had the bends.

# Arrival

She slipped into Scotland riding metal ridges, feeling smooth and free, but a little bored. She noticed a daily paper someone had left behind, and wondered whether to glance through it, but decided against it, not wanting to hear tales of woe or of celebrity today.

With all her heart she hoped that Kade was still at the Sight. She hoped she could take him away, see more places, perhaps go on a waterfall tour of the world and kiss in every one of them. There were so many things to tell him.

It was such a big world. When he left her, she had told herself it would be easy to find someone else she loved as much as Kade, but now she knew otherwise. So many people, each with their own reality. She wanted a reality that had Kade in it. And she was pretty sure Kade wanted her in his world.

The train pulled up. As Brooke alighted she discarded the hard layer she had wrapped herself in to travel safely. She slept on the bus to Kittim and awoke to the roar of the town falls. It was evening when she hailed a taxi and got the same driver that took her to the Sight last time. She recognized him by his belly, moulded by sedentary years into a double bulge sculpted by the steering wheel.

'You here for this cave thing love?' he asked.

'What cave thing?'

'Ye have'ne heard? They reckon they found an underwater cave network. Dead good business for me.'

So it was not a story.

Kade walked unseen from the loch to the willow pool and sat for a long time with his back pressed against the tree's trunk. His hand stroked the bark, his mind slowly re-ran the events of the last year: this time a year ago he had been living with his mother and his mother was living. He'd been happy enough, maybe a bit immature. He'd plucked up the courage to ask Aurora about the Tasting. He'd thought her agreement to take him to the caves would mark a change in him and in their relationship and had not known that it would be such a big change, that she would die. He had known cave diving was incredibly dangerous. That was why he had seen it as a rite-of-passage. He had seen his mother as strong, and yet she had died. Now it was all over. His mourning was over. She was dead. It was in the past.

A breeze lifted the boughs of the willow. He had gone to India, to the biggest gathering on earth, and met Brooke. And lost her. He would not lose her again. The wind picked up, fanning the boughs. He wondered what had happened to all the debris he had thrown away.

The hands! He had forgotten the skeleton hands! They still waved in the graveyard deep below, like freshwater coral. Oh fuck. What could he do? He was so exhausted and it was so deep.

But the hands *were* in the furthest reaches of the cave network. Very deep. Deep enough to escape discovery? Probably too far for a Landhuman to reach without very special equipment. Could he risk it?

He cried out with frustration. When would it stop? The air felt sweet in his lungs. He did not want to go back underwater, to feel the horrible neutrality of the loch without the Waterpeople, and he did not think his body could cope with changing from air to water and air again. He was only *half* Waterman.

He longed for Brooke. She could make him strong again with her warmth, her scent, her voice. He wanted her to meet Stirling and Ursula and for them to chit-chat about nothing in particular by a fire.

So he allowed himself to leave the hands to fate and he braced himself to go to London the next day. First, though, he would rest. His body had a deep understanding of his need for that. As he made his way back to the Sight the familiar route put pleasure in his steps.

# Depth

He asked Ursula and Stirling to join him in his yurt for dinner and told them he didn't want to talk about anything serious. They mentioned they had seen some divers in the loch that day, then respected his request and discussed ketchup containers and weather vanes. While eating the crispy spicy food that Kade had made, Stirling told them of his latest commission, from an ex-pat Scot living in Nairobi who wanted ice-water from the top of Ben-Nevis, which he had climbed as a child.

Kade felt thirsty and left Stirling and Ursula giggling as he went out into the moonlight to draw some water from the well. As he drew up the pail he considered how he would travel to Brooke. Hopefully Stirling would give him a lift to the train. Otherwise it was two hours by bus and then six on the train with noise and brightness, the bustle of thousands of people getting somewhere, not wanting to be where they were. Then he would have to find her house and maybe meet her family. The idea of that seemed harder, at that moment, than all he had been through in the last year. He looked around at the soft night and tried to picture Brooke's face when she opened the door to him.

He poured the well water into a glass bottle. A noise scraped through the air and echoed through the mountains. Kade turned and saw a figure up the hill.

Love charged through her and her body hummed with feeling. He was very close now. Close and real and delicious. As she approached him, Brooke noticed something different in Kade's features. Was it his mouth? His brow? Yes, the furrow between his brows no longer threatened to turn into a canyon. As he came nearer she saw that his mouth was more relaxed, a smile appearing. His hair was longer, with a sheen like moonlit water and his eyes were receptive and open, little no-tan lines fanning out from the edges like sunbeams. In India he had frowned a lot and it seemed as though his crow's feet would become fully fledged, but something had clearly changed.

'Kade?' she asked in both question and confirmation. All other questions felt redundant. With that one word she asked, 'Is it really you? Can I come close? Do you want me? Will you let me love you? Are you ready? Am I welcome here, as your lover, beside you?'

'Brooke,' he said, answering yes to all her questions. He took her hand. It recognised his touch. Their bodies had missed each other as much as their minds had.

On her finger was the diamond ring. 'You found it,' he said.

'Yes.' She smiled. 'It was from you.' She wanted to ask him where he had got it, and why he hadn't given it directly to her, but that could wait. They stared at each other, shining with excitement and relief.

'How are you?' he asked.

'Good,' she said. 'More than good.'

She glanced down at the bottle in his hand.

'Are you thirsty?' he asked.

'Yes.' The touch of his fingers as he passed her the bottle felt like a kiss. Yes, she was thirsty.

'Oh, Kade. I missed you so much.'

Then it became too strong. Their hearts had to be next to each other, and they embraced, chests together, cheeks close. He kissed her, a whisper away from her lips. 'Would you like to stay with me?

Brooke nodded.

'Would you like some food?'

She nodded again. He led her down the hill.

Who was this man who walked next to her? This slightly different, surer, man that she had just fallen in love with all over again?

The air was clear and quiet, the shade of the leaves a couple of months closer to autumn than it had been at the party. Brooke shivered. She had felt so alone that night, the night he did not turn up. Kade put his arm around her shoulders, not pretending to keep her warm, but really doing so.

He led her to a yurt that glowed orange from the fire within. 'This one's mine,' he said. 'There's a couple of people inside. Ursula and Stirling. You met them didn't you?'

'Yes. And I liked them.' Even if they had freaked her out, just a bit.

As he held back the canvas door she thought how nice it was to have a round doorway after a lifetime of oblongs.

Inside smelt wonderful, of Kade and spices. Stirling and Ursula sat on the other side of the fire, as close as lovers. They smiled across the flames.

'Hello Brooke. What a nice surprise,' said Ursula, not sounding surprised at all, but very pleased.

'Hello,' said Brooke and entered, padding onto the soft sheepskins and settling on one that seemed to be reindeer.

'Well,' asked Stirling. 'What brings you back here?'

Brooke brushed her hair out of her eyes. As Kade came to sit next to her she became conscious of the heat of her blushes and the volume of her heartbeat. She was not embarrassed though. She was happy, not ashamed, that Kade did that to her. 'I came to see Kade,' she said, turning to smile at him.

'How are you, love?' asked Ursula. 'How's your hand?'

'All better. I'm good,' said Brooke, and then remembered to ask, 'How are you?'

'Good too. Good to see you two together.'

'Yeah,' agreed Stirling.

Brooke felt their approval as warmly as the flames, or perhaps a lick hotter. She saw that Kade and her being together was significant to other peoples' lives as well as their own. She felt witnessed, and could also feel that slight undercurrent of the

Sight that she had detected before. It had a need to pull people it liked unto itself, to absorb them. This did not make her feel uncomfortable, but she knew that she would not settle here. Her role as a visitor was to remind them of the outside world. 'And I came to find out about these waterpeople Kade mentioned.'

Ursula and Stirling looked with interest at Kade. 'Waterpeople?' asked Ursula.

Kade looked mischievous, then serious. He began to talk in his wonderful voice, as much to the others as to Brooke. 'The Waterpeople are gone now. They had to move on. Maybe you'll meet them one day.'

Brooke could see that Ursula and Stirling had a thousand questions, but knew Kade wanted to be alone with her. Stirling stood, cracked his knuckles and said to Ursula, 'Fancy having a look at the moon on this fine evening?'

'Oh? Yeah. Sure,' said Ursula, grinning at Stirling. They got up, touching Brooke and Kade on the shoulders as they left.

Brooke turned to Kade. The fire swept gold over his irises. 'I would like to have met people that call themselves the waterpeople,' she said.

'I know where they've gone,' he said. 'We'll visit them one day.'


Brooke touched his hand and he saw the ring sparkle. Again, all over again, he had the feeling he wanted to tell her everything. His thoughts leapt around his head, trying to arrange themselves into speech. There was this baby with lights ... I'm half Waterman ... They had this myth ... Floods.

Noticing speech had started, all his thoughts moved forward, queuing to be spoken. But it was so peaceful here, sitting with Brooke by the fire. He pushed the thoughts away. He felt the joy of just being with Brooke, not even having to say anything, knowing that, in a way, she understood. She had come all this way, and she had found the ring.

'Brooke?'

'Yes?'

Wordless, he leaned forward. He kissed her cheek slowly several times and then reached her lips. He kissed gently, not feeling as though he were searching her saliva for information. He knew she felt good and he felt good. The world softened and deepened as she opened her lips and kissed him more, seeming unafraid of what she might reveal. He found all bitterness washed away, and Tasted love, a sweet excited taste, contentment, relief and something else, an emotion with no name that only existed between her and him. He could feel the beginning of her smile.

They sat back from the kiss, momentarily embarrassed at their bodies' forwardness. But they were grateful for it and he smiled at her and she smiled back.

'Kade?'

He liked that because there was no one else there. She was confirming his presence. 'Yes?'

'When I knew you before, you told me lots of stories about yourself and I told you lots of stories about other people.'

Indirectly you told me a lot about myself, thought Kade, but he did not speak. Instead of finding the quickest way to fill the gap between what he and she knew, he wanted to listen to her, and his thoughts and feelings uncurled under her voice.

She leaned into him and flexed one palm out towards the fire. 'So now,' said Brooke. 'I'm going to tell you a story about me.' The silhouette of her hand seemed like charcoal. The fire cracked loudly. She told him about the Tasting she had experienced that night when she was buzzing with energy.

'It was amazing, Kade, to Taste that. Maybe I'll be able to do it again one day. Maybe you're not so strange.' She swept her hair away from her neck. He could not help but kiss her. They tumbled gently sideways and lay next to each other.

'I love you,' he said. He felt admiration too, and pride.

That night they slept clothed, side by side, still shy. They each dreamed of themselves, asleep by the loch with the other.

260

'I love you too,' said Brooke when she woke, entirely refreshed from sleeping in fresh air, next to Kade, with the sound of the river nearby. They touched, waking all the parts that still slept, stroking away shyness. Brooke thought they both knew what they would do next, but she said it aloud anyway.

'Let's go to the willow pool.'

They climbed the gorge without instructing each other, confident of each other's ability, relaxed and excited. Just before they arrived at the willow pool, Kade stopped. He turned towards her. His eyes sparkled. All of a sudden he gathered Brooke to him and kissed her passionately, filling her with warmth, safety and elation. He kissed her all over her face and hands, then held her cheeks with his palms and quietly said, 'You, as a woman are about fifty-five percent water and I am sixty-five percent.' He pointed at a miniature pool the fall had carved into the rock, and took her hand. 'Water is shaped by its container and also shapes it. I want to shape you and for you to shape me.'

They climbed the next cliff and emerged at the willow pool. With Kade it was twice as beautiful. They crossed over to the island. The willow's boughs tickled her as she walked through the pale green room to the pool's small beach. Together they looked at the water. The sun was at an angle that made the reflections disappear and she could see into the pool almost as easily as if there had been no water there. The world looked fresh. Kade's hand felt warm. He stroked her arm and turned to face her.

He undid the sash of her dress and slowly lifted the hem, kissing her legs, her hips, her stomach, her solar plexus, her neck, her lips, as he lifted her dress higher, higher and over her head. The late summer sun kissed her skin.

She unbuttoned Kade's shirt and held him to her, so warm. She could feel him pressing against his trousers. Kade took off the rest of his clothes and gently pushed her knickers down from her hips, then led her down into the water.

Brooke lay naked on the moss next to him, the blue sky reflected in droplets on her chest. He felt calm and gentle, as though he could sleep. Brooke's eyes were closed. One of her hands stroked the moss, the other, fingers relaxed and spread, rested on his chest. A stretch began to travel through her. She pointed her toes, flexed her legs, lifted her hips, arched her back sending the water droplets down, swung her arms overhead, yawned and opened her eyes. Finally she gave him a big sleepy smile. He felt like the prince to her sleeping beauty.

'Kade,' she said, slipping her voice into her heart. 'I like it here, but I want to travel.'

'So do I,' he said. 'With you. Where do you want to go?'

'We could go to the next Kumbh Mela.'

'Definitely. But that's years away. Where else do you want to go?'

'Well,' said Brooke, turning onto her front. 'The Kalabari, who live on twenty-three islands in the Niger Delta ... '

Kade raised his eyebrows.

' ... believe that there are three kinds of spirits that guide our actions. First there are the spirits of the ancestors. Your particular lineage influences you, but not people who are not related to you. Then there are the 'village heroes,' real people who have visited and are now gone. They influence the whole village.'

'I thought *you* might be like that,' said Kade, sitting up. 'I feared I might never see you again. That you were just a beautiful temporary thing.'

Saying nothing, Brooke stood, walked over to the pool and scooped some water into her mouth with her hand. She walked up to him and kissed him, transferring a sip of water into his mouth. He tasted it again, that KadeBrooke emotion.

Brooke smiled and licked her lips. 'Thirdly there are spirits who can manifest as humans or rainbows or pythons. They are responsible for the weather and for extra-ordinary things that happen, good or bad, like innovation, the gain of lots of wealth, deviant behaviour, insanity, great happiness.' Looking him in the eye, she said, 'Those spirits are called the Waterpeople.'

He held her gaze. 'We better visit them, then.'

'The Kalabari?'
'The Waterpeople.'

# Thanks and Acknowledgements

Thank you to www.youwriteon.com and all those who reviewed *Thirst*, and its previous incarnation *Depth*. Finding www.youwriteon.com was like finding a needle of gold in the haystack of the internet.

Thank you to Miranda Anderson, Tamara Alferoff, Mr Collingwood, Lucy and Gillian Rix, Natasha Gilmore, Tara Kelsall, Mike Jones, Sean McDonald and my family. Thanks also to Fleet Frensham Heights, Islington Sixth-form centre, and to Goldsmiths' anthropology and communications departments.

Finally, thanks and gratitude to Masaru Emoto, whose book, *Messages from Water*, is referred to in 'Patterns.' See www.hado.net for more on Dr Emoto's projects.

amberalpha@hotmail.com

www.ingramcontent.com/pod-product-compliance
Lightning Source LLC
Chambersburg PA
CBHW020650030726
47498CB00002B/452